CHRISTOPHER BUSH
THE CASE OF THE UNFORTUNATE VILLAGE

CHRISTOPHER BUSH was born Charlie Christmas Bush in Norfolk in 1885. His father was a farm labourer and his mother a milliner. In the early years of his childhood he lived with his aunt and uncle in London before returning to Norfolk aged seven, later winning a scholarship to Thetford Grammar School.

As an adult, Bush worked as a schoolmaster for 27 years, pausing only to fight in World War One, until retiring aged 46 in 1931 to be a full-time novelist. His first novel featuring the eccentric Ludovic Travers was published in 1926, and was followed by 62 additional Travers mysteries. These are all to be republished by Dean Street Press.

Christopher Bush fought again in World War Two, and was elected a member of the prestigious Detection Club. He died in 1973.

By Christopher Bush

CHRISTOPHER BUSH

THE CASE OF THE UNFORTUNATE VILLAGE

With an introduction
by Curtis Evans

DEAN STREET PRESS

INTRODUCTION

THAT ONCE vast and mighty legion of bright young (and youngish) British crime writers who began publishing their ingenious tales of mystery and imagination during what is known as the Golden Age of detective fiction (traditionally dated from 1920 to 1939) had greatly diminished by the iconoclastic decade of the Sixties, many of these writers having become casualties of time. Of the 38 authors who during the Golden Age had belonged to the Detection Club, a London-based group which included within its ranks many of the finest writers of detective fiction then plying the craft in the United Kingdom, just over a third remained among the living by the second half of the 1960s, while merely seven—Agatha Christie, Anthony Gilbert, Gladys Mitchell, Margery Allingham, John Dickson Carr, Nicholas Blake and Christopher Bush—were still penning crime fiction.

In 1966--a year that saw the sad demise, at the too young age of 62, of Margery Allingham--an executive with the English book publishing firm Macdonald reflected on the continued popularity of the author who today is the least well known among this tiny but accomplished crime writing cohort: Christopher Bush (1885-1973), whose first of his three score and three series detective novels, *The Plumley Inheritance*, had appeared fully four decades earlier, in 1926. "He has a considerable public, a 'steady Bush public,' a public that has endured through many years," the executive boasted of Bush. "He never presents any problem to his publisher, who knows exactly how many copies of a title may be safely printed for the loyal Bush fans; the number is a healthy one too." Yet in 1968, just a couple of years after the Macdonald editor's affirmation of Bush's notable popular duration as a crime writer, the author, now in his 83rd year, bade farewell to mystery fiction with a final detective novel, *The Case of the Prodigal Daughter*, in which, like in Agatha Christie's *Third Girl* (1966), copious references are made, none too favorably, to youthful sex, drugs and rock and roll. Afterwards, outside of the reprinting in the UK in the early 1970s of a scattering of classic Bush titles from the Golden Age, Bush's books, in contrast with those of Christie, Carr, Allingham and Blake, disappeared from mass circulation in both the UK and the US, becoming fervently sought (and ever more unobtainable) treasures by collectors and connoisseurs of classic crime fiction. Now, in one of the signal developments in vintage mystery publishing, Dean Street Press is reprinting all 63 of the Christopher Bush detective novels. These will be published over a period of months, beginning with the release of books 1 to 10 in the series.

Few Golden Age British mystery writers had backgrounds as humble yet simultaneously mysterious, dotted with omissions and evasions, as Christopher Bush, who was born Charlie Christmas Bush on the day of the Nativity in 1885 in the Norfolk village of Great Hockham, to Charles Walter Bush and his second wife, Eva Margaret Long. While the father of Christopher Bush's Detection Club colleague and near exact contemporary Henry Wade (the pseudonym of Henry Lancelot Aubrey-Fletcher) was a baronet who lived in an elegant Georgian mansion and claimed extensive ownership of fertile English fields, Christopher's father resided in a cramped cottage and toiled in fields as a farm laborer, a term that in the late Victorian and Edwardian era, his son lamented many years afterward, "had in it something of contempt....There was something almost of serfdom about it."

Charles Walter Bush was a canny though mercurial individual, his only learning, his son recalled, having been "acquired at the Sunday school." A man of parts, Charles was a tenant farmer of three acres, a thatcher, bricklayer and carpenter (fittingly for the father of a detective novelist, coffins were his specialty), a village radical and a most adept poacher. After a flight from Great Hockham, possibly on account of his poaching activities, Charles, a widower with a baby son whom he had left in the care of his mother, resided in London, where he worked for a firm of spice importers. At a dance in the city, Charles met Christopher's mother, Eva Long, a lovely and sweet-natured young milliner and bonnet maker, sweeping her off her feet with a combination of "good looks and a certain plausibility." After their marriage the couple left London to live in a tiny rented cottage in Great Hockham, where Eva over the next eighteen years gave birth to three sons and five daughters and perforce learned the challenging ways of rural domestic economy.

Decades later an octogenarian Christopher Bush, in his memoir *Winter Harvest: A Norfolk Boyhood* (1967), characterized Great Hockham as a rustic rural redoubt where many of the words that fell from the tongues of the native inhabitants "were those of Shakespeare, Milton and the Authorised Version....Still in general use were words that were standard in Chaucer's time, but had since lost a certain respectability." Christopher amusingly recalled as a young boy telling his mother that a respectable neighbor woman had used profanity, explaining that in his hearing she had told her husband, "George, wipe you that shit off that pig's arse, do you'll datty your trousers," to which his mother had responded that although that particular usage of a four-letter word had not really been *swearing*, he was not to give vent to such language himself.

Great Hockham, which in Christopher Bush's youth had a population of about four hundred souls, was composed of a score or so of cottages, three public houses, a post-office, five shops, a couple of forges and a pair of churches, All Saint's and the Primitive Methodist Chapel, where the Bush family rather vocally worshipped. "The village lived by farming, and most of its men were labourers," Christopher recollected. "Most of the children left school as soon as the law permitted: boys to be absorbed somehow into the land and the girls to go into domestic service." There were three large farms and four smaller ones, and, in something of an anomaly, not one but two squires--the original squire, dubbed "Finch" by Christopher, having let the shooting rights at Little Hockham Hall to one "Green," a wealthy international banker, making the latter man a squire by courtesy. Finch owned most of the local houses and farms, in traditional form receiving rents for them personally on Michaelmas; and when Christopher's father fell out with Green, "a red-faced, pompous, blustering man," over a political election, he lost all of the banker's business, much to his mother's distress. Yet against all odds and adversities, Christopher's life greatly diverged from settled norms in Great Hockham, incidentally producing one of the most distinguished detective novelists from the Golden Age of detective fiction.

Although Christopher Bush was born in Great Hockham, he spent his earliest years in London living with his mother's much older sister, Elizabeth, and her husband, a fur dealer by the name of James Streeter, the couple having no children of their own. Almost certainly of illegitimate birth, Eva had been raised by the Long family from her infancy. She once told her youngest daughter how she recalled the Longs being visited, when she was a child, by a "fine lady in a carriage," whom she believed was her birth mother. Or is it possible that the "fine lady in a carriage" was simply an imaginary figment, like the aristocratic fantasies of Philippa Palfrey in P.D. James's *Innocent Blood* (1980), and that Eva's "sister" Elizabeth was in fact her mother?

The Streeters were a comfortably circumstanced couple at the time they took custody of Christopher. Their household included two maids and a governess for the young boy, whose doting but dutiful "Aunt Lizzie" devoted much of her time to the performance of "good works among the East End poor." When Christopher was seven years old, however, drastically straightened financial circumstances compelled the Streeters to leave London for Norfolk, by the way returning the boy to his birth parents in Great Hockham.

Fortunately the cause of the education of Christopher, who was not only a capable village cricketer but a precocious reader and scholar, was taken up both by his determined and devoted mother and an idealistic local elementary school headmaster. In his teens Christopher secured a scholarship to Norfolk's Thetford Grammar School, one of England's oldest educational institutions, where Thomas Paine had studied a century-and-a-half earlier. He left Thetford in 1904 to take a position as a junior schoolmaster, missing a chance to go to Cambridge University on yet another scholarship. (Later he proclaimed himself thankful for this turn of events, sardonically speculating that had he received a Cambridge degree he "might have become an exceedingly minor don or something as staid and static and respectable as a publisher.") Christopher would teach in English schools for the next twenty-seven years, retiring at the age of 46 in 1931, after he had established a successful career as a detective novelist.

Christopher's romantic relationships proved far rockier than his career path, not to mention every bit as murky as his mother's familial antecedents. In 1911, when Christopher was teaching in Wood Green School, a co-educational institution in Oxfordshire, he wed county council schoolteacher Ella Maria Pinner, a daughter of a baker neighbor of the Bushes in Great Hockham. The two appear never actually to have lived together, however, and in 1914, when Christopher at the age of 29 headed to war in the 16th (Public Schools) Battalion of the Middlesex Regiment, he falsely claimed in his attestation papers, under penalty of two years' imprisonment with hard labor, to be unmarried.

After four years of service in the Great War, including a year-long stint in Egypt, Christopher returned in 1919 to his position at Wood Green School, where he became involved in another romantic relationship, from which he soon desired to extricate himself. (A photo of the future author, taken at this time in Egypt, shows a rather dashing, thin-mustached man in uniform and is signed "Chris," suggesting that he had dispensed with "Charlie" and taken in its place a diminutive drawn from his middle name.) The next year Winifred Chart, a mathematics teacher at Wood Green, gave birth to a son, whom she named Geoffrey Bush. Christopher was the father of Geoffrey, who later in life became a noted English composer, though for reasons best known to himself Christopher never acknowledged his son. (A letter Geoffrey once sent him was returned unopened.) Winifred claimed that she and Christopher had married but separated, but she refused to speak of her purported spouse forever after and she destroyed all of his letters and other mementos, with the exception of a book of poetry that he had written for her during what she termed their engagement.

Christopher's true mate in life, though with her he had no children, was Florence Marjorie Barclay, the daughter of a draper from Ballymena, Northern Ireland, and, like Ella Pinner and Winifred Chart, a schoolteacher. Christopher and Marjorie likely had become romantically involved by 1929, when Christopher dedicated to her his second detective novel, *The Perfect Murder Case*; and they lived together as man and wife from the 1930s until her death in 1968 (after which, probably not coincidentally, Christopher stopped publishing novels). Christopher returned with Marjorie to the vicinity of Great Hockham when his writing career took flight, purchasing two adjoining cottages and commissioning his father and a stepbrother to build an extension consisting of a kitchen, two bedrooms and a new staircase. (The now sprawling structure, which Christopher called "Home Cottage," is now a bed and breakfast grandiloquently dubbed "Home Hall.") After a falling-out with his father, presumably over the conduct of Christopher's personal life, he and Marjorie in 1932 moved to Beckley, Sussex, where they purchased Horsepen, a lovely Tudor plaster and timber-framed house. In 1953 the couple settled at their final home, The Great House, a centuries-old structure (now a boutique hotel) in Lavenham, Suffolk.

From these three houses Christopher maintained a lucrative and critically esteemed career as a novelist, publishing both detective novels as Christopher Bush and, commencing in 1933 with the acclaimed book *Return* (in the UK, *God and the Rabbit*, 1934), regional novels purposefully drawing on his own life experience, under the pen name Michael Home. (During the 1940s he also published espionage novels under the Michael Home pseudonym.) Although his first detective novel, *The Plumley Inheritance*, made a limited impact, with his second, *The Perfect Murder Case*, Christopher struck gold. The latter novel, a big seller in both the UK and the US, was published in the former country by the prestigious Heinemann, soon to become the publisher of the detective novels of Margery Allingham and Carter Dickson (John Dickson Carr), and in the latter country by the Crime Club imprint of Doubleday, Doran, one of the most important publishers of mystery fiction in the United States.

Over the decade of the 1930s Christopher Bush published, in both the UK and the US as well as other countries around the world, some of the finest detective fiction of the Golden Age, prompting the brilliant Thirties crime fiction reviewer, author and Oxford University Press editor Charles Williams to write: "Mr. Bush writes of as thoroughly enjoyable murders as any I know." In 1937 he became, along with Nicholas Blake, E.C.R. Lorac and Newton Gayle (the writing team of Muna Lee and Maurice West Guinness), one of the final authors initiated into the Detection Club before the outbreak of the Second World War and with it the demise of the Golden Age. Afterward he continued publishing a detective novel or more a year, with his final book in 1968 reaching a total of 63, all of them detailing the investigative adventures of lanky and bespectacled gentleman amateur detective Ludovic Travers. Concurring as I do with Charles Williams's encomium, I will end this introduction by thanking Avril MacArthur for providing invaluable biographical information on her great uncle, and simply wishing fans of classic crime fiction good times as they discover (or rediscover), with this latest splendid series of Dean Street Press classic crime fiction reissues, Christopher Bush's Ludovic Travers detective novels. May a new "Bush public" yet arise!

Curtis Evans

The Case of the Unfortunate Village (1932)

IN LATE SEPTEMBER 1931, according to *Witchcraft and Black Magic*, one of eccentric English scholar Montague Summers's many tomes on the occult, a Finnish farmer drawing water from a well in a dark and gloomy wood outside the city of Helsinki made a passing gruesome discovery: "an arm which had quite recently been severed from a human body." Upon draining the well police discovered additional horrors: "mutilated human remains—heads, arms and legs." Local authorities concluded after investigation that more than forty graves in a nearby cemetery had been violated by the cemetery caretaker, a mortician by the name of Saarenheimo, who had in his possession a small library of volumes concerning necromancy (including a tome, printed in England, which detailed the making of magical lotions from the body parts of corpses), photographs of dead bodies and a membership card in an English occult society. With Saarenheimo refusing to answer questions about the grotesque affair (according to a newspaper account he occupied his time in his cell intoning cabalistic hymns), Finnish police appealed for help from Scotland Yard in discovering a naturalized Englishman whom they believed headed this purported occult society, thereby sparking a nine days' nightmare in the British press, which doubtlessly detected an attention-grabbing alternative to yet more news about the impending General Election. (See my introduction to Christopher Bush's *Cut Throat*.) "Finnish Horror," "Black Magic in Finland" and "London Search for Satanist" screamed the papers, darkly proclaiming that a "society of devil-worshippers" was "scattered all over Europe" and that a Satanic high priest lurked somewhere in London. The next year three men and three women plead guilty in a Finnish police court to the crime of practicing black magic, but it does not appear that any supposed English ringleader was ever apprehended.

In September 1932, a year after the UK's Satan scare, Christopher Bush published his eighth detective novel, *The*

Case of the Unfortunate Village (1932), a tale which concerns, in part, the suspected existence of a coven of witches in the formerly bucolic Sussex village of Bableigh. In speaking in the novel of "the existence of Satanism and the cult of the Black Mass," Ludovic "Ludo" Travers, Bush's lanky and bespectacled gentleman amateur sleuth, confidently declares: "There we are not dealing with non-existent things. You may remember the discovery last year of a considerable number of Satan worshippers in Helsingfors [the Swedish variant for Helsinki], when the Finnish authorities called in the help of Scotland Yard because they suspected that the chief priest was an Englishman. After that it's surely not too much to assume the possibility of there being a nest of such people here?"

Two years earlier, mystery author Cecil John Charles Street under his "Miles Burton" pseudonym published *The Secret of High Eldersham* (1930), a novel much praised by the late scholar Jacques Barzun and recently reprinted by the British Library. In the novel, Street, a keen student of European folkways, drew heavily on sociologist Margaret Murray's once popularly influential (though now thoroughly debunked) tome, *The Witch-Cult in Western Europe* (1921), which posited the existence of an organized witch religion throughout Europe. Other detective novelists who during the Golden Age drew on Margaret Murray's work, so perfectly tailored for mystery fiction, were John Street's close friend John Dickson Carr--see especially *The Burning Court* (1937) and *The Crooked Hinge* (1938)--and, in looser fashion, Agatha Christie, in her highly sinister village tale *Murder Is Easy* (1938). It seems not at all unlikely that Murray's sensationalistic theories, possibly filtered through *The Secret of High Eldersham*, influenced as well Christopher Bush in *The Case of the Unfortunate Village*.

In the novel Ludovic Travers, who has just come off the publication of *Millions for All*, his latest book of popular economics and doubtlessly a hopeful title after the onset of a global economic depression, is prevailed upon by an old public school friend, Henry Dryden, big pot and local magistrate in Bableigh, to investigate (with the assistance of his friend John

Franklin, head of the Detective Bureau of Durangos Limited, the consulting and publicity firm of which Travers is a director) both the origins of the pall of disquiet that has fallen over the formerly placid Sussex village and the gunshot death, ruled an accident, of Dryden's friend Tom Yeoman, the local squire who had fallen on hard times. Even after Travers and Franklin arrive in Bableigh, however, the spell of unfortunate village "accidents" continues, making the novel something of a forerunner, not only in its milieu but in its plot, to Agatha Christie's *Murder Is Easy*.

In an unusual device which presages the classic English deduction board game *Cluedo*, Bush gives his village characters allegorical surnames reminiscent of John Bunyan's *Pilgrim's Progress*, a book the author had read by the age of seven. Hence there is the late squire, Tom Yeoman; vicar Lyonel Parish; devout churchgoer Miss Faithful; consumptive daily Martha Frail; and a mini Arts Colony--about whose rather free sexual habits Bush, like Gladys Mitchell with her village denizens in her 1932 detective novel *The Saltmarsh Murders* (published the same year as *The Case of the Unfortunate Village*), seems decidedly non-judgmental--comprised of widowed sculptor Ashley Mould; "ultra-impressionist" painter Marian Crome (Her "Woman in a Bath" the traditionalist Dryden denounces as "two obscene-looking breasts and a monstrously distorted navel," while he dismisses her "Aphrodite" as "a mound of yellowish paint like a breast, with a dab of vermillion on it."); and two middle-aged former living companions, avid gardener Agnes Rose and potter Harriet Blunt. Could a coven really have been formed among these people? Artistic temperament is one thing, witchcraft surely quite another!

At one point in the novel Bush, who recently had settled with his companion, Marjorie Barclay, in Beckley, Sussex, has Henry Dryden rhapsodize his Sussex village, Bableigh, as follows:

> Bableigh has trees everywhere. The pasture land is sandwiched between woods. The valleys are green lakes, and when the sun's right they're blue hazes. Visualize a place like that, Mr. Franklin, clean off the track, its

houses peeping out at you, and its little lanes pitching into the valleys each side of the ridge. Think of it, remote, peaceful and basking.

Can Ludo Travers and John Franklin solve the mystery of the strange malaise that has afflicted the unfortunate village of Bableigh and return the community to its previous state of pastoral grace? Read this bewitching tale and see!

THE PROBLEM

CHAPTER I
THE TALE OF A VILLAGE

IF NINE MEN out of ten had spoken as Henry Dryden had spoken, Ludovic Travers would have hunted about for a means of side-tracking the conversation, but Dryden was the tenth man. A stranger would have respected anything Dryden had seen fit to bring into a conversation. There were things about him that made for implicit confidence; the John-Bullish massiveness of his frame, for instance, and his short, curly beard, which between them gave not only an impression of solidity but the possession of those stable virtues which one instinctively associates with an Edwardian appearance. But Travers was no stranger. He had been at school with Henry Dryden and had never lost sight of him the forty-odd years of their lives. He knew him, even more surely than the world knows him through his poems and essays, as one whose outlook was as serene and sane and kindly as his private life, and that in spite of the intense mysticism that permeates most of his work.

In the same way the number of people to whom Dryden would have spoken as he had spoken to Ludovic Travers could have been counted on the fingers of one hand. And yet a stranger would have been puzzled over Travers. His long, lean body and finely cut face gave him the appearance of the perfect intellectual, and the horn-rimmed spectacles and the delightful voice would have confirmed that impression—and then there might have come something elusive and puckish that would have made one pause. There was certainly nothing of the Edwardian in his make-up. Outward appearances he had no use for, and the fact that every question has two sides was for him merely an incentive to hunt for a third. You see it in his best-known books, "The Economics of a Spendthrift" and "The Stockbrokers' Breviary," and you may recall that chapter in his latest work, "Millions for All," which bears the intriguing title, "The Tin-Whistle," and turns out to be an inquiry into the origin and application of the expression, "to whistle for one's money"!

Travers had run into Dryden in the Strand just after midday and had been asked to lunch. It was during the meal that the talking had been done, though when they entered the grill-room of the Fraggiore, Dryden had had no intention of mentioning either

Bableigh or the curious happenings that had been troubling him. Then Travers had asked about the village and had mentioned Tom Yeoman, whom he had met once at Dryden's house, whereupon Dryden began to talk and had kept it up for the best part of an hour. Travers had been fascinated for a variety of reasons; moreover, he was trying to guess just how far Dryden would be prepared to go. At length he leaned across the table with a smile and a question that were both very tentative.

"To get clean down to bed-rock, Henry, am I right in saying that you sensed something wrong with this village of yours? Call it something sinister or ominous if you like, but you certainly sensed it?"

Dryden hesitated. "I don't think I'd go so far as that. You're pushing me too far, Ludo. A lot of it's so nonsensical that it's probably only my nerves and not the village at all. Even that last business."

"Yes," said Travers reflectively. "That last business." He gave the coffee quite a lot of stirring before he looked up again. "But you will admit, Henry, that the whole thing has got on your nerves."

Dryden nodded. "Yes, I'll admit that. I know I'm a fool for letting it; still, I'll admit it."

Travers leaned forward again. "Then why not consult us—confidentially?"

"Us?" He was clearly at a loss.

"Yes. Durangos Limited."

Dryden's face fell. Travers would have bridled up if anybody else had shown the same casual toleration; as it was he smiled somewhere inside and prepared to be patiently explanatory.

"I'm afraid you've rather got us wrong, Henry. I admit we used to be a bit noisy. We used to encourage jokes about ourselves as Ford did about his cars, but they were thundering good cars for all that, and we're a thundering good firm, though I say it." He dismissed all that with a wave of the hand. "If you want my opinion in a friendly and private capacity, it's this. Do what I should do under the same circumstances—consult Durangos."

The other looked the least bit uncomfortable. "You're still carrying me too far. I'd be ashamed to consult anybody about such ridiculous nonsense."

"But what about the dog?"

Dryden stopped short. "Yes . . . the dog. As you say, you can't get away from the dog. Unless Yeoman did it himself?"

"Impossible!" said Travers decisively. "But in any case, Henry, there'll be no harm done if you do consult us. John Franklin, who's in charge of the department concerned, is a particular friend of mine, so we'll make the whole thing unofficial. You'll like him, Henry. He's extremely able and he's got a way with him that'll be as good as a tonic for you. What do you say? We'll go along and have a chat?"

Dryden got out the first word of a further protest. Travers hopped up like a shot.

"I knew you'd agree. I'll get hold of Franklin while you're clearing up."

They walked back to the Strand, and though he made no comment Dryden was considerably impressed when he saw for the first time the immense building towering above Charing Cross station. He liked the huge waiting-room with its reticent decoration and atmosphere of unhurried importance; he liked the lift-boy and he liked the airy corridor into which he stepped.

"The whole of this suite is the Detective Bureau," said Travers, then cut short the comment with a brisk tap at one of the doors. A noise came from inside and he waved Dryden through.

There never was any pose about Franklin. He was working at the desk, and as he pushed the papers aside and got to his feet he

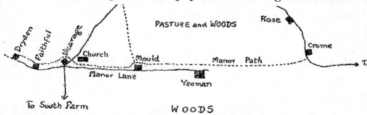

looked rather annoyed at being caught out. Dryden took a liking to him straight away, and he found him unusual. What he had anticipated was a human ferret; what he saw was a man as tall as himself, with a manner that rather recalled Harley Street, and a complexion so dark and eyes so staringly black that one knew at once there was something foreign in his near ancestry. Then as soon as he spoke, Dryden knew that that, of course, was all wrong;

the voice was very English, and pleasant, and definitely reassuring, as Travers had predicted.

"Sorry! I'm afraid I didn't expect you so soon. And this is Mr. Dryden?"

The smile was almost boyish. In less than no time they were settling themselves in the easy chairs, and as the May afternoon was a bit chilly the electric fire was switched on. The cigarettes were passed round and Dryden owned up to being a chain smoker.

"I'm afraid Mr. Franklin is going to be very annoyed by the time I've finished talking," he said. "This room has never heard such a farrago of nonsense."

Franklin smiled. "Don't you believe it. In any case, Job would have found this room his spiritual home."

"I expect he would," said Dryden. "He might, of course, have missed the potsherds." He shook his head diffidently. "I really haven't the pluck to begin at all. What shall I say, Ludo?"

"Just ramble on, Henry, as if you were in your own study. When it's all over we'll get Franklin here to give his opinion on things in a purely private capacity. After that it'll be up to you."

Dryden still hesitated. "I'm really wasting Mr. Franklin's time. Still, I'll tell him about the dog."

"No, you won't," said Travers patiently. "The dog's the wrong end. Begin with the village and the people."

"Oh, but Mr. Franklin doesn't want to hear about that."

"Of course he does." Having dragged Dryden to the water, Travers was determined to make him drink. "Besides, everything's inter-related. You can't separate Yeoman and Parish—and there's Mould."

"Ah, well!" Dryden heaved a sigh and gave Franklin a look of commiseration. "Perhaps Mr. Franklin will allow me to collect my thoughts for a moment."

"Do, please," said Franklin quickly. "And if you don't object I'll take shorthand notes. It may save subsequent questions."

It was all very friendly and homely. The chairs were comfortable and the fire made the room less business-like. Travers's long legs stretched well across; Franklin leaned back with the pad on his knee, and Dryden sat forward, looking into the fire, cigarette held in a curiously old-fashioned way between the tips of index finger and thumb.

"Bableigh is the village I'd like to talk about, Mr. Franklin. It's quite close to Northurst. Do you know it?"

Franklin shook his head.

"Well, it's really a hamlet perched on top of a ridge. There's a church, vicarage, tiny school, post-office-shop and the usual cottages—and, of course, the inevitable inn. After that the village opens out. There's a large farm to the south—"

"Pardon me a moment," interrupted Franklin. "Would it be possible to draw me a little map to illustrate all these places?"

"A capital idea!" He took the sheet of paper and roughed out a plan. From time to time during his story Franklin passed it across again for additions to be made.

"Before we look at the village," he said, "we might notice how it lies. Take a capital H. The upstrokes are the main roads from London to the coast. The cross stroke is the unpretentious road that runs through Bableigh—the one drawn here—and that cross stroke is about two miles long, with Bableigh in the middle.

"I live here at Old House, and that's about a mile from the main road to the west. Then comes one cottage, as you see, then the vicarage and the village huddling round it. All I've indicated along the Northurst Road is the last cottage and that's occupied by the woman who works for Miss Crome, and she's worn her own path from the back garden to join Manor Path by Mould's house. Manor Path is a short cut for pedestrians to rejoin the Northurst Road after it makes the curve. You'll remember everything very easily if you think of Tom Yeoman's house, which is Manor House. The lane going down to it is Manor Lane. The path which goes past it is Manor Path. Mould's house is Manor Cottage because it used to be the cottage for the gardener at Manor House, to which it belongs.

"As I was saying, Bableigh's merely a hamlet perched on top of a ridge. South Farm is in the southern valley and there's a smaller farm or two in the northern valley. Manor House is where Tom Yeoman used to live. Old House is where I've lived myself since the war, and where my people lived for generations before me. Then there are one or two oldish places that have been restored and modernized, just where Manor Path rejoins the Northurst Road. Windyridge is owned by a Miss Crome; the other, called The Pleasance, is owned by a Miss Rose. You might think of those two houses and Manor Cottage as a kind of Art Colony, don't you think so, Travers?"

"Excellent description," came Travers's voice from the depths of the chair. "Tell Franklin all about them."

"Right, then. Ashley Mould the sculptor. Have you heard of him, Mr. Franklin?"

Franklin smiled as he shook his head. "You'd better make up your mind to regard me as a perfectly hopeless low-brow."

"All the better." He lighted another cigarette, this time from his own case. "Ashley Mould's an important character in this very rambling story. Tom Yeoman got into financial difficulties and had to get rid of his gardener, keeping only an odd man from the village, and as Manor Cottage was free he advertised it to let unfurnished. Ashley Mould took it on a two-year agreement, and that was a year ago last January. He made certain alterations and had a wooden studio built at the end of the garden by Manor Path. I ought to say he probably came to live in Bableigh because he was on friendly terms with Marian Crome of Windyridge; at least I always understood she knew the Moulds pretty well. She bought her house the previous September. She's an artist and—luckily for her, I'd say—has sufficient money to be independent of what she might get from her art work. The Pleasance is now occupied by Agnes Rose, who used to share it with her friend Harriet Blunt. They've been in the village over three years now." He leaned across solicitously. "I'm afraid it's all very confusing. Still, if you just think of those three households, Mr. Franklin: Mould the sculptor, a very clever man indeed, even if he is highly modern; Agnes Rose, who's fond of gardening and used to share the house with Harriet Blunt, who's a potter; and finally Marian Crome the artist, who's an ultra-impressionist."

Travers suddenly sat up in his chair. "Marian Crome!" He laughed as he turned to Franklin. "We've seen an effort of hers. Don't you remember, John? A week or two ago when we were going past the Conard Gallery? You know—the supposed-to-be woman in the non-existent bath!"

"My God, yes!" said Franklin, then apologized for the blasphemy.

"Perfectly excusable," said Dryden, but he didn't laugh. "I think I remember the one you mention. She called it 'Woman in a

Bath.' Two obscene-looking breasts and a monstrously distorted navel. Utterly horrible. Perhaps you'll keep that in your mind too, because it might help a lot. And there's just one more person to add—Lyonel Parish, the vicar. That makes four houses to keep in mind. You know what a really beautiful Sussex village is like, Mr. Franklin? You'll pardon the question."

"I've seen plenty," said Franklin. "Travers's sister lives at Pulvery, and they're often good enough to ask me down for the weekend. What I associate with all the villages is gorgeous views across valleys, and fine old cottages with long, low, tile roofs."

Dryden nodded vigorously. "You've got it. And Bableigh has trees everywhere. The pasture land is sandwiched between woods. The valleys are green lakes, and when the sun's right they're blue hazes. Visualize a place like that, Mr. Franklin, clean off the track, its houses peeping out at you, and its little lanes pitching into the valleys each side of the ridge. Think of it, remote, peaceful and basking. Above all, go back to it a year and more ago when the Moulds first came.

"I'm a bachelor, Mr. Franklin, but I'm gregarious by nature. The coming of all those people to Bableigh was a great joy to me. I spent hours in their houses. I would go out and call when the fit seized me, and I was always sure of a welcome. It might be the Moulds or Marian Crome, or the two at The Pleasance, and I spent many a whole evening with Parish and the Yeomans." He shook his head and an expression of pain seemed to pass quickly over his face. "We were a friendly lot of people; different in most things, perhaps, but human and interesting. That was Bableigh just over a year ago."

Travers had been watching the ash of Dryden's cigarette, and how it lengthened. Now it dropped on the curly beard and he pushed forward an ashtray. Dryden appeared not to notice.

"I want to be unprejudiced," he went on. "I'd like to know whether the things that happened were the result of some single actuating motive, or were merely isolated occurrences. More than once I've even dared to wonder if some evil and devastating blight struck the village itself."

"I take it you don't mean the village, but the part with which you were socially identified."

Dryden seemed impressed by the pertinence of Franklin's remark. "You're quite right. It's these four households that I've mentioned that we're concerned with."

"And just one other question. How was it that all the people you've mentioned seemed to arrive in your village at much about the same time? I mean, none are old inhabitants."

"Merely luck," said Dryden. "Manor Cottage I've already explained. Windyridge and The Pleasance came into the market on the death of their owners—quite old people. One was a distant relation of Marian Crome."

"Sorry," said Franklin. "I just like to have things clear, that's all. You mentioned an actuating motive. I wondered if any such motive had caused them all to assemble in Bableigh, as it were, within the space of three years. Carry on, Mr. Dryden."

"Well, we'll take Marian Crome first. She's the masculine type and about forty. When she first came to the village—in the September, you'll remember—her work struck me as merely puerile. It was a vapid, impressionist sort of landscape. Even now I can't quite fathom her audacity in sending a picture to a London gallery for—"

"Galleries exhibit anything," interrupted Travers. "It's all a question of payment."

"I expect that's it. In any case, it doesn't matter. The important thing is this. I can't explain why I have the exact dates in my mind, but within a very few months—it'd be February when I first noticed it—her work underwent a sudden and curious change. She began to vary her childish interpretations of landscapes with pure impressionism—the sort of thing you saw in that distorted navel affair." He turned to Travers. "I'm very hazy about terms. Would you call it 'impressionism'?"

Travers shrugged his shoulders. "It's a good enough term, Henry."

"Well, whatever the pictures are, these particular ones seem to me to be masses of paint that paw at you. Her landscapes merely excited risibility. When I saw them they actually made me cheerful; they gave me the kind of pleasure that one gets on seeing the naïve efforts of one's nieces and nephews in the nursery. But now her rooms are speckled with these other monstrosities, which to me are utterly repulsive and even bestial. If I could do it I'd buy every one she paints and burn it so as to have the house what it used to be. Parish told me the same thing one day, though he didn't take them as badly as I did. I'm not exaggerating when I say that the house has become impossible while these horrible things leer at me. I'm afraid to go into it.

"But the really curious thing is that she doesn't seem to have altered much herself. A slight pretence at being frivolous, perhaps, but nothing more. She's a reasonably normal person, the tiniest bit spinsterish, but sympathetic and generous. But this is the main fact I would impress on your mind, Mr. Franklin, since you're good enough to listen to me. One house in my village has closed its doors on me. One person in it has changed, and changed inexplicably."

He looked anxiously at Franklin to see how the recital was being taken. Franklin nodded gravely.

"Now we'll take Ashley Mould," went on Dryden. "He came down last January twelvemonth, and I, of course, called. His wife was a very charming woman, though rather an invalid; she died, as a matter of fact, after only being with us a few months. I can't say I ever liked Mould himself overmuch because he had a certain affected cynicism that jarred on me. Still, he was always agreeable and informatively original. At the end of March Mrs. Mould died, and she was buried in Bableigh churchyard. They had no maid at the time, and he never troubled about getting one afterwards. Then suddenly, a month or two later, he shut himself up and developed into a very annoying kind of hermit. They say he used to drink a lot. What he did was to have things left at the back door and pay the tradesmen when he thought of it. His garden, and it used to be a lovely place, hasn't been touched since, and they tell me it's a wilderness. I believe he used to leave the village occasionally by going along Manor Path to the Northurst Road and so to the bus, but he never took a walk in the village itself. He called on nobody, and his looks were unpleasant.

"I put it down to grief at the loss of his wife, but two things seemed to cut across that theory. He didn't commence this amazing way of living till some time after his wife was dead. Also, it had never struck me when I was there that he had any special affection for his wife. In other words, I've wondered if it was some outside influence that changed him, and it is a very definite change. I called there three or four times, and he refused to open to my knock, though I'm perfectly sure he was in the house. The last time I called—and that'd be just before Christmas—I saw him looking at me through the window with an expression on his face that I should call fiendish. After that I left him alone, in spite of the fact that now the report is that he's becoming normal again. I haven't actually met him abroad, but if I do I'm wondering whether to risk a snub or an insult. Oh! and something I should have said. Parish, the vicar, had much the same experiences with Mould as I had myself. By the way, I'd like you particularly to remember that Parish was quite a jolly fellow in those days—"

"He changed too?"

"He did, and his change was the worst of all. But we'll come to that later. It was just after Christmas that Parish told me he'd had another go at Mould. He went to the back door, and when Mould opened it, thinking it was a tradesman, Parish shot his foot in it and made his way in. He tackled Mould roundly. Asked him what he meant by treating his neighbours and himself in that way. Mould heard all he had to say, and when Parish had finished he showed him out politely and told him to go to hell."

Franklin smiled. "A stout fellow, your parson!"

"Yes," said Dryden. "He was . . . in those days. And when he told me about it he seemed immensely tickled. There was one thing he said which I've often thought about since. He chuckled away as he was telling me. 'You leave him to me, Dryden,' he said. 'I've got a most uncommon method of attack I'm going to try out on Master Mould.' What his idea was I can't imagine, or why he was so bursting with delight when he foreshadowed it. However, that's not the point. In spite of the fact that Mould is recovering from his bout of whatever it was, it still remains that yet another house in my own village is closed to me, and a second person has undergone a violent change."

Franklin rubbed his chin reflectively. "Most interesting. Any other changes, Mr. Dryden?"

Dryden lighted yet another cigarette. "I'm afraid there are, but of a less complex type. Agnes Rose and Harriet Blunt lived together at The Pleasance, as I told you. Both are spinsters and in the forties. Before they came to Bableigh the position was this: Harriet Blunt was showing some pottery at an exhibition, and met

Agnes Rose there. The two got friendly, and as Agnes is a person of sudden and tremendous enthusiasms, she decided to take up pottery too, as an amateur, of course. I don't think Harriet Blunt has much money, and I know the pottery work is for her a serious thing on which she depends for a living. She's a most interesting woman, whereas Agnes Rose is the type that's full of gush and superlatives, though a good enough soul at heart. Well, the two women came to Bableigh. The house is the property of Agnes Rose, and they shared the expenses. Harriet Blunt has her kiln at Northurst, sharing it with another professional potter who has his headquarters there.

"I used to call at The Pleasance quite a lot. They made a very interesting and always refreshingly amusing couple—Miss Blunt so forthright and the other so volubly helpless. Then about a year ago Agnes tired of the pottery craze, and tired very badly. She had a new enthusiasm. Somewhere she'd seen the most marvellous rockery, and she determined to have one of her own like it. That meant she neglected her share of the work and the household duties, and you can imagine what happened. The two quarrelled and separated; Harriet with a very genuine grievance. She moved to the school cottage, which she now shares with the young schoolmistress, who's away at the week-ends, and she carries on with her work under rather awkward conditions. Agnes Rose has become a self-centred fool of a woman with a craze that will soon die out for a new one. But you see my point. Together these two women were miraculously complementary. As a pair they were perfect, one setting off the other so admirably. As things are at the moment, yet another house is closed to me. Agnes Rose by herself is unbearable. Yet another person has undergone a change for the worse." He looked round somewhat helplessly at the two listeners. "Just what it all means I can't convey to you. I know it must sound trivial, and I can't re-create the atmosphere without being melodramatic."

"Keep to the facts," Franklin told him. "The atmosphere will look after itself."

"Well, if you don't mind. . . . And now we come to the vicar—Lyonel Parish. Faithful, our old vicar, died at a great age two years ago. Parish was once a missionary in China, then had an illness and came home to a church in one of the new suburbs of London.

There he later had some kind of breakdown, and when he recovered he came to us. I liked him straight away. He had none of the ordinary vicarial reticences about him. Please understand me. I'm not commenting on religion; I'm merely claiming that by the very nature of his calling a parson's not every man's man. Parish is a shortish, spare man, and he used to have a pair of twinkling eyes. He's the only man to whom I could apply that overworked adjective, 'whimsical.' He loved jokes—even practical ones. He was friendly with everyone, and accessible. He had two foibles; at one he used to laugh himself, and the other he took far too seriously.

"The amusing one is that he claims descent from the poet, Thomas Parnell, who lived at the time of Queen Anne. You're familiar with him, perhaps, Ludo?"

"Can't say I am," said Travers. "Wait a minute though. Isn't he the author of the oft-quoted 'Pretty Fanny's way'?"

"That's right. The amusing thing is, as I used to point out to him, that Thomas Parnell, according to the biographies, left no descendants. He used to laugh at that. Over his mantelpiece he used to have what was reputed to be a portrait of Parnell, which was left him by an aunt. But the thing Parish never would stand being chipped about was his own verses. He used to contribute poetry to the local papers; just religious snippets and very innocuous, like those of his supposed ancestor. Parish himself took them very seriously, however. He once talked of having them collected and published, but that was just before he changed."

Dryden paused to contemplate the dead end of his cigarette, and it was noteworthy that he made no attempt to light another.

"His was the worst change of all. If you'll allow me to anticipate somewhat, he changed after Tom Yeoman's death, and that was three months ago. *He's become two new men.*"

He looked at Franklin apprehensively as he made that statement. Franklin never moved a muscle.

"You remember I told you he used to be a happy and genial soul. He loved a joke. He had a fund of quaint utterance. Now all that *natural* gaiety has gone, and in its place is a forced geniality that seems to remember it once was natural; a kind of chattering, unnecessary geniality that forces itself to the surface."

He paused and shook his head perplexedly. Then he swivelled round in the chair.

"I do want you to realize this tremendous change, Mr. Franklin. It's a false and loathsome geniality that he now shows. The original man no longer exists. Let me tell you how he affects me. Mould's face, that day I saw him looking out of the window at me, was horrible. The other day I met Parish, and when he was talking to me on trivialities and emanating this ghastly new geniality of his, his face suddenly seemed to me to be worse than the face of Mould. It was a skull, aping life and grinning mechanically."

He shook his head again, then fired the question almost passionately.

"You think I'm nerve-ridden, perhaps? That I'm imagining things?"

"Oh, no!" said Travers quickly. "You're sensitive, Henry, and you've felt these things more deeply than some of us would have done. I know there's something remarkably queer behind all these experiences of yours. Are you going to tell Franklin about the other side of Parish? The second man he's become?"

"I thought I'd bring that in with Yeoman."

"The very best place," said Travers. He nodded over at Franklin. "That really concludes the story of the strange changes that came over the village of Bableigh."

"All I'd say to Mr. Dryden at this juncture is this," said Franklin. "Mr. Dryden mentioned the possibility of one central motive actuating the changes in all these people, and I'm wondering what there might be in it. If I might give an illustration which is frankly absurd. Suppose all these people had been affected by the slump and national crisis of last year. Mould might have lost a lot of money and have brooded over the loss. The same thing might have made Miss Rose unnaturally irritable. Miss Crome might have lost money too, and have tried this new style of painting as a means of making money. Your vicar might have been affected in some similar way. That's merely an illustration of the kind of general actuating force you've had in your mind. Either these happenings are unconnected occurrences, or they're part of a whole. If they're connected, one of your problems is to find what connects them."

"Wait till you hear about Yeoman," said Travers. "That may change your views."

"That was some sort of sudden death?"

Travers made a face. "It certainly was sudden. I'll say it's ten to one it was murder."

CHAPTER II
THE TALE OF AN ACCIDENT

DRYDEN PAUSED again for an apology before he resumed his story.

"I'm afraid I must be rather long-winded if you're to understand everything about the Yeoman affair, Mr. Franklin."

Franklin waved the apology aside. "That's all right, Mr. Dryden. Tell the story in your own way."

"Well, Tom Yeoman lived at the Manor House. Once it had quite a lot of land with it, but everybody doesn't like that sort of thing nowadays, and all he kept when he bought it was about two acres of gardens and the orchard. The man who farms South Farm let him have the run of his land for rough shooting.

"Tom Yeoman was one of the finest men I've ever met. He'd spent most of his time in India, where he had financial interests, and he came to Bableigh just after the war. He was then about forty and recently married. His wife was a perfectly delightful woman, and later on they had a boy and a girl. They kept a large indoor staff and a couple of gardeners, though they were what I'd call a domesticated pair. You got the idea of sincerity and absolute simplicity as soon as you stepped inside the door.

"Tom was vicar's warden, but he wasn't the bigoted sort. He was just a good-living fellow and as good company as a man would wish for. In winter he loved pottering round with the gun and a tough old Airedale called Sam. The point about the dog is interesting. You see, he didn't care a rap what sort of a dog he had with the gun. He told me he thought Sam was as much entitled to a day's fun as anybody else."

"You thought a good deal of this Mr. Yeoman?" Franklin asked quietly.

"I did. You see, he was a better man than I'll ever be. There was something enormously lovable and attractive about him. You saw it most when things began to go wrong and that bad business in India hit him hard. He mentioned it himself, quite casually and as if it were an ordinary occurrence, that he'd have to go very quietly for a bit; let Manor Cottage and do with a daily gardener; let the chauffeur go and keep only a couple of maids. What I didn't know then was that most of his private fortune had already gone into the breach to steady things.

"At the beginning of this year I knew he was in a bad way. Then he told me he hated the idea like blazes, but he'd have to sell Manor House and take a much smaller place. Parish had a word with me about it later. Those two understood each other remarkably well, and as Parish is a bachelor he used to spend a lot of time round there. You will remember that Parish was what I call normal in those days, and I may as well make the statement here in case I forget it, namely, that if Tom could come to life and see his old friend he wouldn't know him. Pardon the insistence, but perhaps you'll keep that particularly in mind.

"The two thought the world of each other. There was a deeply religious strain somewhere in Tom, though nothing would have made him confess it. Still, as I was saying, Parish told me confidentially that Tom was in a very bad way. Practically everything had gone, and all he could be certain of was a small house and enough to live on very quietly, but there'd be no public school for the boy, and that hurt him a good deal. Moreover, he was insured for ten thousand and he was very worried about keeping the payments up. Parish was almost desperate about losing the Yeomans. He was always a man of the most generous and charitable nature, and he'd have given Tom money surreptitiously if it could anyhow have been done. Indeed, the afternoon before Tom's death I met Parish and he told me he thought he saw a way out. I taxed him with having some scheme for lending money, but he laughed it off. I should say that he looked none too well that afternoon, and he owned up that he'd been worrying a lot about things. The next evening, and that was three months ago, Tom Yeoman was found dead. I can show you the full report of the inquest, but I'll tell you now what happened.

"He must have gone out for a bit of rough shooting. His way lay due south through his own orchard, and then he stepped into the wood that runs down the slope. There's a sort of track through the wood for about a quarter of a mile, then you come to a stile set in the fence that shuts the wood off from the pasture land. He didn't tell his wife that he was going, but the village man who was working in the gardens happened to come across near the orchard for something and saw him go through the orchard gate carrying the gun, and the dog was trotting alongside him. The gun was under his arm—the old-fashioned type of gun with exposed triggers and trigger-guard.

"Shortly after—the man couldn't be sure how long after, but it seemed as if it was after the expiration of the normal time to reach the stile—the man heard a shot. Then he began to hear quite a lot of shots, and these were the farmer himself and his brother-in-law doing a bit of rabbiting for themselves. Now just at the time when we judge Tom left the house, Parish called and asked to see him. Mrs. Yeoman said he was out somewhere and probably pottering about in the garage. Parish looked for him there and then went straight home, as he wasn't feeling any too well. As a matter of fact, he had to turn in with a chill. But Mrs. Yeoman thought, when her husband didn't come in to lunch, that he'd gone somewhere with Parish and that's why she didn't worry. In the afternoon she sent the man to the vicarage, where Parish was in bed, though of course he had no idea where Yeoman was. When dusk came on Mrs. Yeoman was alarmed and sent the man to South Farm to see if he was there. The man found his master lying on the far side of the stile with the top of his skull blown about.

"The inquest showed that everybody was satisfied it was an accident of a not uncommon kind. Brambles were trailing all over the stile. Nobody ever used it but Yeoman himself, and he must have tripped over a bramble, and as he fell the trigger caught too and the shot got him in the head. The posture was natural; the doctor was implicitly satisfied and that was the official end of the affair. The insurance company paid up after some brief inquiries of their own. In any case, everybody knew it couldn't have been suicide. Tom Yeoman wasn't the man to take that way out. Mrs. Yeoman is now living with friends in the North and Manor House is for sale."

Dryden paused as if to dismiss all that into the past. Ludovic Travers, who knew what was coming, sat up in the chair and began polishing his glasses.

"Let me own up," went on Dryden. "I was grossly dishonest over the matter. From the very beginning I thought it wasn't an accident, but I lied all the way through—not to myself, but to everyone else. I was scared lest the insurance company should hold things up and make more trouble for Mrs. Yeoman, who was nearly off her head as it was. I thought that if I, as a magistrate, hinted and doubted, people might begin to talk about suicide after all and the company might not pay." He looked round at Franklin. "Even now I'm wondering if my attitude was right."

"Every man's entitled to his own thoughts," said Franklin. "You're outside the law—unless you deliberately concealed vital evidence."

"That," said Dryden, "is the very point. Let me tell you what I *did* think. In my opinion he was the last person in the world to have an accident of that kind. He knew the peculiarities of the stile and he was one of the most careful people I've ever known."

"He might have been particularly worried and absent-minded that morning," suggested Travers.

"I know. I'm not giving you evidence, I'm telling you my own thoughts. But certainly it wasn't suicide—the wound proved that. The muzzle, it is true, was almost touching his head when the gun went off, and if you take myself as illustration as I'm now sitting, bolt upright, the shots followed a line parallel to the floor. They entered behind the left ear, as if a left-handed man had committed suicide clumsily with a revolver. But Tom wasn't left-handed and he wasn't using an easily manipulated revolver, but a heavy gun, and he couldn't have used any apparatus to fire that gun or that apparatus, however simple, must have been found. Add what I've already told you and I think you'll agree that we can dismiss the idea of suicide utterly from our minds."

"Which leaves accident or murder," said Franklin bluntly. "And as you don't favour accident, we come to murder pure and simple. Why do you think he was murdered?"

"Well, tell me this. Wasn't it amazing that the gun should go off and discharge the shots so accurately behind the ear and straight through the skull?"

"Amazing, perhaps," said Franklin, "but not impossible. Even the billion-to-one chance happens. The incredibility would lie in its dependence on yet another billion-to-one chance." He smiled suggestively. "The rest of your evidence, for instance."

Dryden nodded heavily. "Yes. I suppose that is so. But the rest of my evidence is far less vague. It concerns the dog, which went out with its master that morning and hasn't been since seen by anybody. The idea was that it ran off and somebody stole it. I didn't think so. It was an extraordinarily faithful animal and I was certain it would have stayed by the body and prevented any stranger approaching."

"We must look at things fairly and squarely," put in Travers. "It is possible, you know, that the dog had become dangerous and he took it out and killed it, intending to tell his wife about it later."

"Just a moment!" exclaimed Franklin. "You're supposing that the dog *is* dead."

"I think you'll see in a moment," said Dryden quickly. "The dog was my first real doubt. I've done all sorts of things in connection with the death of Tom Yeoman, but I've spent most of my time over the dog. To be perfectly frank, I found its body . . . two days ago."

"Really!"

"Yes. You see, my theory was that if Tom was murdered then the dog would have attacked the murderer, who'd have been forced to kill it and dispose of its body. So I made a sharp-pointed stick and poked about in the vicinity, and finally I found it buried in shallow leaf-mould. I covered it up again. Then I thought the matter over and decided to get away from Bableigh for a day or two and think things over. That explains . . . well, this afternoon."

"Quite. And what did you ultimately propose doing?"

Dryden tugged at his beard. "Well, I might have informed the authorities—or I might not. The dead dog is no real evidence of murder, and now Mrs. Yeoman has got used to the idea of an accident, why lacerate her feelings again and bring notoriety into the lives of the children?"

"Exactly!" said Franklin, and refrained from mentioning the question of justice.

"The immediate necessity is, I take it," said Travers, "to see if the dog was murdered—if I may put it that way. Find out how it was killed, or how it died, and you'll be on the way to finding evidence about the death of its master."

"If I might ask a question or two," said Franklin. "You say the doctor was implicitly satisfied—about the wound and the quantity of blood and the position of the body and all the other important facts?"

Dryden lighted another cigarette before replying to that. "I like to be fair," he said, "and fairness makes me say I don't think he had too many ideas about it all. He's an excellent fellow is Sawyer, but he's old and obstinate, and even if I'd been so minded I'd never have dared to make a suggestion to him or question his opinions."

Franklin smiled. "I think I know the type. And you know the exact time the shot was fired?"

"Approximately ten-thirty."

"Then assuming it was murder, if you have any suspicions of anybody we might inquire into alibis."

"No, no!" said Dryden hastily. "We mustn't do that. We can't run the risk of any gossip in the village. Besides," and he looked up hopefully, "it's surely far too long since the affair for such inquiries to be possible."

"Perhaps you're right," said Franklin. "But *had* he any enemies?"

Dryden hesitated rather curiously and he fidgeted in his chair. "I suppose this will be in strictest confidence?"

"The whole success and credit of this firm depends on confidence," said Franklin quietly.

"Thank you. Thank you." He shuffled again for all that, then decided to speak. "Well, I'll get it off my mind. Yeoman certainly had no enemies, but two of the people I've already mentioned were not on the best of terms with him. Mrs. Yeoman called on Marian Crome one day and was very shocked at one of those new-style pictures which was shown her. Yeoman himself saw it afterwards and forbade his wife to call again."

"The picture was indecent?"

"Heavens, no!" said Dryden, and still he didn't laugh. "It's hard to say. Marian Crome doesn't intend them to be either indecent or suggestive. It's difficult to explain, Mr. Franklin. She's quite a decent soul herself, and I know she was incredibly shocked when she suspected what had happened. She spoke to me about it and I smoothed things over." He shook his head lugubriously. "I'm afraid it didn't stop her continuing to paint that sort of thing, however. You see, she'd never understand how people like myself find this impressionist work of hers not only sexual but repulsive."

"Anything special in the one that shocked Mrs. Yeoman?" asked Travers.

"Well, I know what Yeoman told me and I know what I thought myself. It was called 'Aphrodite,' I believe, though all I could see was a mound of yellowish paint like a breast, with a dab of vermilion on it."

"Pardon me," said Franklin, "but unless you imagine Marian Crome committed murder, aren't we wandering from the point?"

"Perhaps we are," said Dryden. "Only, you see, Marian Crome might have mentioned the matter to Mould and he was on bad terms with Yeoman. About a week before his death he was passing and Mould began abusing him about the dog. He said if it ever snarled at him again, or if he caught it in his garden, he'd heave a brick at its ribs. You can guess what Tom thought about that. All the same, if I've been harbouring an unjust thought I'd rather forget it altogether."

"Exactly." Franklin scribbled something on his pad. "I was to recall to you the second of those peculiar changes in your friend the vicar."

"Oh, yes," said Dryden, but seemed more concerned with collecting his thoughts. "Yes . . . the vicar. Do you know, I think I can tell what you're going to say. If he's changed it's because of the shock of his friend Yeoman's death."

Franklin smiled. "I admit I was going to raise the matter. And what are the objections?"

"Well, I told you that Parish had had a breakdown before he came to us. I submit that if he had been influenced to that extent by Yeoman's death he'd have had a similar nervous breakdown—which is the very thing he hasn't had. For instance, if you were to meet him without having heard a thing about him, you'd probably notice nothing unusual. To you he'd merely be a country vicar of a not very human type. But the difference to me is what he used to be, and for that you can only take my word."

"I understand," said Franklin. "The first change you observed in him was this forced geniality. The second was?"

"The characteristics of that second man are a strange way of looking clean through you as if he were concerned not with you but with something away and invisible in the background. Often, too, he gives you a very limp and utterly unresponsive hand to shake. I seem to imagine there's some kind of religious connection with these peculiarities; I mean, he's most like that when he's talking religion, and he's now got the habit of introducing religious matters into any conversation I have with him when I meet him in the street. It's most distressing."

"Religious mania?"

"No!" said Dryden emphatically. "There's no mania in the man. It's something devilish and inexplicable. He insisted on conducting the funeral, and got up from bed to do so. As far as I could judge he was normal though frightfully pale. I had no chance to speak to him that day, but the following morning I was going round to the vicarage for a chat when I met him. He began to refer in a very peculiar way to Yeoman's death. I forget what words he used, but he mentioned—quite unnecessarily, of course—a power that shapes our ends, and he harped on the inscrutability of providence. It was all so ghastly that I was struck with a sudden horror. As I said, he's become two new men, and both are inexplicably terrible. I'm forced to avoid his company. His house is closed to me. And one remarkably curious thing is that although I used to spend so much time round there, he never refers to it now. You'd expect him to say, 'You never come to see me nowadays,' or something like that."

"You're sure his reason's not affected?"

Dryden shook his head. "You will be the judge of that. When you see him and speak to him, dismiss from your mind what I've been saying, and I'm positive you'll be of the opinion that he's normal." He raised his hand with a gesture of despair, "But you can never know what a fine thing he was before he became what he is now."

"Has anybody else remarked on the change?"

Dryden looked at him quickly, then down at the fire. "I'll tell you something of which I should be ashamed. You can have no idea how tremendously I've missed his company, and how much I've wondered if by any chance there was some explanation to be found in myself. I wondered if the village had noticed anything, so I spoke discreetly to Jimson, my man. Every evening from nine to half-past he's a modern Doctor Johnson at the village inn—The

Roebuck. Jimson says the village has noticed that Parish has aged with Yeoman's death, and that's all. The people have a great liking for him because they feel he's sincere, and he's most generous, as I told you."

Franklin rang through to the office, then smiled across at Dryden. "A cup of tea won't do us any harm."

"Best thing in the world," said Travers, and rose and stretched his legs. "By the way, Henry, harking back to that earlier problem of all the houses that became closed to you, did I understand you to say that Parish had worried a lot about that, too?"

"Well, he was very puzzled about Marian Crome's pictures, and very distressed. Like myself, he was a lover of the plain man's art. He liked Harriet Blunt's pottery, for instance. He was also much upset about the split between the two women at The Pleasance. I don't mind saying that when I told him before Tom Yeoman's death that in my opinion something was radically wrong with our particular circle—as it certainly was—he agreed, and said he had been puzzling his head over the same thing."

They left the case to look after itself during tea, then all at once Dryden became aware of the time and bestirred himself.

"I had no idea it was so late." He turned to Franklin, and it was quite a different man who put the question. The obvious tension and the uneasiness of the earlier afternoon had gone. "What do you think I ought to do about all this, Mr. Franklin?"

"You wish me to be perfectly frank?"

"Most certainly I do."

"Well, then, what I'll say is this. Still speaking unofficially and among friends, I'd very much like to run down to Bableigh and see the actual ground where the supposed accident took place. I'll also make arrangements, if you wish it, to see what the dog died of. That's the second part of your story. As for the first part—what I might call the evil blight that suddenly fell on all your friends—to be perfectly candid it's beyond me at the moment. You say you've sometimes sensed the presence of evil. If you'll pardon the remark, I'm a plain, ordinary man. I can sense nothing unless it's solid and under my nose. I'd be unfair to you if I claimed to be anything else. But to deny that there are people who can sense things not purely material would be impertinent and absurd."

"That's plain speaking," said Dryden, "and I'm grateful for it. When will you come down and see us?"

"No time like the present. To-morrow suit you?"

"Splendidly." He looked remarkably relieved. "Come back with me in the car. Stay a few days."

"And what time?"

"Ten? Or ten-thirty?"

"Ten-thirty it is," said Franklin. "Outside here. I shall have to bring a man with me; not to stay, but to bring back the dog."

Dryden seemed delighted as he held out his hand for the fare-well shake. Travers accompanied him to the ground floor, then strolled with him towards his hotel.

Half an hour later Franklin was still before the fire, chewing on his pipe. He looked round as Travers entered, and pulled him up a chair.

"Well, what did you think of him?" Travers asked.

"I liked him enormously, if that's what you mean. There's something homely and . . . bucolic about him."

"He's a fine chap," said Travers with a nod of agreement. "He's also my exact conception of Jupiter when the gods were in their best fettle. That bronze beard, for instance—" He broke off. "What's on your mind?"

Franklin roused himself. "Sorry. I don't know that there's anything much—unless it's everything!" He went off at a tangent. "The great Henry Dryden doesn't talk much like a poet."

"Shakespeare didn't spout blank verse at The Mermaid," said Travers enigmatically. He laughed, then his face straightened. "What you've got to accept, and I say it very seriously, is that Dryden's a man of curiously alert spiritual perceptions. Let me give you an illustration. It's not in that volume I lent you, it's in another which I'll find when we get home. It's a magnificent piece of prose, and it's important from the point of view of all that business at Bableigh.

"The gist of it is this. He called at a house and was introduced to a girl who had just come in from a walk and was wearing a tweed costume. She was full of life and vitality, but while she was talking to him he saw her as dressed in a single white garment, and her face was a deathly grey, and both their voices seemed to be coming from a remote distance. A week later that girl was killed in an accident."

He paused for a moment. "That sounds very silly as I relate it, but I happen to know it was true, and for a reason quite different from the one that it was Henry Dryden who wrote it. In my second year at Halstead there was a new master who was amazingly popular. He was a Rugger international, and the smaller fry, myself included, indulged in hero-worship. I could never get Dryden to say a good thing for him, and finally he told me, confidentially and rather sheepishly, that there was something in this man that frightened him. At the end of his second term that man dropped out. I didn't know why then, but I do now. No wonder Dryden was spiritually frightened."

"Yes," said Franklin lamely. "That's all very well, only you see you can't expect me to have eyes of that sort. I could see you believed all that business about there being something wrong with a section of the village, and I knew Dryden believed it himself. Would you like to know what I saw?"

Travers grinned. "Why not?"

"I saw the usual small village with people treading on each other's toes and quarrelling. Miss Rose is explained like that. Mould got fed-up with it all and decided to become a temporary hermit. The parson's upset about the death of Yeoman, and he'll soon get over it in all probability."

"And what about Miss Crome's pictures?"

Franklin shrugged his shoulders—and changed the subject. "Is Dryden's way of life normal?"

"Perfectly. Naturally he's the great man of that immediate district, but that doesn't affect his simplicity. He has a delightful old house, full of lovely things and books and comfort. A very homely couple—old family servants—look after him. Jimson does anything that's wanted, and his wife's cook-general. Dryden's a man of normal tastes; he eats beef and drinks beer, and he snores—because I've heard him. He's got plenty of money in the sense that he doesn't spend anything like his income."

"That's clear enough," said Franklin, and seemed to show a certain relief, "You going to Pulvery to-morrow?"

"I suppose so," said Travers, who hadn't really given it a thought.

"Then why not come down with us? Have lunch, see what there is to see, then push on."

Travers rose to it at once. "You sure I shan't be butting in?"

Franklin knew him far too well to answer that question. "Then you'd better ride with me and Dryden and let Palmer drive your Bentley and have my man with him. Is Dryden staying at an hotel? If so, why not call him up and tell him about it?"

"You do it for me, there's a good fellow," said Travers. "I'll give you his number. There's something rather important I wanted from Main Inquiries."

"You needn't worry," said Franklin unconcernedly. "I've got most of it already."

Travers's eyes opened. "Most of what?"

"Oh—er—information about those people. There's nothing available about Marian Crome. The vicar and Ashley Mould you'll find notes of on the desk there."

Travers gave a guilty look at an unresponsive back, then took off the receiver.

THE FIRST PHASE

CHAPTER III
ON THE SPOT

IT WAS RARELY that Travers was late for an appointment, but the following morning Dryden and Franklin waited for at least five minutes outside Durango House till the Bentley came up. Travers nodded cheerfully to the two, then sprinted to the commissionaire and handed him a small parcel. Another minute and he had made his apologies and was at the wheel of Dryden's car.

The morning was certainly not in tune with death or murder. When Tonbridge was passed and the morning began to wear on, the sun grew hot for the time of year. The trees, too, were flecked with their first green, and the hedges were in full leaf, and whatever Franklin's professional mind was anticipating, Ludovic Travers was enjoying what had been an extremely pleasant journey, and was looking forward to an excellent lunch at the end of it. A mile short of the village he waved a motor-coach past and took a side road.

"We've just left the down stroke of the H, if I remember rightly," remarked Franklin.

"That's right," said Dryden. "We're now on the cross stroke and clean away from everything. There's nothing for trippers to see at Bableigh, and the roads are pretty narrow, as you see. There's the church!"

Franklin caught sight of the tower, then it was gone as the car ran between the woods. Travers slipped into, second and began the long climb up the narrow lane. Franklin glanced back and saw the Bentley following close behind, Palmer driving, and his own man, Wilson, alongside him.

"All your roads like this?" he asked Dryden.

"Much about the same. You see, we're on that ridge, and you've got to climb to get to us. One lane, the one that goes to South Farm, is terrifyingly steep. It's probably one in three, and there's a bend and a brick wall at the foot."

The car breasted the hill. Just short of where the road made a bend and was lost to sight, Travers drew the car in. He got out with an air of complacency.

"Well, here we all are. And though I say it, I've rarely been better driven."

"Not so bad," said Franklin, stretching his legs. His eyes opened as he caught sight of Old House; the pair of gigantic yews at the gate, the length of mossy, bricked path, the timbered gable that fell almost to the ground, the bulging walls and lop-sided windows, and the sweep of the tiled roof.

"Wonderful old place," said Travers at his elbow. "This is Jimson, asking about luggage."

Dryden's man was short and plump; a handy enough fellow by the look of him. At the moment his black clothes indicated that he was present in his capacities of butler, footman and personal servant; later on, as Dryden told them while the bags were being taken in, he'd probably be in dungarees in the garage, or putting in an hour or two in the garden.

"Have a look at that view," said Travers, and Franklin had a look. Across the road to the south the ridge fell away steeply, and far away to the right was the grey line of the South Downs, and then a greyer and more tenuous line that was either cloud or sea. In the middle distance of the valley bottom a farm and buildings could be seen.

"That's South Farm," Dryden told them. "See that wood running up from it on the left? That's where we're going after lunch." He turned his back on the valley and pointed out the red roof just visible among the trees towards the bend. "There's that one cottage, you may remember, then the vicarage and the village proper." He smiled, obviously at some pleasant recollection. "A most delightful old lady lives there. I believe I told you. I always call her my neighbour. Miss Faithful, she is, the sister of our old vicar."

Once through the gate Travers took on himself the duties of showman, and waved his hands at carved barge-boards and ancient glass and twisted chimneys and intricate timbering. Franklin had seen nothing quite so intimately old as that lovely house. His own bedroom was a sheer joy with its view over the south valley. There was even a reading-lamp on the bedside table.

"Bribery and corruption," said Travers. "You'll never get rid of him, Henry."

"It is a charming room," and Franklin beamed. "I had no idea you had electric light."

"Most of the larger houses about here used to have their own plant," said Dryden. "Then the company brought the light down the main roads, so we canvassed the village and got enough names for it to be worth while to bring the wires through. The posts run across the meadows at the back of the house."

When lunch was over and Jimson had finally withdrawn to make a fourth at the kitchen table, Franklin got something off his mind.

"By the way," he said to Travers, "what were you up to this morning, keeping us all waiting?"

Travers flushed slightly as he fumbled for his glasses. "The fact is, I only managed this morning to get hold of the name of the firm who handle most of Mould's work, so I slipped along and bought a small figure." He beamed apologetically at Dryden. "It won't go on the bill, Henry even if there is one."

Franklin smiled to himself. Travers, as usual, was going into the fray with sleeves well rolled up.

Dryden frowned as he thought of something. "Mould worries me", he said. "After what's happened I can't possibly call. And I would have liked you people to see him."

Travers flushed again, and this time removed the glasses. "I should have told you something else. I think Mould's vagaries can be explained—I mean, his rôle of hermit. His brother was telling me about it last night—"

"His brother!"

Franklin received a somewhat pained look. "Don't you remember those notes of yours about Ashley Mould, and how his brother is Wilfred, the education crank?" He explained to Dryden. "Wilfred once consulted us about some investments, and I'd met him once or twice at a certain club. To be brief, I had a short gossip with him last night, and the name of Ashley happened to be mentioned. I'm glad to report that Wilfred hates him like sin. He tells me he had two spells in a home—for tippling, you know—though he didn't know he'd broken loose since his marriage. Also he says Ashley suffers from protracted fits of the sulks, and these fits are the product of a tremendous vanity. The last one was because he quarrelled with an art group with which he used to be associated. They didn't make enough of him, it appears."

Dryden clicked his tongue. "Well, I must say he wasn't long in showing us the worst side of his character. A pity. A great pity to let temper get the better of one like that." He caught sight of the time. "You might be glad to know that Jimson tells me the gardener won't be at the Manor this afternoon. He's laid up with lumbago."

"But I thought the place was shut up," said Franklin.

"So it is," explained Dryden, "but there must be a man there to keep the gardens from getting too wild. When I said he was away I meant we could go where we liked without fear of gossip."

"You'd call this a gossipy village?"

Dryden shrugged humorously. "Find me one that isn't!"

"But we'd better take the Bentley, don't you think?" said Travers. "It'd rather clinch the idea that we're inspecting the house as prospective buyers."

"We shall want it for the dope," added Franklin.

"The dope?" Dryden looked puzzled.

"Dry chloride of lime for the corpse," explained Franklin. "We've also got a gallon tin of the solution. That dog's been buried the best part of three months, and Wilson's going to take it to town in a public conveyance."

When they set off, then, it was in the Bentley. Round the bend, fifty yards past Miss Faithful's cottage, the village came into sight, huddled beyond the church. Franklin recognized the three prongs of the fork—the main road running left towards Northurst, the centre lane which they took, and on the right a lane that ran sheer and south to the farm. Manor Lane was over three hundred yards in length; on its left the pasture land and woods in which the back gardens of cottages could be seen, and on its right the great wood that fell away with the valley. Half-way down Manor Lane they passed on the left an old cottage with yew hedge in front.

"That Mould's house?"

"That's it," said Dryden. "Now you see why he might have been annoyed by the dog. Yeoman had to pass Manor Cottage every time he went to the village."

On the right the hedge that bounded the wood was badly gapped. Then came an ancient brick wall. A few yards and it was broken by an archway and gates, and as the car drew in they saw the house—a black and white Tudor building, much larger than

Old House and more showy. But it turned out to be a lovely place with a view far over the valley to the last line of hills that fronted the sea.

Franklin stowed the dry chloride in his pocket and carried the tin of solution. Travers took over the small sack and the water-proof wrappings. Short of the main gate Franklin stopped.

"I rather gathered there was a back way round by the garage. Might we try it?"

"By all means." Dryden looked surprised. He looked still more so when Franklin had surveyed the back buildings and was making his suggestion.

"I put it to you. Somebody could easily have followed Mr. Yeoman to the wood without being observed. This back way is invisible from the house, and you say the gardener was working out of sight over there in the walled garden."

"But, my dear sir! Who was to know he had gone to the wood?"

"Your vicar came here to the garage. He might have seen Yeoman disappearing along this path and through that gate. He might have followed him."

Travers smiled dryly. "You're not putting up the parson as the murderer?"

Dryden shook his head impatiently. "Come, come! Let's be serious."

"Sorry," said Franklin. "You see, I merely thought that what was possible for the vicar was possible for anybody else. I know you said the vicar looked in the garage here and then went straight home." He picked up the can again. "Shall we go through to the wood?"

The orchard was already falling sharply with the hill. They went through what Dryden called a private gate, and just inside the wood Franklin set the can down again and surveyed the scene. "And we're now going to take the exact road that the dead man took that morning. Is that right?"

"Perfectly right," said Dryden. "At least I know of no reason why he should have left the track."

They moved along on what was barely discernible as a path. The trees were fairly dense and there was little undergrowth, so that one could see all that stirred within compass of fifty good yards. Their feet left no trace on the leafmould, and the wood fell so steeply that when he raised his head from watching his going, and saw the sky above the trees, Franklin had the feeling of rising to the surface of a pool. Before they reached the stile he had stooped down to pick up something and place it in his pocket, and then the hedge came into sight and the pasture land beyond it. The stile itself was a simple affair of three rails and two stepping-pieces set in the low, straggly hedge.

Franklin steered his foot between the brambles that trailed across and stepped down on the other side. He smiled as he picked up something from the ground, then took out the other stubs and showed them to Dryden.

"A trail of your cigarette ends. Maroulis, with the red band."

"Dear me, yes!" He looked very confused till Travers laughed.

"Henry, you're in the same class as myself when it comes to sleuthing."

"I'm afraid I was rather careless," Dryden remarked ruefully. "Not that it matters, I suppose?"

"I don't suppose it does," said Franklin amusedly. "Unless, of course, the wood was set alight and they'd traced it to you." His face straightened. "Now, Mr. Dryden, would you mind coming over here and showing me precisely how the body lay when the man found it. We'll put this sheet to protect your clothes. This stick will do for the gun."

Travers leaned on the stile and watched. "Seems perfectly natural," was his verdict when it was all over. "The stile's a bit tottery, and these brambles are enough to trip an elephant."

"It certainly *might* have been an accident," agreed Franklin. "And what about clothes, Mr. Dryden? Were they particularly dirty or disordered?"

"Neither. Damp, of course. The knees were a bit dirty, but that was probably how he fell."

Travers picked up the tin of solution. "And what about the dog?"

"Never mind the dog," said Franklin. "Let's get rid of one thing before beginning another."

"Good enough," said Travers amiably. "We've agreed it might be an accident. What next?"

"Let's look at it in the light of sheer horse-sense," said Franklin. "If it was an accident, I might as well go home. Mr. Dryden isn't going to employ me to discover what he already knows to be the verdict of a jury. To say that it might have been an accident is absurd. But Mr. Dryden himself insists that it wasn't suicide. All that's left, then, for us to discuss is murder, so we'll consider that. If it was murder it was either planned or unplanned. Either the murderer lay in wait here for him or else he met him here by accident. Any objections to assuming the murder was planned?"

"Yes," said Dryden. "He was killed with his own gun."

"How do you know?"

"There was a discharged cartridge in it."

"And a full one?"

Dryden shook his head. "Only the empty one. The left barrel."

Franklin raised his eyebrows. "That's interesting. If a man's going shooting he slips in two cartridges. . . . I wonder."

"Wonder what?" asked Travers brazenly.

"Well, one cartridge might have been used for shooting the dog, and if so the murderer would have removed it." Travers smiled. "Then why not exhume the dog?"

"All in good time," said Franklin imperturbably. "The dog won't disappear, and the thread of a perfectly good argument might. And now this question of the gun. Any other guns in the village?"

"Only two," said Dryden, "and they're accounted for. The farmer and his brother-in-law who were shooting in the hedges round the farm that morning, if you remember."

"Good! Then we'll assume he was killed with his own gun. But there couldn't have been a struggle for possession or his clothes would have been disordered."

"The murderer might have asked to see the gun," suggested Travers. "I know that means he was an acquaintance of the dead man; still, he asked to see it, and that's how he got hold of it. He faked the body to make it appear an accident."

"Right or not," said Franklin, "we'll discard any theory of a struggle, because it's not borne out by the state of the clothes, and as Yeoman was a powerful man there'd have been very much of a scrap before anybody wrenched the gun away from him. But to get on. The shot's been fired. The body's placed in position and the gun's alongside it. But the dog keeps yapping at the murderer. By the way, did the gardener hear it?"

"Never a sound. He neither saw nor heard the dog after it went through the gate with its master."

"Well, it mightn't have made much noise. It might merely have set itself and shown its teeth—"

"It wouldn't have done that if the murderer was well known to it," interrupted Travers.

"Then why was it killed?" asked Dryden.

Travers shrugged his shoulders.

"We'll assume the dog *was* about to come for him," went on Franklin, "so he groped for the gun, let the dog have the second barrel, whipped out the cartridge, replaced the gun, then looked round to see where to put the dog's body.... And where was that?"

The question was so dramatic that Dryden looked startled. Then he pointed to a holly clump twenty yards back in the wood and ten yards off the path.

"Just behind that clump on the far side."

Franklin treated himself to a satisfied nod. "The very place. He nipped over the stile with the body, scraped a hole in the soft leaf-mould out of sight behind the clump and then sneaked out of the wood."

Travers stooped for the tin of solution. "Which brings us to the exhumation of the dog."

"Just a moment," said Franklin. "We've got a bit muddled. We're assuming the murder was unplanned and arose out of a casual encounter. We haven't discussed the other theory—that it might have been deliberately planned." He looked round at the lie of the land.

"That presupposes two things; first that the murderer knew he was coming this way at a certain time. What about it, Mr. Dryden? Had he regular shooting days and hours?"

Dryden shook his head. "Even his wife didn't know he was going out shooting that morning. The only one who happened to see him go was the gardener."

"Did he see the gardener?"

"The gardener said he didn't." He noticed the look that flitted across Franklin's face. "The gardener didn't do it. You've only to see him to know that."

"You should know," said Franklin. "But we'll deal with the second point. Whether or not the murderer knew he was coming this way at that particular time, he must have concealed himself. He lay in wait—but where? There's no tree large enough near the track. This hedge would have been leafless—and it's too thin. There isn't a ditch or a hollow. Also the dog'd have nosed him out." He looked at them for confirmation. "I don't think the murder could possibly have been planned, do you?"

"I quite agree," said Dryden. "And if you'll pardon my saying so, Mr. Franklin, I've tried to think out something of the sort for myself. One thing I've always come up against. If the murderer fired those shots—indeed, if he committed murder at all—he ran a very big risk. The hedge at Manor Lane is very gapped, as you saw. The older women often come here sticking—dead boughs, you know. I know the lane's a quarter of a mile away from here."

"May I put up something?" Travers hooked off his glasses and blinked away as he polished them. "Assume Yeoman met here by accident the man who killed him. That man asked to try the weight of the gun, then drew his attention to something over there, and when he turned his head, shot him. I admit it would have to be a quick piece of work, and I don't quite see how the bullets were to enter behind Yeoman's ear and pursue a course parallel to the ground—unless the murderer were well above him; standing on the stile, for instance. But once he had fired, the murderer was as safe as houses, *whoever came up.*"

"How on earth do you make that out?"

"Because he could say he had run up *just in time to see Yeoman kill himself.*"

"But that supposes he knew Yeoman was likely to kill himself."

"And it supposes," added Dryden, "that he knew his story would be believed."

"Well, why not? Do you suppose the whole of this gossipy village didn't know he was in serious financial difficulties. The fact was evident as soon as he reduced expenses." He looked at them inquiringly. "I think that theory holds good, don't you? Even when he shot the dog he knew he was perfectly safe."

"Why?"

"Well, nobody knew which shot was fired first, so to speak. He could have said that he saw Yeoman kill his dog—to accompany him to the happy hunting-ground, as it were—and then shoot himself. All he had to do was to bury the dog, fake the suicide and get out. If he met anybody he might have pretended to be bringing the news of Yeoman's death." Travers stooped once again to the tin. "All of which may be verified by the dog!"

"Right," said Franklin. "As you say, the dog's the main thing. Was there much of a smell when you uncovered it, Mr. Dryden?"

"To tell the truth, I didn't notice. I just uncovered enough to know what it was, then I spread the mould over agin."

There was no wind down there in the wood. Franklin handed Travers the powder, then put on rubber gloves.

"Now, Mr. Dryden, we'll see what we shall see."

Dryden showed the exact spot behind the clump. Franklin spread out the sheet, laid the sack ready and sprinkled the chloride lavishly. Then he got to his knees and began scooping out the mould. In less than a minute he stopped.

"How deep is this animal buried?"

"Just below the surface," said Dryden, and peered round the evergreen clump. Then he stared at Travers.

"Why, it . . . it doesn't seem to be there!"

Franklin got up and dusted his knees. "Unless you've made a mistake about the site, Mr. Dryden, it certainly isn't there." He smiled wryly. "All that there is . . . well, there's two things."

"What?" asked Travers quickly.

Franklin smiled. "Another of Mr. Dryden's cigarette ends—and a certain amount of smell."

CHAPTER IV
FORGET-ME-NOTS

TRAVERS PUT his usual question: "Well, what now?"

Franklin recovered from his disappointment with extraordinary rapidity; indeed, his "Now we know where we are" seemed, under the circumstances, just the least bit unnecessary, till he enlarged on the theme.

"The dog's gone, therefore somebody was interested in seeing it gone. If it wasn't a casual removal, then we're entitled to assume it wasn't a casual death. You remember Mr. Dryden told us it was assumed at the inquest that somebody had stolen the dog. If the dog died at that person's hands, or if he got the wind up and poisoned it, where would he have buried it? Well, if he chose this wood it'd have been up there by the lane, just inside one of the gaps. The fact that it was buried here—and Mr. Dryden knows that to be a fact—proves it was buried just after the murder."

"Then you're sure of murder," said Dryden.

"Not by any means," Franklin told him. "I'm more inclined that way than I was when we first set foot inside here; all the same, I'm a long way off certain. All I'm getting at at the moment is that somebody must have been interested in the dog and where it was buried—sufficiently interested to have been aware of your own movements, Mr. Dryden. Also, it's not too much to assume that the dog's been removed because it might have been proved from the corpse that Yeoman didn't die in quite the way the jury imagined."

Dryden looked down his nose at the reference to his own investigations. "I'm afraid I've made rather a mess of things—"

"Not at all," Franklin assured him. "The probability is that this person paid a precautionary visit to the dog's grave and there saw your cigarette end—or shall I say ends! That alarmed him. Whoever it was, therefore, must have known the cigarettes were a brand smoked by yourself. All the same, I don't think there's any danger to you."

"Danger?"

Franklin smiled. "Another billion-to-one chance. If there is a murderer and he thinks his neck is in any danger from you, then he might think of removing you too."

Dryden drew himself up instinctively. "I don't think I'm particularly perturbed."

"All the same, Henry, it's just as well to know," said Travers genially. "And in that context, why not fill up the excavation and get out of the line of fire?"

Franklin stopped him just in time. "Wait a moment. I'll collect all the soil that was under the body. If it was sufficiently decomposed, and if it really was shot, a pellet or two might have dropped through."

He put on the gloves again, scattered the lime and filled the small bag. The whole of the solution was emptied over it till the neighbourhood reeked of chloride; then the surplus was trodden out and a parcel made with the waterproof sheet.

"Put the empty tin in the hole," said Travers. "If the bloke pays another visit, it'll give him a nasty shock."

He superintended the job himself, fetched more mould and smoothed the site over.

"And what now?"

"Home, I think," said Franklin. "Unless Mr. Dryden can think of anything else?"

Dryden seemed hopelessly undecided what to do. "The whole thing is inexplicable to me. I mean, the dog's removed and . . . well, you think it's murder. The curious thing is, you know, that now we're really faced with something, I can't possibly believe it. Who on earth would want to kill Tom Yeoman? He couldn't have had an enemy in the world."

"You never know," said Travers oracularly. "The best of us have skeletons in the cupboard."

"To come nearer home." Franklin lowered his voice. "There's that matter of Ashley Mould and the quarrel over the dog. He's right on the spot, as it were—"

"Quarter of a mile away," put in Travers.

"Well, on the spot comparatively. He's only to cross the road and he's in the wood. By the same argument he's the one who could get out of it the easiest."

Dryden began to look anxious, as if afraid of that insinuation developing into some definite action; and while he was hesitating Travers had a suggestion to make, and he made it very diffidently.

"I take it nothing can be done at the moment. I mean, we're absolutely up a gum-tree, now there's no evidence, but in the meanwhile, Henry, I wonder if you'd mind my calling on Ashley Mould?"

Franklin was used to Travers's apparent eccentricities, but even he was taken aback. Dryden was positively startled.

"But, my dear fellow, I told you. . . . It's out of the question!"

"In what way, Henry?"

"Well, I absolutely refuse to accompany you myself, and surely you can't go alone."

Travers smiled knowingly. "You never can tell. I rather think I can manage it."

Franklin tucked his package under his arm and began to move off up the slope. "I don't think it's wise to stay here. All the same, Ludo, I don't see what you're driving at."

Travers pretended surprise. "I'm not driving at anything, my dear fellow. I'm merely proposing to call on Ashley Mould, who, as Dryden here told us, has practically recovered from his protracted fit of the sulks. It will be a private visit for the purposes of talking art. I suggest, therefore, that you two people take the car back and leave me to walk."

"Just what do you expect to find?" asked Dryden.

"Why . . . Ashley Mould!"

"I see," said Dryden dubiously. "You merely wish to look at him."

"That's it. I shan't drop any bricks, Henry, if that's your anxiety." He smiled ingratiatingly. "You know, from what you said at lunch I rather gathered that you were anxious to have him looked over."

"So I am," said Dryden quickly, but he shook his head all the same. "You don't see my point of view. Everything's so difficult."

Franklin knew the trouble. Dryden the magistrate and Dryden the friend of the dead man Yeoman were two vastly different people. The friend had been worried, driven to distraction by the doubts that had tormented him; the magistrate was aghast at the possibilities which an inquiry threatened—the scandal, the furtive questionings, everything, in fact, that was at variance with his own quietly ordered life. That was why Franklin poured oil on the waters. Travers, he said, would be viewing Mould from a perfectly disinterested angle. Once Travers got to know Mould he would have a foothold among the very people who had been causing a certain amount of bewilderment in Dryden's mind. At the house, then, Travers remained behind and Franklin drove off sedately in the Bentley.

Travers was feeling on remarkably good terms with himself. What he was to look for in Ashley Mould, should he succeed in seeing him, he hadn't the least idea. All he knew at the moment was that the visit meant a mild excitement, and breaking new ground, and a chance for Machiavellism of a mild and not too dangerous kind. All the same, it was with an air of sober unconcern that he opened the front gate and strolled to the twenty-yard-distant door.

He knocked, then looked about him. The garden seemed in a state of heartbreaking forlornness. What had once been a centre-piece of turf was overgrown with weeds and coarse grass, and as for the flower-beds that surrounded it, they seemed past praying for. Still, lawns and garden weren't everybody's money. Mould might be too busy a man to tend to them himself or too wrapped up in his own grievances to be aware that anything was wrong.

Having made those reflections Travers knocked again. There seemed to be no sound from inside, and the house had that peculiar atmosphere of emptiness about it. Another knock and a minute's wait and Travers was looking round for the back entrance. There it was—a door set in a partition to the right, and a gravel path leading round from where he stood.

But as soon as he set foot inside that door he had the shock of his life. In front of him was a forty-yard garden, broad as the whole frontage to the road. At the far end, where the hedge ran alongside Manor Path, was the studio—a wooden building with a glass roof. The centre of that garden was lawn as yellow and straggly as a neglected meadow, and all round it was what had once been a border, from six to nine feet wide. Here and there could be seen green clumps that were perennials in various stages of growth. But what made his eyes nearly pop from his head were dense masses of blue that now filled the whole of those surrounding borders. Forget-me-nots they seemed to be, so thickly packed that the few perennials that rose above them must have forced their way through to light and air.

He knocked at the back door, then turned for another look One part, at least, of Dryden's information had been wide of the mark—unless it had been the front garden to which he'd been referring, and not the back. True that grass needed cutting, but instead of the garden being neglected it was sheer perfection. Only a genius could have achieved that mass of gorgeous blue. It was dazzling and yet amazingly harmonious. Against the green of the hedge and the blue of the sky the effect was that of blue-bells in a vista of wood. And then Travers realized he had been standing here for a matter of minutes and there had been no answer to his knock.

His eye fell on that building that backed the final splash of blue. Perhaps Mould was in the studio—in any case there'd be no harm in having a look. The flowers straggled across the weedy path, so he chose the grass. Just short of the studio he turned to survey again that mass of celestial blue as it melted in some uncanny way into the subtle mauve of the walls and roof of the old house, and as he wondered at which end the door would be, and stepped down to the path that led to a gate and the meadow, he found himself looking through a window. Again he stopped short.

Within a foot of the glass and standing on a pedestal table was a clay figure at which the sculptor had probably been working. It was more than a bust since it began just above a hairy waist, and its height would be about ten inches. The face was the face of Lucifer, the forehead tipped with horns, and its expression either overwhelming agony or diabolical hate. One thing was certain— the effect was devilish and repulsive.

It would be no more than a second or two that his eyes rested on that amazing figure, then they went beyond it to the back of the one large room. Two people were there, a woman and a man. The woman he could see clearly, though her head was bent back and her eyes were shut. Of the man all he saw was broad, stooping shoulders and a frizzy mass of hair as bald in the middle as if it had been tonsured. Travers backed to the grass again, then went almost at a run across to the partition door. A pause for one last peep at that heavenly blue of the forget-me-nots and he turned to survey the contrast of that overgrown and neglected front. A shrug and a grimace and he slipped across the grass to the front gate, where a precautionary peep showed the coast was clear. Five minutes later he was back at Old House.

Before the Bentley had reached the end of Manor Lane Franklin could see that Dryden was still rather nervous about what was likely to happen at Manor Cottage.

"I don't think we need worry about Travers," said Franklin, who always had to do a chuckle somewhere inside when he thought of his colleague's infinite stratagems. "I very much doubt if Mould will throw him out of the House."

Dryden smiled faintly at the thought, then his face fell again. "I hope he'll be tactful. We really mustn't begin arousing suspicion till we've something very definite to bring forward."

"Travers knows that as well as we do," Franklin assured him. "He won't let us down."

The other seemed relieved; at any rate he made a comment on the weather and pointed out the poles that carried the electric wires. Then from the gate of the cottage next his own an old lady was seen to be looking out. She turned back, then looked again, as if uncertain of something.

"Pull up a moment, will you?" said Dryden. "I'd like you to meet Miss Faithful."

As Franklin got out he saw the daintiest old lady he had ever fallen in love with at first sight. She must have been well over seventy, and her cheeks were almost a transparent white, and though her hair was like snow her eyes seemed quick and alert. Her clothes were as charmingly old-fashioned as herself, and her voice had an elusive quality that was old-fashioned too.

"I thought it must be you, Henry," she said as Dryden went towards the gate. "And yet I couldn't recognize the car."

Dryden laughed and waved back at Franklin. "You don't know Mr. Franklin, do you? This is Miss Faithful, my neighbour. She's going to show us her garden."

Franklin thought for a moment she was going to curtsy, but it was only one of her quick little motions. She fluttered back from the gate to let them through.

"There's nothing much to see except the bulbs. And such a lot of weeds. Somehow I haven't felt equal to them this year."

Dryden was all concern at once. "Not your heart again?"

"Nothing very much. It varies, you know. Hearts are like that, don't you think so, Mr. Franklin?"

He felt strangely gratified that she'd remembered his name, though he was unprepared for the question.

"Well, you see, I haven't a heart. . . . . I mean medically. But I'm sorry to hear you've been unwell."

She smiled gently. "But I'm not—really. When the sun gets stronger I'm going to set about these weeds in earnest."

An old-fashioned basket, quaint as herself, a trowel and a pair of gloves were lying on the path that led through the tiny border to the front door. The cottage with its creeper and roses looked dainty too, so did the late daffodils and the aubretias and the tulips in full bloom under the windows. But Dryden wouldn't stay to tea—much too early, he said; besides, he'd never dream of giving her all that trouble. Franklin thought what an unusual couple they made, each evocative of an earlier generation.

"You must bring Mr. Franklin in again, Henry," she said as they stood by the gate.

"I'd love to come," said Franklin, and meant it.

Dryden shook his head at her and smiled roguishly. "Mr. Franklin doesn't know that it's all wicked and sinful pride. You want him to see the wireless set."

Modernity and Miss Faithful seemed strange bedfellows, and Franklin said so in rather a different way.

"But this is something special," laughed Dryden. "It's the only all-electric set in the village, and we're all very proud of it. How many stations is it you can get?"

She refused to be drawn and shook her head at them as if they were a couple of schoolboys.

Dryden turned for a last wave as the car moved off, and Franklin couldn't resist the question: "Is she a distant relation by any chance?"

"Lord, no!" His laugh was as burly and healthy as himself. "I sometimes wish she were. She often reminds me she saw me an hour after I was born. She's a lovable soul."

"Perfectly delightful. . . . She kept house for her brother?"

"That's right. How old do you think she is?"

"Seventy?"

"Nearer eighty. Mind you, she's aged a lot recently. I happen to know that heart of hers is much worse than she imagines. That's why I didn't like to worry her about tea, and Martha didn't seem to be about."

"Martha?"

"The woman who does the housework. She shares her with Marian Crome."

They took Wilson and the package of leafmould to the main road to wait for the London bus. When they got back to Old House there was Travers sprawling in an easy chair. Dryden pushed the bell for tea and asked what had happened.

"Nothing," said Travers brightly. "The gentleman wasn't seeing visitors—officially."

"Why the 'officially'?" asked Franklin.

"Ah!" said Travers. "That's too long a tale—and here's tea."

Jimson deposited the heavy tray and began arranging cups and things. Dryden scurried him off at once.

"You're really a most exasperating person sometimes, you know, Ludo," he said. "Any sugar?"

"Two," said Travers. "And the callous effrontery with which you bring that charge against me, Henry, distresses me very much. You're the person who's exasperating. You've deliberately misled me on two points."

It was hard to say if he intended to be taken seriously Dryden stared at him.

"I say, I'm very sorry. . . ."

Travers helped himself to toast. "That's all right, Henry. But you did give me to understand that Mould had rather been off work for some time, didn't you?"

"On the contrary," said Franklin, "Mr. Dryden distinctly assured us that he was getting normal again."

"The explanation is accepted," said Travers gravely. "You'll both be glad to hear that he's working again. He's modelled a remarkably fine body and head. A small thing but masterly."

"What of?"

"Well, some would say one thing and some another I'm pretty sure it was Old Nick."

Dryden's eyes opened. Franklin laughed.

"But I'm perfectly serious," protested Travers. "But with regard to that other point, Henry, you can't deny that you told us his garden was a wilderness."

"Isn't it?"

"If it is, it's the sort of wilderness I'd like to own. Think of forget-me-nots; odd little plants scattered about among the tulips. Not very impressive, are they? Then think of mass after mass of them, banks of them, yards of them; forty yards of blue on your left hand, forty yards on your right, and then another bank in front of that studio. Stupendous, Henry, and you spoke of a wilderness!"

Then, of course, he had to say what had happened. One thing only was omitted—the second person in the studio-room.

"That was certainly Mould," Dryden said. "The bald spot on his head is uncommonly like a tonsure. But those forget-me-nots puzzle me very much. Of course he might have sown them in memory of his wife."

Travers smiled. "You told us, Henry, that the relationship between the couple wasn't such as to suggest he would sow forget-me-nots, even if he were half tight and maudlin."

"Well"—and he hesitated—"I can't say they were a demonstrative couple. I'd even say he was rather off-hand at times. Yet I must admit he was desperately upset at her death. I never saw a man more struck down."

"That may be so. Wilfred told me he'd sulk for days if she dared to disagree with him—"

"If we must discuss this horticultural riddle of yours," put in Franklin, "might I suggest that as the previous occupier was a gardener, the flowers are the result of self-seeding coupled with neglect. Moreover, Mould might have chucked some seed broadcast to save himself the trouble of touching those borders at all. But what was that you were saying about Old Nick?"

"Merely that he'd completed a portrait of the gentleman. After all, we can't very well quarrel with him about that."

"What I can't understand is why you didn't call after all," said Dryden. "You say he was in the studio."

Travers looked up. "Perhaps I was rather foolish. I got a sudden feeling, a sort of psychic revelation, that the occasion wasn't really propitious. Besides, I thought of something better. I'll be more conventional and call on Monday morning."

"Why Monday?" asked Franklin.

"Pure kindness of heart," said Travers. "I'm calling back here for you then to take you to town. By the way, will you have the report on the leafmould by then?"

"To-morrow probably."

"I see. Well, the idea is this. His brother told me he was a man who flourishes on adulation, and Henry has rather confirmed the same thing. This morning, as I told you, I managed to acquire an example of his work. If it hadn't been for the sudden impulse that made me come away without seeing him this afternoon, I should probably have traded on that. As it is, I shall write a letter from Pulvery, recall an imaginary meeting, say I think he is a genius; add that I have only one example of his work, but can't resist the chance of seeing him as I happen to be reasonably near. The letter will reach him first thing on Monday morning. If my guess is correct, by the end of the morning we'll be sworn brothers. The latest news about Old Nick and the forget-me-nots should be at your disposal—as well as anything else I happen to acquire."

Dryden looked at him queerly, then smiled. "You've certainly got a way with you, Ludo. Though how far it will lead us . . ." He shrugged the rest.

"That's all right then." He looked at his watch, then got up. "I think I'll be getting along now. What's your own programme for to-morrow?"

"I thought I'd take Mr. Franklin to see a few people," Dryden told him—none too confidently.

"That'll be very nice for him," said Travers. "By the time you've finished you'll be the unblushingest liar in Bableigh."

Dryden wondered—then thought he saw it. "You don't mean to say you've been making up all that you've been telling us about Mould!"

Travers smiled. "Now you're hurting me again. Highly coloured, perhaps, but not made up!" He changed as suddenly to earnest. "One thing I wish you would do. Leave Mould to me. Don't approach him at all."

"But how could I do anything else?"

"Merely a precaution," said Travers enigmatically. "By the way, when trying to recall all you told us yesterday afternoon, Henry, I found I couldn't visualize Miss Crome. Is she tallish? Dark hair cropped closely at the back?"

"That's it. Rather masculine in appearance."

Travers nodded. Franklin thought he saw through that particular subterfuge, and when Dryden left the room ahead of them, looked inquiringly. Travers whispered heavily:

"She was in that studio . . . surreptitiously . . . with Mould!"

Franklin's eyes opened.

"They were embracing . . . rather enthusiastically!"

He nodded with a world of meaning, then began to prattle nothings for the benefit of Dryden.

CHAPTER V
BABLEIGH ON PARADE

FRANKLIN AWOKE the following morning with a wonder what the day would have in store. His evening had shown him Dryden the host, the excellent companion, the formidable chess-player and the raconteur, and of Henry Dryden the author and latter-day mystic nothing whatever had obviously been visible. Franklin, then, was already of Travers's mind, that Dryden was a man extremely sane in outlook and sympathies, and little likely to suffer from delusions or hysteria. If, then, Dryden was about to exhibit certain neighbours of his whose very presence and habitations were enough to fill him with immediate and unmistakable aversions, then he—John Franklin—looked like being in for an unusual time. One of those people looked particularly intriguing—and that was Marian Crome.

Dryden himself awoke with some words of Travers's in his mind; a prophecy that he now knew to be true. He was indeed about to become the biggest liar in Bableigh. He and Franklin had gone into the matter overnight, and it was late before they had settled on the nature and sequence of the whitish lies that would serve not only as the reason for Franklin's being in the village at all, but also for the particular reason for the visit that was being paid to any individual person. The opening move, they decided, must be a lie clad in the very whitest of garments. Mr. Franklin really came to have a look at Manor House. After that conversations could reasonably be expected to look to themselves.

But if Dryden was unhappy about those subterfuges, justifiable though they were, he was perfectly happy about Franklin. He liked his blunt sincerity, his absence of pose, his caution and his frank confession of limitations. Then there were all sorts of unexpected and likeable touches that made him understand why a wealthy intellectual like Travers should confess that Franklin was the one man with whom he always felt at home.

It was after breakfast, when Dryden was showing him over the main gardens, that Franklin made his first mention of shop for that day.

"I'd rather like to have a look at that extraordinary garden of Mould's if we can manage it not too conspicuously."

"Perfectly easy, my dear fellow," said Dryden. "Have a look at that map if you've got it on you."

Everything was very easy, as Franklin could see for himself. A back path led from the gate near where they were standing, past Miss Faithful's back hedge, and emerged by the vicarage just along the Northurst Road, a few yards past the acute angle made by that road and Manor Lane. If you crossed the road then, and went through the churchyard, Manor Path went over the meadows and skirted the back of Mould's studio. From there it went on to rejoin the Northurst Road in the neighbourhood of Windyridge.

It was about ten o'clock when the two set out by the back way. Franklin stopped for a moment outside Dryden's gate to admire the view across the north valley, then followed his host along the path. As they reached the trim hedge that bounded Miss Faithful's garden, a woman suddenly emerged from the gate with a heavy pail. In the act of scattering its contents beyond the path, she caught sight of Dryden and checked the action—but it was too late. Then she smiled sheepishly.

"Well, Martha, you're doing it again, I see," said Dryden, none too seriously.

"Yes, sir . . . I forgot, and that's the truth."

"Well, you mustn't forget," he told her in his best official manner. "You're encouraging flies, you know, and making a bad smell. Bury the rubbish if you can't burn it."

"Yes, sir." She was so fragile that Dryden could have lifted her with one hand. The face was thin to emaciation, and the high cheek-bones were flushed. As she stood there wiping her fingers nervously on her apron, Franklin had to smile at the sight of the law confronting so desperate an offender.

Dryden nodded. "You must remember what I tell you, Martha. And how're you keeping nowadays? Pretty fair?"

"I can't grumble, sir. The winter's gone, and that's my bad time."

"I know. I know." He nodded again, paternally this time. "You must take care of yourself, you know."

"That was Martha Frail," he explained to Franklin as they passed on. "Miss Faithful, as I believe I mentioned shares her with

Marian Crome. Nice woman in her way, and a good worker, only she will throw the household rubbish where it's the least trouble."

"Consumptive, is she?"

"Yes." He shook his head. "She had a spell in a sanatorium last year—I ought to say that Parish insisted on it and paid all the expenses. They patched her up, but—" He shrugged his shoulders ominously.

They skirted the eight-foot wall of the vicarage garden and came out at the road. Franklin looked left to the small cluster of houses.

"We'll come that way back," said Dryden, and crossed to the churchyard gate. They made a steady progress along the path—the stones were far too interesting to be hurried past—and then just through the meadow gate Dryden stopped.

"I ought to have asked you if you'd like to see the inside of the church."

"When we come back, I think, don't you? Those fellows seem to be enjoying themselves!"

He pointed to a small collection of urchins who were playing cricket with a home-made bat and a pile of coats for wickets. Then Dryden stopped again to identify the backs of the gardens for him; that one was the inn, that the shop, and the very last cottage of all on the right-hand side of the Northurst Road was, if he remembered, Martha Frail's, where she lived with an only child, her husband having died two years before. Franklin could see the path she had worn as a short cut from her back gate to Manor Path and Windyridge.

"The husband was consumptive, too?"

"He was," said Dryden. "It's a peculiar thing, you know, that theirs is the only case of tuberculosis in this immediate district, and his family and hers were both afflicted with the same thing. The results can be imagined. They had three children, and two have already died of it. The little girl that's left looks certain to go the same way."

"And I suppose all her brothers and sisters and her husband's brothers and sisters have married, and are filling the district with tubercular descendants?"

"Not so bad as that," said Dryden. "Martha and her small daughter are the only ones left." His voice lowered. "We're now at the garden."

The hedge which shut them off from Manor Lane now split in two, and the path curved with it. The roof of the studio could be seen, and then the gate which led to Mould's garden. The two men paused instinctively before they reached it, and through the opening caught a glimpse of the untidy lawn and then of the border that surrounded it, and though Travers had prepared them for something out of the ordinary, the sight of that perfectly amazing bank of blue came as a shock. There was something unnaturally fresh and dainty about such a mass of colour, and something incongruous in its uniformity.

Franklin moved on past the gate and the length of the studio to get a more comprehensive view through the hedge, then found it too dense to be seen through. He looked round to catch Dryden's eye, and they moved on again.

"Well, what did you think of it?" he asked. "Ever see anything more extraordinary?"

"Remarkable," said Dryden. "Like seeing an albino with immense blue eyes."

Franklin smiled. "And a blue necktie. I don't know whether I liked it or not. Of course we didn't see it as Travers did."

Dryden tugged at his beard. "It's curious, as you say. A small thing, but typical of all the small things that have been making me uneasy these last few months, Mr. Franklin. . . By the way, we're almost at Windyridge. I wonder if I remember what I'm to say."

Windyridge was thatched, and its timbering lay concealed beneath yellowish plaster. What had looked like a hole in the roof turned out to be a huge window that was taking the place of a dormer.

"That's her studio," said Dryden. "We'll go round by the back, then you'll see all there is to see."

That turned out to be very little. The long garden ran north and was nearly all grass, and a large, brick outhouse stood well clear of the kitchen. Marian Crome came out to meet them, and seemed unaffectedly pleased to see Dryden.

"I saw you coming across the meadows and I couldn't believe my eyes!"

Dryden took the hand she had extended long before she reached them. He looked what she thought was guilty, and what Franklin knew to be uncomfortable, as he introduced the stranger and said his piece.

"So we're likely to be neighbours!"

Nothing affected about that, Franklin decided. Dryden's term "spinsterish" had surely been rather harsh. And she was a remarkably attractive woman. "Unfortunately, no," he said. "The Manor's far too large for me. But I'd very much like to see your pictures, if I may."

Then all at once she became girlish, and the masculinity of her appearance made it the more embarrassing.

"Of course you may. Mr. Dryden is a horrible man. He says the most monstrous things about my work."

"Come, come!" protested Dryden.

"Well, you think them. That's the same thing." She gave him a look that had not a touch of malice in it. "Of course you don't want to see them?"

They were already in the brick-floored kitchen. Dryden produced a hearty laugh and his cigarette-case.

"I'll stay here in front of this jolly little fire. You and Mr. Franklin run along."

He drew up the grandfather chair alongside the sleeping cat. She made a face at him and led Franklin off to the room she called the lounge, where about a dozen things were to be seen on the walls. As she explained, she worked only when she really had an overwhelming urge to put something on canvas; moreover, she worked very slowly, and some of her things were in town, and quite a few she had given away. She was afraid she didn't take her art too seriously, being little more than an amateur.

Franklin had an anxious time as he nodded at this and postured before that and dexterously avoided speaking; and yet he was amazed at the ease with which he could distinguish those particular pictures that had caused all the trouble. The landscapes, it was not too hard to see, were landscapes—the kind of things a child might have done and coloured crudely. But the others—there were two of them—were so utterly inexplicable that they might have been elaborate jokes. She looked at him rather anxiously as they stopped at the "Aphrodite"—that mound of ochre with its red daub which had so upset Mrs. Yeoman. Franklin felt he ought to say something.

"How do you get the inspiration for this sort of—er—subject?"

She clasped her fingers and looked at it, head on one side.

"I couldn't really say. It's just the urge, you know. When it comes I feel I have to let myself go—just let the brush do its own work." She waved her hand at the ghastly result. "I can no more explain it than you can. It's a sort of personal inspiration. Poets get it, you know."

"Yes," said Franklin feebly. "I suppose they do. But it's not everybody's money."

She seemed most thankful—or at least so he thought—that he'd said nothing worse. And then when the circuit of the walls had been made she assumed a sort of jauntiness.

"Well, that's the lot. I don't know if any of them are any good to you."

Franklin hesitated artistically. "I very much doubt it. You know what people are. It's difficult to see with the eyes of one's clients."

"You're a dealer?"

"Hardly that," said Franklin vaguely, and made a step in the direction of the kitchen. "Still, it was extraordinarily good of you to let me see them."

Dryden rose as they came in, and picked up his hat.

"You're not going already?" she asked. "Let me make you some coffee."

"Very good of you," said Dryden, "but Mr. Franklin is in rather a hurry and we have to make some other calls."

"And why haven't you been before, you naughty man?"

Franklin winced, but Dryden stood up to it well. "I'm afraid I've been rather remiss. But I must see more of you." He sighed diplomatically. "Time seems so short nowadays."

She walked with them to the front gate, holding in her arms that fluffy cat which had been sleeping on the rug before the kitchen fire. Twenty yards along the road towards the village they looked back and received a last wave of the hand.

"A great friend of the Moulds, was she?" asked Franklin out of nowhere.

"Why yes, she was. I think she knew them before they came here. What'd you think of her?"

"In a way I was disappointed," Franklin told him. "I was expecting to see a mannish creature, fingers daubed with paint; the ultra-Bohemian type, in fact." He smiled to himself. "She's quite a taking woman, in a way—and most contradictory."

"How do you mean?"

"Well, she's a fine figure of a woman, masculine in type and with just that deep voice. She wore a collar and tie and that close-fitting jumper thing, tweed skirt, rough stockings and brogues, and her hair was cut close at the back. That was one side of her. But she had two little curls like fronds, coming coquettishly from behind her ears, and she had on that charming bead necklace and had used some adorable scent. And she had a voice rather more soprano than her natural one that she assumed when she wished to be less masculine." He gave Dryden a quizzical look. "If I were making a wild guess I'd say that woman is preparing to emerge from a period of masculinity. She's re-feminizing herself. And why?"

Dryden seemed amused at both theory and question. "I'm no authority. What do you suggest yourself?"

"Well, she might be in love!"

Dryden chuckled. "I can't imagine a situation like that."

Franklin joined him hypocritically. "Still, as Travers says, you never know. A dangerous age the forties—at least, so I'm told."

Dryden was still chuckling as they slowed down before another house that looked like a double cottage, cunningly restored. The small front garden only was visible, the back sloping south down the incline.

"Miss Rose's place?"

Dryden nodded and his face grew solemn in a flash. "The same opening, and I'm to mention that we've seen Miss Crome and now you insist on seeing the famous rock-garden. Is that right?"

An untidy-looking servant-girl showed them in and at the same moment there was an outburst of yapping and a couple of white Pomeranians came bounding into the hall. Franklin, who had a horror of pet dogs, drew back as the girl began to shoo them away; then a voice was heard from somewhere beyond.

"Peter! Bingo! Stop it at once, you bad dogs!"

The owner of the voice arrived with its echoes. She was a plump little person, fluffy-haired, all rings and bracelets, and the perfect owner of a voice which had recalled a stage parent mechanically chiding a family which makes no longer even the pretence of being interested. She raised her hands with rapture on seeing Dryden.

"Well, what a surprise! So long since we've seen you."

Dryden said his recitation. Franklin washed his hands once more of the Manor House, and claimed to have an intense admiration for rock-gardens.

"Don't tell me you're one of those clever people who know all the names of things!" She made a gesture of helplessness that was most amusing. "I always forget them. Besides"—with perfect inconsequence—"the garden's very trying. I don't seem to have the energy I had—and my maid's so stupid. This tiresome weather, don't you think?"

However, from somewhere she summoned sufficient energy to take them out to the back. Then she was suddenly all of a flutter again and positively hustled Dryden round to the corner of the house.

"Do tell me, now. We've had such arguments about it. Is there room here for a teeny weeny garage, or not? Just an Austin, you know?"

"Heaps and heaps," Dryden assured her. He smiled. "So you're going to have a car! Do you all the good in the world."

That seemed to please her enormously and she prattled away down the path and round and round the mazes of the rock-garden. That, frankly, was a disappointment. It was definitely unfinished, and shamefully neglected, and even Franklin could see it had been too elaborately planned and too haphazardly constructed. And that was a pity, for here and there it had clumps of wonderful colour. Still, he and Dryden followed discreetly at the heels of its owner, who talked unceasingly and went off at the most amusing tangents, and Franklin had quite an enjoyable time, though when it was all over and they were back in the drawing-room again, it was much more domestic and far less entertaining. Poor Dryden grimaced and grappled with the obvious, and Franklin's head swam with his efforts to find answers. When at last they were clear of the house he let out a breath.

"I know," said Dryden feelingly. "I fear she's a very great strain at the moment. And yet I do assure you that when she first came down here with Harriet Blunt she was a pleasant, amiable soul."

Franklin suddenly laughed. "I know who she reminds me of—Mrs. Feather. Perhaps you're not acquainted with that good lady."

"No," said Dryden absent-mindedly, then he smiled too. "Curious how after this visit with yourself I can see the funny side of things. When one is alone it's hard to achieve a right perspective."

"It is," said Franklin. "I ought to congratulate you, by the way, on your judgment of character. You said she'd soon get tired of that rock-garden hobby, and she has . . . if she's serious about having a car."

"You never can tell with a woman like that." His voice lowered again. "That's the school-house we're now coming to. The mistress is away at week-ends, so we should find Miss Blunt alone. You're interested in pottery this time. That's right, isn't it?"

From what he had gathered Franklin was expecting to find a woman of a vastly different type from the two he had already met that morning, and this time he was not to be disappointed. Harriet Blunt looked like a mother who knows how to manage a family and retain a sense of humour. She was an older woman than Agnes Rose, slim, snub-nosed, black-haired and with twinkling brown eyes. She seemed a woman of tremendous drive and vitality—the sort that has a living to get and makes no fuss about it. Franklin was surprised at the strength of the grip she gave him.

"You *would* bring Mr. Franklin on a day like this, when everything's upside down!" she said to Dryden, who rather seemed to enjoy the way she treated him. "Still, come along in, the pair of you, and see what there is."

The table of what was apparently the work-room was stacked with ornamental pottery—bowls, vases, jugs, plaques and a figure or two. She waved at them.

"There they are, all ready to pack, as you see. But if Mr. Franklin should happen to like anything, he's welcome to it."

"That's very good of you," said Franklin. Harriet Blunt was a woman after his own heart, but for all his assurance he knew she saw through all his pretences when he picked up this and handled that and ventured on what must have been the tritest of remarks. When he had seen everything he set aside a small bowl for himself and a really delightfully modelled old woman for Travers's sister "Charming, aren't they?" and he exhibited them to Dryden. "How much do I owe you, Miss Blunt?"

"The bowl—ten shillings; the figure—thirty. Two pounds the two and that's as much as I'm ever likely to get from my agent." That was a plain assertion and there was nothing aggressive about it.

"You are sure that'll pay you?"

She laughed. "My good man, if it didn't you wouldn't be taking them out of this house! I'll find a box to pack them in."

There was something so naturally humorous in the way she said it that Franklin laughed too. Dryden shook his head portentously. It was curious how he could slip so naturally into the position of god-parent to the village, and even more interesting that everybody was willing to take him as such.

"You know, you shouldn't be living here like this." He indicated the books and the general untidiness.

"Rubbish! Besides, it's the vicar's day for Mrs. Clark or it wouldn't have been like this."

He shook his head again. "Getting your own meals and so on. It's a pity you and Agnes Rose—" He stopped. "Perhaps I shouldn't have said that?"

"Oh, I don't know. I think the same thing sometimes." She gave a humorous sort of sigh and went on with the packing. "I know you won't believe me, but I'm still remarkably fond of that woman!"

"I rather think you are," said Dryden solemnly. "And I've more than a shrewd idea she's sorry that fuss ever came about."

She handed Franklin his parcel. "Want a receipt?"

"Oh, no! I mean, I've got the goods."

"Splendid." She laughed again. "Now you two run along, and if Mr. Franklin isn't going away too soon, Mr. Dryden, bring him in again. Only, give me fair warning." She held out her hand with a smile that was suddenly shy. "Good-bye, Mr. Franklin. I'm ever so grateful."

When they got out to the road again it was Franklin's turn to do the chuckling.

"Like a breath of fresh air. There's one house you can go into with pleasure."

"Hardly as things are," said Dryden. "Rather a lot of people about this morning."

There did seem a considerable amount of excitement for so small a village. Just beyond the churchyard gate, where they now stood, a group of people were talking excitedly. Children were hanging on the outskirts and a small knot of women were there too, aprons on, as if they had just come from their cottages. Dryden looked again, then held the gate for Franklin to pass through.

"What about the key?"

"The door's always open during the day," said Dryden, "though I don't suppose anybody goes in more than once in a blue moon."

Even then, when Franklin turned the heavy handle, he expected to find it shut, but it opened easily enough and they stepped through to the fibre mat. Their feet made no sound as they moved along on the coco-nut matting. Franklin paused for a moment to survey the timbering of the roof. His eyes fell to the colour of the east window, then dropped to the altar with its glint of brass and the red of the velvet. He made a step forward, then stopped again. Dryden saw the same thing and stopped too.

Kneeling on the altar step was a man dressed in black. The absence of vestments, the comparative darkness of the interior and the fact that he was the length of the building from where they stood, made him at first unrecognizable; then Franklin knew it must be Parish, the vicar. But it was the extraordinary attitude of the man that had made him stop short where he now stood. His arms were extended and his body seemed convulsed with some tremendous struggle, as if he were pleading despairingly or writhing in agony. All the time there was no sound, and it was this silent laying bare of a man's soul that struck Franklin with a kind of terror. Then, as he turned to go, the hands smote the breast and the face lifted to heaven. Then as suddenly the shoulders stooped and the head was buried in the hands, while the whole man shook with the intensity of the emotion that was tearing him.

Franklin felt on his arm the grip of Dryden's hand and stepped back quietly to the porch. He drew the door to gently and followed him along the path.

"That was Parish?" he asked.

"Yes," said Dryden, curtly or angrily, and either it was Franklin's imagination or he was trembling himself. And he said nothing else till they were through the gate and on the road again. Then he stopped.

"You saw that?" The words were like a challenge.

"Yes," said Franklin, rather shamefacedly.

"What did you think of it? Didn't you sense something wrong?"

Franklin was feeling more and more self-conscious. "Perhaps I did . . . though I couldn't say what. . . . I mean, it's not a nice thing to blunder clumsily into another man's intimacies."

Dryden stared, then his face lifted. "Yes . . . perhaps that was it." He looked away for a moment before moving on again.

The chattering groups were still there at the fork of the roads and Franklin thought there were curious glances cast at himself and Dryden; the usual curiosity, perhaps, at the sight of a stranger.

But he was wrong. As they drew level with the main group a man detached himself and came towards them. He touched his hat to Dryden.

"Beg pardon, sir, but have you heard about the accident?"

"What accident, Boyce?"

"Young Clark, sir. They say he's broke his neck at the foot of the hill."

"Broke his neck!"

"That's right, sir. Dashed clean into the wall. They've just took his body to the farm."

CHAPTER VI
PROVIDENCE REMAINS INSCRUTABLE

FOR THE FIRST three hundred yards of its length that hill was the steepest Franklin had ever come across in an English village, and it was narrow, and with a surface that was none too good. But it was only at the foot of the sharp descent where it made a sudden bend that it could be called really dangerous, and then not to a careful driver who knew its peculiarities. After that, till it came to an end at the farm, the lane fell placidly like the lower reach of a torrent which widens to a lake.

A policeman, a tall, raw-boned man with heavy moustache, stood in the middle of the road just short of the bend. At the moment he was keeping at a distance half a dozen boys and a grown-up or two who had come to see whatever there was to be seen.

Franklin, turning his head, saw more of the curious hurrying down the hill in their own wake.

"That your local constable?" he asked.

"We haven't one to ourselves," said Dryden. "We share him with a neighbouring village. You'll find him much more intelligent than he looks."

The constable saluted as they came up. The sightseers drew in closer. Franklin, running his eye round, saw that the wall was not a wall but a brick embankment to shore up the hill where the lane cut back. Leaning against it was the constable's bicycle. On the ground at the opposite side lay what had once been another bicycle. On the bricks, four feet from the ground, was a horrible spatter of red.

"What happened, Parker?" asked Dryden.

"That I don't know exactly, sir," the constable told him. "When I got here he was lying over there. Coming down that hill a bit too quick, I should say, sir. Still, you know him, sir, as well as me."

"Yes. Perhaps I do." As he fingered his beard Franklin knew what he was thinking. "Has the doctor seen him?"

"He's just gone along to the farm, where they've taken him," he grunted. "Not that he can do much good, sir. He was dead as soon as he hit that wall. You never saw such a sight, sir. Blood—"

"All right, Parker, all right!" said Dryden quickly. He turned to Franklin. "I think I'll go on to the farm and have a word with Doctor Sawyer."

"I'll wait for you here," said Franklin. He watched him stride off round the bend, then took out his pipe. The group above them edged still nearer.

"This the first accident you've had on this hill?"

"I don't know that it isn't, sir," said Parker cautiously. "For one thing it isn't a real road. Nobody uses it who don't go to the farm."

Franklin nodded. "An errand-boy, wasn't he?"

"He was, sir, and in a way he wasn't." He proceeded to explain. "He did odd jobs for Lucas at the shop, only after to-day he wouldn't have done. His time had expired, so to speak."

Parker was evidently a bit of a character. Franklin waited for him to explain still further.

"Between ourselves, sir, and seeing you're a friend of Mr. Dryden's, and a magistrate, I shouldn't be surprised, sir?"

Franklin nodded unblushingly.

"Then I don't mind telling you, sir, he'd got the sack, expiring to-night. He was a bad lot, sir, as you probably know. He'd have been up before the bench last December, sir, if Mr. Dryden hadn't settled it out of court on account of his poor mother. Then Mr. Dryden and Mr. Parish between 'em got him this job with Lucas, and he got suspicious a few days ago and had a word with me about it. Last Monday he caught him out proper."

"Stealing?"

"Stealing it was, sir. He'd have sacked him on the spot, only we thought it'd upset the poor old girl, so Lucas agreed to let him go on the short notice. Between you and me, sir, it isn't a bad thing for her he is laying down there at the farm. He's been nothing but a worry and a trouble ever since he went to school, and she's one of the most respectable women in the village. She's slaved herself to death for him. She paid back all he took the last time—from a shop in Hastings, that was—and she'd have done the same again."

"Much was it?"

"Runs into pounds, so Lucas tells me. You see, sir, people had been paying him, and he was keeping the money."

Franklin nodded. "Mr. Dryden was telling me much the same thing. It's a curious thing, you know, Parker, what mothers'll do for children, even when they know they're not worth it."

Parker heaved at his belt. His voice lowered. "Well, sir, what you'll think of the statement I don't know, but I'm not fretting about *him*. He was bad right through, and he'd never have been anything else. If you ask me, sir, it was providence, that's what it was."

"You should know," said Franklin. "But what I can't understand is how it happened. Harum-scarum young devils like that usually ride their bicycles like circus performers. How'd he come to lose control?"

Without waiting for an answer he went across to the wrecked bicycle. Parker talked as he followed.

"Something went wrong with the brake, sir. That's always liable to happen. Not that we shall ever know what did happen, because we shan't."

"But a bicycle has two brakes!"

"This one hadn't," said Parker, and pointed to the bent front forks. "As you can see, he'd been tinkering it up with wire."

The bicycle was a very old one, though its frame had been dabbed here and there with black enamel. The pedals were a very old type, and the saddle was practically springless. As Parker said, there was no hind brake, though it had once had one. The front brake had been wired from the lever to the brake-shoe, and the force of the impact had snapped this wire clean off. Even then Franklin wasn't satisfied.

"If the force of the impact smashed the wire," he said to Parker, "then the brake was functioning up to the last moment before it hit the wall. If so, why wasn't the one brake enough to hold the bicycle?"

"There's only one answer to that, sir," said Parket promptly. "It *wasn't* enough. How else did he come to lose control?"

Franklin smiled. "That's fairly sound logic. There is one other solution. The wire might have snapped under the strain. It doesn't look any too robust." He stooped and felt the rigidity of the carrier, which still remained attached to the frame behind the saddle. "But tell me this. Why was he coming down here at all?"

"Why, on an errand, sir!"

"Yes, but what errand? Here's the carrier, and it's empty. Had he anything in his pockets?"

"Not of that sort, sir."

"I'd make a note about it if I were you," Franklin told him. "And I'd see Lucas personally."

When they turned round it was to find the group of people increased to twenty, and not more than ten yard away.

"I'll send them off, sir," said Parker. "We don't want them hanging about here."

"Ask first if anybody saw him," was Franklin's advice.

As the constable moved towards the group a car was seen coming round the curve. It drew up just short of the crowd. Dryden got out first and was followed by an elderly man who looked like the doctor. The chauffeur remained at the wheel, and at the back was a sobbing woman with her apron to her eyes. The doctor popped his head in again.

"Drive Mrs. Clark home and wait for me there." He looked round and saw a woman whom he recognized in the small crowd. "Mrs. Long, you get in the car and go with Mrs. Clark!"

There was quite a commotion for a moment or two as the car went through, then Parker asserted himself and sent the spectators packing, except one boy whom he brought along.

"This boy says he saw him, sir, just before it happened."

Dryden nodded down, and the urchin got out his story headlong. He had been one of the small party playing cricket on the meadow by Manor Path and had seen the dead boy twice. The first time he had been coming from the direction of the Manor. Shortly after that the ball had been knocked into Manor Lane, and there he had seen Willie Clark swing across the road on his bicycle and disappear in Farm Lane. Parker wrote it all down.

Before Franklin had been in Doctor Sawyer's company five minutes he knew that Dryden's description had been a charitable one. He was a loose-limbed old fellow, not far short of seventy, with hook nose, beetling eyebrows and mutton-chop whiskers. His manner was blustering and aggressive, and Franklin was soon following Dryden's lead and letting him have entirely his own way. The blame for the accident, he said, was to be put on one man, and one man only—Lucas, the shopkeeper. He ought to have had a new bicycle long ago; what was more, the doctor proposed to give him a piece of his mind. Then when it was suggested that the dead boy was coming from Mould's house, he pooh-poohed the idea, and he glared at Franklin when he confirmed Dryden's theory by adding that Manor Cottage was the only place he could have come from when he had first been seen, since the Manor itself was empty.

Dryden called Parker over. "You must let me have my own way about this," he said to Sawyer with a placatory smile. "Parker, you take over the bicycle, and see it's produced on Monday; then go to Manor Cottage and see Mr. Mould, and ask him if the boy Clark called there this morning." He turned to Sawyer. "I don't think there's anything to keep us further, do you?"

They began to climb the ascent, and in a couple of minutes Sawyer was grumbling because he hadn't had the sense to tell his chauffeur to come and fetch him.

"If you care to wait," said Dryden maliciously, "we'll send him down for you. . . . Hallo! this looks like Parish coming."

The vicar it was, coming down the hill like a man floating through space, chest well back and legs swinging away from under him. Dryden's description had been accurate. He was a shortish, spare man, his hair grey with a queer tinge of its original sandy colour. His eyes were a clear blue, as striking in their way as that massed fringe of forget-me-nots round the green carpet of Ashley Mould's garden. What his complexion was like ordinarily Franklin had no idea, but now his face was pale and drawn. Then when he took his hand he had that exasperating feeling of gripping something warm and yet not alive, and while Parish was speaking his eyes were looking through and beyond. And yet his voice was hearty and full of life, and there was nothing clerical about his greetings.

"Terrible business this," said Dryden, nodding back.

"Deplorable. Deplorable." His hands came together across his breast. "Most distressing." He shook his head ponderously, then looked round at the three of them. "But don't you think our duty's to the living rather than the dead?"

Sawyer darted a look from under his eyebrows. "What's the idea?"

Dryden's face had flushed. "If you mean his mother, and the expenses of the funeral—"

Parish broke in quickly. "No, no! I'll see to all that."

"Come along," said Sawyer impatiently. "I must be getting back. You staying here, vicar?"

"I thought I'd see his mother," said Parish abstractedly. "That's really what I meant when I said our duty was to the living." He smiled gently and curiously apologetically into space. "*My* duty, I should have said."

"You won't find her down at the farm," Sawyer told him bluntly. "I sent her back in the car. She never ought to have come, and I'd like to know the damn fool who told her."

"I think it was I who told her," said Parish quickly. He frowned. "Did I tell her?" It seemed as if he were talking to himself, and but for the earnestness with which he put the question and groped for the answer, the absent-mindedness would have been laughable. "She was at the vicarage. It was Saturday, you see." He nodded quickly. "Yes, they brought the news there. I remember now. It was I who broke it to her. Mrs. Hopper was there too."

Dryden gave Franklin a quick look. Sawyer shuffled even more impatiently, but Parish seemed still loth to leave the spot. He glanced back again.

"He died quickly? No pain?"

Sawyer grunted. "He died as quick as I'd like to. He didn't know a thing about it."

They had a breather or two going up the hill, and when the top was reached the doctor mopped his forehead. Dryden was blowing a bit too, and the fittest man among them seemed to be the vicar. He held out the same limp and unresponsive hand to Franklin and smiled away into space.

"If you'll excuse me, I'll leave you all. Unless you're coming my way, doctor?"

"Not at present," Sawyer said curtly.

The three stood there, just short of the cross-roads, and watched the vicar float away. His steps were quick, and at each stride he seemed to lift himself on the ball of his foot.

Sawyer nodded. "Weird mixture, that chap! And one of the best-hearted men I know." He rounded on Dryden. "I wish to God he wouldn't be so damn pious with it."

"We can't all be alike," said Dryden gruffly. "You don't understand him, perhaps." It was more of a question than anything else.

"Why *should* I understand him?" fired the doctor. Then he held out his hand. "I've got patients waiting for me. See me in Northurst this afternoon." He shook hands with Franklin, gave him a nod, and was off.

"Thank God he forgot about seeing Lucas," said Dryden. "I think we'll see him ourselves, if you don't mind." He made no attempt to move, and his eyes still followed the retreating figure of the doctor. "You see, Parish has even got on Sawyer's nerves."

"I don't think it takes much to do that!" was Franklin's retort. "By the way, did I understand from what the vicar was saying that Mrs. Clark works there?"

"She does work by the day," explained Dryden. "The vicar and Miss Blunt share her between them. The housekeeper at the vicarage is rather old, and Mrs. Clark does the rough work."

"The housekeeper would be the Mrs. Hopper the vicar mentioned."

"That's right, I expect Mrs. Clark won't be doing any more work to-day."

The comment seemed to come from the fact that the doctor, as they could see, had just emerged from the cottage gate, and was getting into his car. There were still a few people in the street, but Lucas's shop was almost empty. When the last customer had gone, and Dryden began to question him, he was most apologetic. He wouldn't have had it happen for the world, even though the boy was what he was. It wasn't his fault if the bicycle was out of order. He told the boy he wasn't to ride it, but he would keep on doing so. Customers weren't so far away that a bicycle was needed.

"Don't worry yourself about all that, Lucas," said Dryden. "We know all that. The thing is, did you send him to the farm?"

Lucas was most indignant that a story of that sort should have got about already. He had no idea the boy had gone to the farm. He had no right to go to the farm. He'd been sent with an order to Manor Cottage and should have come straight back. Lucas had wondered why he was so long, and the next thing he had heard was that he was dead.

"That's all right then," said Dryden kindly. "I don't expect you'll be wanted at Monday's inquest, Lucas, but Parker will see you about that."

They were standing for a moment outside the shop when the vicar appeared again. He would have passed without seeing them if Dryden had not called out:

"Just a moment, Parish! We're going your way."

The vicar came over. From the expression on his face they gathered that something had happened.

"And how's Mrs. Clark?" asked Dryden. "More settled down?"

The vicar raised his hand. "I was able to tell her something that must have set her heart at rest. I was the last person, probably, to see her son. I spoke to him firmly and I think his heart was touched. He promised me amendment, and I believe he meant it." He paused impressively. "A few seconds later he was dead!"

Franklin was startled at Dryden's sudden flash of anger. "Good God, Parish! Why didn't you tell us this before? You might have put us in the very devil of a hole."

Parish looked puzzled. "In a hole?"

Dryden made a gesture of hopelessness. "Where did you see him exactly? And when?"

"Let me see." He frowned with tantalizing solemnity. "I was by the gate there"—he pointed to his own gate that opened on the road not twenty yards away—"when the boy came up. He was going to ride his bicycle up to the back door and I told him he ought not to do that and he left it just inside the gate."

"Excuse me, vicar," broke in Franklin. "Did you notice if the brake was working when he got off the bicycle?"

Parish looked at him blankly. "The brake working?"

"All right," said Dryden quickly. "And what happened then, Parish?"

"Well, he went to the house. It might have been to see his mother or it might have been for the weekly order. Lucas, you know. When he came back I spoke to him again. You can imagine what I said to him, Dryden. I pleaded with him for his mother's sake, and I think the lad was touched at what I said."

"You didn't send him to the farm?"

"Why of course not!"

"He didn't mention he was going to the farm?"

Something seemed to be coming back to the vicar's mind. His mouth opened and he went through the facial agonies of a man who tries desperately hard to remember something. Then he gave it up.

"I thought I remembered something." He clicked his tongue. "Dear, dear! Perhaps it was somebody else."

Dyden frowned slightly, then his face cleared as he held out his hand. "That's all right then, Parish. You'll be wanted on Monday, of course, at the inquest."

"Did I do anything wrong?"

Dryden seemed a trifle off-handed. "I don't think so. A pity, perhaps, you didn't mention it sooner." He let the limp hand fall. "Still, just repeat what you've just told us at the inquest."

"Ah!" His face fell again. "Yes. The inquest." He nodded once or twice, standing there rather forlornly, and Franklin began to feel uncomfortable. Then he moved away along his garden path.

Dryden took out his watch. "Past two. Mrs. Jimson will be very annoyed. We must hurry."

And yet Dryden looked remarkably abstracted too as they walked back to Old House. Franklin stole a look at his face, and wondered.

"There's one good thing about this morning," he said, "we know it could have been nothing but an accident."

Dryden answered so quickly that Franklin knew he had guessed what had been worrying him. "Are you sure of that?"

"Well, not sure. It might have been designed, but that's too fantastic for words."

"How might it have been designed?" Dryden asked soberly.

"By tampering with the brake."

Dryden stopped in his tracks. "But why should Mould tamper with the brake?"

Franklin smiled. "He didn't. I'm merely talking nonsense. Mind you, somebody *might* have tampered with the brake. Not a person at all. Those boys I was thinking of. You know what boys are like. They're thoughtless young devils when they're up to mischief. There's Parker waiting for you. You might do worse than ask him to make inquiries."

The policeman was leaning on his bicycle by the gate.

"I saw you talking to Mr. Parish, sir, and I didn't like to interfere, so I thought I'd wait here, I've seen Mr. Mould sir."

Dryden looked at him. "And what happened?"

"Well, sir, he told me straight away that young Clark had been there, and he gave him sixpence to go to the farm for him to see Rogers, and ask him to see him without fail as soon as he knocked off."

"Rogers?" said Dryden reflectively. "That'd be about gardening," he explained to Franklin. "Rogers does gardening in his spare time. When Mrs. Mould was alive he used to work at Manor Cottage sometimes on the Saturday afternoons." He coughed nervously. "How *was* Mr. Mould, Parker?"

Parker knew the drift of the question. "He was all right with me, sir. A nicer gentleman you wouldn't want to speak to." Parker's face suddenly expanded to a broad grin. "Have you seen his garden recently, sir?"

Dryden coloured. "Why do you ask?"

"Well, sir, he took me round the back and showed me a whole lot o' forget-me-nots all over the place. 'Look at that damnable sight!' he says. 'No wonder I want a gardener.' And he wasn't so far wrong, sir," Parker added. "You never saw such a sight in your life."

"About the boy Clark." Dryden's cold voice brought the policeman back to earth. "Was there a sixpence in his pocket?"

"Oh, yes, sir!" said Parker, "And we know Mr.Mould sent the message. The baker told him about the accident and Mr. Mould sent another message to the farm by him. I just saw Rogers. He's working at Manor Cottage this afternoon."

Dryden was very perplexed about Mould. As he told Franklin at lunch, he could understand neither his geniality with the policeman nor his sudden urge to have that garden of his swept and garnished. The curious absent-mindedness that had been exhibited by the vicar that morning worried him still more.

"That's really a new side to his character," he said to Franklin. "He honestly seemed to have forgotten what happened."

"You nearly always get that left over after break-downs," Franklin told him. "I had the misfortune to be that way once myself, and I know that for months I was forgetting names and places and all sorts of things. Even now I get annoying fits of it."

"Undoubtedly that is so. I've heard it said before." He gave Franklin a look that anticipated the diffidence of the question. "And what did you think of him?"

"That's a difficult question," said Franklin thoughtfully. "Of course I couldn't help noticing what you'd described as his trick of being in two places at once"—he smiled—"though that's nothing derogatory to a man's character. I think perhaps, I liked him . . . and yet somehow I know I'd never feel really at home in his company. My fault, perhaps, but I don't think we should have much in common. As for abnormalities, frankly I didn't see any—beyond the one mannerism I've mentioned."

Dryden tugged reflectively at his beard. Again the question was diffidently put. "Why did you like him?"

Franklin smiled slightly. "Well, you'd already prejudiced me in his favour by mentioning his kindness of heart and generosity. This morning I saw two instances of that—his anxiety for the mother and his immediate taking over of the funeral expenses; what I might call Christianity practical and applied. And as soon as it flashed on me why . . . well, it's difficult to refer to, but I mean what we saw in the church—"

Dryden put the question so suddenly that Franklin was taken aback. "Why was he in the church?"

There was something so unnecessary about that question that he hardly knew what to say. "Well—er—where would a man go—I mean a man of deeply religious feeling; where would he go if it wasn't to the One Person who can hear and sympathize? I take it he was terribly shocked when he heard of the boy's death, and after the strain of breaking the news to his mother, he went across to the church."

There had been something so foolish about that explanation of the obvious that Franklin gave him a quick, questioning look. But Dryden was still tugging at his beard. Franklin leaned across the table.

"May I put a personal question? Between you and me there's somewhere a tremendous difference, Mr. Dryden. To be blunt, you see and sense things which I have no means of either seeing or sensing. You were very distressed, for instance, at certain changes that came over your vicar. To you he's abnormal. I find him normal enough. Now I put it to you. For the very first time he has been under the eyes and observation of both of us at the same time. You told Travers and myself that when you were in his presence the effect on you was that of something repulsive. You see my point? If you could describe to me just what effect he had on you this morning—*while I was with you*—I might have a better chance of trying to see with your eyes."

Dryden seemed very much struck by that. "I'll tell you," he said, "and I'll tell you quickly, because it's so easy. You may have noticed that I virtually courted his company this morning. I'll own up that I deliberately thrust myself on him in order to see how he would react." He shook his head perplexedly. "What I experienced was something I'd never experienced before. I felt an overwhelming pity. I couldn't keep my mind from what he used to be—the real man of whom you saw nothing but vestiges. I felt nearer to him this morning than I've done since Yeoman's death. When I saw him groping for words and standing there with Sawyer looking sardonically at him, it was almost too much for me." He paused. "And yet, a few moments before, I had felt that same repulsion."

"In the church?"

Dryden nodded, and Franklin saw something in his face that made him leave that matter where it was.

"Well, Mr. Dryden," he said, "it would be presumptuous of me to give opinions or advice, but I would like to say this. Why not take your change of feeling towards him as an augury for the future? Your old friend has had a severe shock, of that I'm positively certain. The death of your mutual friend was too much for him. *But*, the fact that you felt that overwhelming sympathy this morning surely shows that he himself is slowly recovering from the shock that made him so different—I may even say so repulsive to you." He smiled across sympathetically. "Take it from me, in a few weeks you'll both be laughing at all this. And pardon my impertinence in—er—"

"I'm grateful to you," said Dryden quickly. "Very grateful. I think perhaps I'll try to see more of him help him along a bit. Perhaps I need some help too."

They had a long walk before lunch the next day, then idled away their time till evening. When the solitary bell began to toll, Franklin pricked up his ears. Dryden caught his look at the clock.

"You'd like to go to church?"

"I think I would," said Franklin. "Sure you don't mind?"

"I'll go with you." But he glanced down at his clothes and Franklin protested, and they argued it out till Dryden owned that perhaps he would feel happier where he was.

Franklin drifted in with the very last strokes of the bell and found a pew at the back. He had come, he told himself, in no irreverent spirit. Perhaps that was why he joined his ragged baritone to the singing and kept a check on his thoughts. It was during the sermon that he found the task most difficult with his eyes on the preacher's face. But it was no special sermon, written with the previous day's tragedy in mind, and there was nothing unusual in the vicar's manner. Then, at the very end, there was a pause. In that moment he seemed to Franklin to become something like the ideal he had preached—a man among common men—and his voice lost much of the intonation that had dehumanized it.

"I feel," he said, "that I should not be doing my duty as shepherd of this small flock of ours, as its spiritual shepherd and its friend, if I made no reference to that terrible affair which came as such a shock to all of us yesterday. All I would say is this. The Divine ways are not our ways. When we think God is hard, or unjust, or perhaps merely just, let us all think of that. We see, as the apostle says, through a glass darkly. But we cannot see the ways of the Divine providence, and the ways of providence are inscrutable."

He made a gesture that was indescribably apt; a resigned perplexity that was also a blessing. It was then that Franklin knew Dryden must have been wrong. Whatever the peculiarities that had got on Dryden's nerves, Parish was a man of the deepest human sympathies. Then the voice resumed its old monotony. "And now to God the Father . . ."

Franklin and Miss Rose recognized each other in the church porch and he strolled with her as far as The Pleasance. When he got back to Old House, supper was in.

"My dear fellow, please don't apologize," said Dryden concernedly. "I've been so busy that I've only just finished. . . . Many people at church?"

"Very few. I don't know the average, but I'd say no more than thirty all told." He laughed. "Something extraordinarily amusing happened just now. I heard an organ playing and a congregation singing, and I wondered if they were having a choir practice at the church. Then it struck me that they hadn't even an organ at the church, but only a harmonium. Then I wondered if there was a chapel I hadn't heard about. Then it dawned on me!"

Dryden didn't see it.

"You haven't got it. Well, it *was* a church organ, and it *was* a congregation. It was Miss Faithful's wireless set giving out a broadcast service from somewhere! She must have had her window open."

Dryden laughed. "Of course! But you could hardly expect me to guess that. . . . But then Miss Faithful couldn't have been at church."

"I suppose she would really have had time to get home before the wireless service began. But she certainly wasn't there tonight."

"Curious," said Dryden. "I always understood she never missed a service. Perhaps her heart's bad again." He pushed the bell and Franklin wondered why, till Mrs. Jimson came in.

"Oh, Susan," said Dryden, "do you happen to know how Miss Faithful is? I understand she wasn't at church to-night."

Susan Jimson, arms folded across her generous waist smiled with the familiarity of a servant of many years standing. "It's that wireless of hers, Mr. Henry. Not that I blame her. The best place for her these dark nights, I say, instead of traipsing off to church at her age. And it's all religion, sir."

Dryden smiled. "I suppose it is, Susan."

So much for that interlude. Then in the middle of supper Franklin happened to remark that Miss Rose had been at church.

"And how was she?" asked Dryden.

"Rather subdued," said Franklin, and his own face took on quite a serious expression. "Between ourselves I don't think anybody could have been very volatile to-night. The vicar spoke very impressively about yesterday's affair. Just a few words at the end of the sermon."

It was remarkable how prejudiced Dryden seemed to be where the vicar was concerned, and yet he appeared to be perfectly unaware of it. That in itself was strange in a man who, as Franklin knew, was generous-minded to a fault. Somehow Franklin was irritated at what seemed a petulant remark. And what had become of that resolution that Dryden had made the previous day—to be more sympathetic with Parish and to lend a helping hand?

"Made a comment, did he? Then I hope he didn't allude to the inscrutability of providence."

"The inscrutability of providence?" Franklin's mind flashed back to the Thursday afternoon and Dryden sitting in the easy chair, arms on elbows, and speaking of Parish and the death of Yeoman. "Curious you should say that. When I heard that phrase in church to-night I wondered where I had run across it before!"

CHAPTER VII
THE DOG ONCE MORE

"WELL, find any pellets?" was Travers's first question as he entered the room.

"Devil a pellet," said Franklin.

"Hm!" said Travers. "That's bad." He realized all at once that he had blundered with cheerful inconsequence into an atmosphere that seemed as decorously subdued as that which overcasts a household on the morning of the funeral of a distant relation. "It's not that that's upsetting you all?"

Then, of course, he was told about the week-end happenings. When they came to mention the beginnings of regeneration in Ashley Mould they were surprised to see Travers looking most uneasy. It was then ten-thirty, and Dryden was due at South Farm at eleven for the inquest.

"Do you know," Travers said, "I think I can explain about Mould. You see, he got my letter on the Saturday morning."

"But you said you were going to time it for this morning!"

"I know I did. Only, you see, we happened to have something go wrong with the battery, and as we were in Lewes I thought I'd have it seen to at once. Being rather foolishly excited about the letter, and having my writing case with me, I wrote it while I was waiting." He looked round apologetically. "You don't think it an extravagant claim on my part that I should be the cause of the spring-cleaning?"

Dryden's face lost some of its solemnity. It was difficult to be too serious when Travers was otherwise.

"I'd hardly like to express any opinion, Ludo, where you're concerned. But you haven't had a reply from him?"

"Oh, yes, I have! I had a telegram on the Saturday afternoon. I'm to be there at midday."

Dryden shook his head. "I doubt if you'll manage it. He's at the inquest, and it all depends. Besides," and here he began to experience a difficulty in finding his words, "I've been thinking things over. There's no doubt I've been rather absurd—hysterical, if you like—about all this business. The report on the leafmould has made a difference. You see, there's nothing at all for us to go on now, as Mr. Franklin agrees. About people and so on; well, I've been looking at things in a different way—or Mr. Franklin has made me see them in a different way." He smiled diffidently. "A long rigmarole, I'm afraid, but if you do see Mould, you'll make the visit purely a private one?"

"My dear fellow!" Travers's protest was as dignified as Franklin knew it to be ironical. "Didn't I assure you I never intended it to be anything else? And if you imagine he'll see some connection between my letter and that accident of Saturday, may I remind you that that's impossible. My letter arrived the first thing on the Saturday morning."

"And he's not likely to take *you* for a detective," said Franklin quietly.

Dryden laughed; then they all laughed, and the air was cleared. Travers saw the pair of them off at the gate, and as a kind of afterthought put the ticklish question:

"You won't object, of course, Henry, if I mention your name? Merely that I know you, and am lunching here to-day." Then, very quickly, "I knew you wouldn't mind. See you at lunch then." And that was that.

Travers was, in fact, much like a dog who has been taken out for the rarest of runs, and knows that at any moment he is likely to be called in and put on the leash. That story which Dryden had related in Franklin's office had seized on his imagination, and he was prepared, not only to believe it implicitly, but to add to the problems of the village of Bableigh certain experiences of his own when he should have had time to make them. The affair had burst in upon his humdrum and ordered life. It was something to do, and something that suited to a nicety his romantic and inquiring mind. It was a problem, and it was adventure, and no foolish weakening on the part of Henry Dryden was going to make him relinquish what had scarcely begun.

He set off just short of noon. Palmer, grey-haired, black-coated, and more like the family solicitor than ever, gave an air of respectability with which the sporting lines of the car rather conflicted. Just inside Manor Lane Travers cocked an ear, then nodded. It *was* a lawn-mower, and the sound was coming from Mould's garden. As he stepped inside the front gate, there was the man waiting for him. He touched his hat.

"Are you the gentleman Mr. Mould was expecting, sir?"

"I expect so."

"He told me he might be a minute or two late, sir, and would you mind waiting?"

"Not at all." He took out his cigarette-case. "Have a cigarette."

The man gave him a quick look. "Thank'ee, sir, I don't mind if I do."

Travers held the lighter for him, then got one going for himself. "You're making things very smart here?"

"Well, sir, it's better than it was," the man told him. "Mr. Mould let it go too far, sir. I had to put the scythe over it afore the mower'd touch it."

"Really!" Travers was most sympathetic. He pointed to the newly dug bed under the long window. "What are you going to put in there?"

"I told Mr. Mould he ought to have antirrhinums, sir."

"A capital idea!" The partition door was open and he strolled over.

The man followed him through.

"Excellent garden you've got here!"

The man gave him another quick look. Whoever the gentleman was, he was a queer sort of gardener to show enthusiasm at the sight of a yellowish lawn surrounded by a bed of newly dug earth, through which protruded sickly patches of perennials like hulks in a shallow sea.

"Well, sir, Mr. Mould left this too long as well. It got sort of overgrown, smothered all over with them old blue flowers. It took me a rare time getting 'em out."

"I expect it did. You're the regular gardener here?"

"Not lately, sir. I used to come here occasionally when Mrs. Mould was alive. Rogers is my name, sir. Mr. Mould got me here special this morning, as he wanted the place clean and tidy, so he got me the morning off." Some connection made him pull out his watch. "I should have been finished long before this, only I had a job of burying to do."

"Burying?" Travers smiled.

"Yes, sir. Someone threw a dead dog under that front window, and Mr. Mould didn't know it till it was stinking the place out. He scraped a hole and buried it himself where it was laying, then this morning he remembered it and told me to make a job of it. He didn't want it mentioned, sir, because he wouldn't like whoever did it to have the laugh on him, if you understand, sir."

"But how extraordinary! Someone put a dead dog under his window?"

"They certainly did, sir. You never know what them young devils o' boys are up to nowadays. If I had my way, sir, I'd give one or two of 'em a damn good hiding. That young Clark, him what got killed, did it, I shouldn't be surprised."

"And you've reburied it?"

"I have, sir. Just here by the shed corner."

Travers nodded ponderously. "Well, I mustn't keep you from your work."

"That's all right, sir." He threw away the stub of the cigarette. "Two or three minutes'll see me finished. You won't mind staying here alone till Mr. Mould comes?"

"Not in the least," Travers assured him. "You push along home. I shall be all right."

He watched him finish, and cursed his deliberation. The lawn mowings were placed in a trench, the blades of the mower were wiped, the spade and fork were polished with wisps of grass, and then at last the tool-shed door was locked and the key hung on a nail at the side.

"You'll tell Mr. Mould I've gone, sir?"

"I'll tell him all right," said Travers, and followed him out to the lane.

Before the man was ten yards away he was speaking to Palmer.

"Any wraps of any kind in the locker?"

"Only the best rug, sir."

"Right. If that chap comes back, or if you see anybody else coming this way, give the horn a touch."

Travers risked the back path. In any case he was working in the shelter of the shed. Five minutes later, accompanied by a noticeable stench, he was thrusting something into the back locker. Palmer sniffed unobtrusively. A lifetime's experience of Travers had taught him to be surprised at nothing, and if that gentleman had appeared with his head under his arm it is doubtful if Palmer would have shown more than an inward perturbation. Travers leaned negligently on the door and watched the road.

"Palmer, there's a considerable portion of a dead dog in the rug."

"Indeed, sir!"

"Go to the village shop and buy a bottle of Jeyes. They always keep it. Drive half a mile on the road home, draw off some water and soak the dog well with the disinfectant. Make a compact parcel of it and come back here for me."

"Very good, sir." His eye caught the unusual condition of his master's boots, and as he pushed the starter he handed over the duster from the pocket. "Your boots, sir."

Travers went back and surveyed his job and put the finishing touches to it and himself. Then he sniffed. As far as he could judge, both himself and the atmosphere were odourless. Five minutes later Mould arrived full of apologies, and blaming the dilatoriness of certain people who had arrived late. Except for a particularly sensual underlip, he was the very spit of his brother; the same heavy jowl, sagging cheeks and paunchy body. His manner was brisk and urbane, and whatever dislike Travers took to his person, his voice was cultured and attractive.

"And what happened at your inquest?" Travers asked when the apologies were all over.

"Only what was to be expected. Purely an accident. Still," and he made a gesture of indifference, "the law's got to be satisfied. Come along in, Mr. Travers."

It was an oak-floored room with rugs here and there. Travers set one foot inside, then nearly came a cropper. Mould, who was at his elbow, clutched him just as the slide began.

"Hallo! Ankle gone?"

Travers rubbed his ankle gingerly. "I think I must have trod on something." Then he saw the cause of the trouble and slipped it unobtrusively into his pocket.

Mould was most concerned, though his examination of the floor produced nothing. However, Travers reported the ankle perfectly sound, and as he seemed inclined to laugh at the affair as due entirely to his own clumsiness, Mould breathed again.

It turned out that the sculptor was quite aware of who he was. He recalled an occasion when they had met some years before, though Travers had long forgotten it. He was a man, too, of extensive reading, as Travers soon appreciated, and he had a biting tongue. Travers was, in fact, quite content to let him do most of the talking, while he listened and nodded and let his eyes rove round the room. It looked remarkably clean—effeminately so; the set of the chintz curtains, the placing of the cushions and that bowl of crimson pyrethrums on the window table. Then Mould got up in the middle of a sentence.

"But you don't want to discuss the neo-Serbians. You'd like to see some of my latest?"

Travers followed Mould along the garden path, fascinated by the proximity of the pinkish circle of bald skull and its coquettish fringe of frizzy hair. The studio was uncommonly clean, he thought, as he ran his eye over it, then Mould showed him over to the exhibits.

There was no doubt whatever about Ashley Mould being an important man. There was an economy and directness about his work that Travers liked enormously, and he made no bones about saying so. And it was definitely distinctive; at least it was wholly outside Travers's extensive experience. Two things he liked particularly: the head of an old man done in beech, and a door-knocker in bronze, fashioned like a centaur—a *jeu d'esprit*, as Mould was careful to describe it. The price was pretty stiff.

"You'll not repent it," Mould said as he took Travers's cheque. "I don't mind telling you in confidence that Alternayer's of Bond Street and Meister's of Paris will take everything I'm doing at the moment. One of these days you'll ask three times what you gave, and you'll get it."

"I think you're right, though I shouldn't say it." He looked again at the larger piece. "My car should be here now. I think I'll take them with me."

"You're sure?" asked Mould. "Then I'll make a neat parcel out of this box. Sorry I can't ask you to lunch—"

"You *are* married, aren't you?" Travers was rather annoyed with himself for putting the question so quickly.

Mould looked up, but saw nothing but a polite inquiry. "No," he said, and his face fell. "I'm a widower. I lost my wife just over a year ago. It was a great shock,"

"I expect it was," said Travers lamely. "But it was good of you to think about lunch, all the same—not that I could have accepted your kind invitation. As a matter of fact, I'm lunching with an old friend who happens to live here. He tells me he's a friend of yours, too. Henry Dryden."

Mould's face flushed. "Dryden! Oh, yes. I haven't seen much of him lately." He laughed inanely as he included the studio in one general wave of the hand. "Too much work, you know. Distractions are bad for one." Then he sighed. "And there was that business of my wife."

"I know," said Travers. "By the way, I oughtn't to say it, but he has the most tremendous admiration for your work. But for that inquest he'd probably have come here with me this morning."

"Really!" He seemed rather bewildered. "I had no idea, you know." Another gesture. "Any time, of course, I'd be delighted to see him."

"I'll give him your message," said Travers as they went out.

Mould locked the door and turned to find his visitors surveying the garden.

"Your man told me you were a bit backward this year."

"Yes." He gave a titter. "How it happened I don't know, but one morning the whole place was smothered with the most damnable blue; what I call 'milk-maid blue.' A sort of putrid insipidity. Forget-me-nots!"

Travers was suitably amused. "They arrived by magic?"

"Oh, they grew all right," said Mould. "The thing was I didn't really notice them till they began to erupt." He took the short cut across the grass, "A gardener had the place before me. He probably had a passion for them."

As Travers put the parcel in the back locker, he noticed an odour of disinfectant and shut the door to quickly. Mould apparently smelt nothing unusual. Then, in the very act of saying goodbye, Travers appeared to remember something.

"I wonder. Could you put me on the track of a Miss Crome? Marian Crome I believe the name is. Dryden was saying she was a painter. I thought, perhaps, while I was down here, you know . . ."

"Yes." Mould spoke dubiously. "I know her very well. I don't think perhaps you'd care very much . . ." He broke off. "You thought of going there now?"

"Well, yes—if it isn't too far."

"Mind if I get a hat and come with you?"

Travers's face lit up. "I'd be delighted."

Mould gave directions, and in a couple of minutes the car drew up before Windyridge.

"Perhaps you'll be so good as to give her a word of warning," said Travers tactfully. "I'll be turning the car round."

When he had his first view of Marian Crome it was at her front door with Mould at her elbow. She seemed the least bit nervous as she shook hands, but he had her at her ease in no time, and Mould, too, for that matter. As for his inspection of the pictures, that probably represented the finest piece of acting of his career, with its curtain the final mixture of gratification and considered judgment with which he chose the "Aphrodite." The price was most modest.

He glanced at his watch. Half-past one! With the vision of two hungry men waiting for their lunch, his perturbation was genuine. Miss Crome hoped he'd come again. Travers, stowing the picture where he hoped the Jeyes might do it good, said he'd love to.

As the car slipped along towards the church, he caught Mould's eye. There seemed to be some amusement in it.

"And you liked her pictures?"

Travers took a chance, and won. "My dear Mould the world is overstocked with truth already. You and I can afford a little—er—tact."

Mould laughed, then sobered down almost as quickly. "The curious thing is that you and I may be wrong. I mean, even Galileo was laughed at."

"I know. . . . Quite a charming woman, don't you think?"

"Oh, quite," said Mould off-handedly, then asked for the car to be stopped at the cross-roads.

Travers gave a most courteous farewell, said he'd remember to give that message to Dryden, then shot the car off again. At the gate Palmer opened the locker door.

"You wish all these taken in, sir?"

"Not all," he was told. "Leave that picture in and shut the door on it."

Travers was grateful for his host's unaffected good humour in the matter of the lateness, and forthwith staged the carved head on the serving-table as part apology and excuse. Franklin expressed himself as far too hungry to be artistically minded, but, as soon as he had eaten his soup, condescended to say it wasn't bad. Dryden got up specially and made another inspection. He gave an appraising nod.

"I expect I'm all wrong, but I think it's extraordinarily fine."

"Then we're all agreed," said Travers. "When you call next time, Henry, get him to show you some more."

He looked so surprised that Travers explained.

"But, my dear fellow!" expostulated Dryden. "Really, you shouldn't, you know. Making appointments and—" Words failed him. "Besides, how do I know what you've said?"

"We'll soon remedy that," said Travers cheerfully, and did so. Then he shook his head mournfully. "You're very hard to please, you know, Henry. I've reopened one door to you in your own village and you raise all sorts of objections. But you will go round, won't you? Seriously, I'm sure he'll be glad to see you." He produced the door-knocker from his pocket, and caught Franklin's eye. "Here's something else of Mould's, for your front door."

Dryden fingered it lovingly. It really was a most delightful piece of work.

"Did I hear you say *my* front door?"

"That's right, Henry. A little gesture from Franklin and myself." He waved aside the thanks and protestations. "And now tell me all about the inquest."

There seemed to be nothing to add to Mould's curt summary except one thing, and that arose out of the vicar's evidence.

"He really spoke most convincingly," Franklin said. "A perfectly clear account and no absent-mindedness. And then what do you think he did at the end of it? After saying what he'd said to the boy and what the boy said to him, he looked at everybody as if he were in the pulpit and told us we were all in God's hands. You never saw anybody look such a fool as the coroner."

"I really must manage to meet him," said Travers with a faraway look. "And did I gather you went to church last night?"

"An excellent sermon and a very quiet, pleasant little service," was Franklin's summary, and then Dryden, with more than a shrewd idea that the two might like some sort of conference, remembered that he had something most important to attend to, and wondered if they'd excuse him. No sooner was he out of the room than Travers produced a grey bead, large as a marble.

"Know anybody who wears a string like that?"

"Yes. Marian Crome. Why?"

"I nearly broke my neck over it this morning," said Travers, and told him all about it. "Not only that: the house was clean and decorated—a large bowl of pyrethrums tastefully arranged on a side table, for instance. Marian Crome had some in her garden that were the very spit of them." He laughed. "The only other thing that happened was that I finally relieved her house of the famous picture that has caused all the trouble. I bought the 'Aphrodite.'"

Franklin smiled dryly. "If it were anybody else but you, I'd say something about a fool and his money." He thought for a moment. "And what's all this amount to? That Mould wanted to have his place reasonably tidy for your visit, and got Marian Crome to do it. Further, the two are on exceedingly close if not intimate terms. And when all's said and done, that's their own business, and nobody else's. We're where we were when we started."

"Surely a rather pessimistic view," protested Travers, "There's still that matter of the forget-me-nots—which, by the way, Mould did *not* plant—and there's the fact that that figure of Old Nick was not produced for my inspection this morning, though I kept insisting that I'd like to see everything he had." His eyes suddenly opened. "Good Lord! I was forgetting to tell you about the dog!"

When Dryden returned the pair were puffing away on opposite sides of the empty fireplace. Travers looked up smilingly and pulled in another chair.

"Here you are, then. Don't say you've been calling on Mould!"

"No," said Dryden, and quite seriously. "Later on, perhaps." He fidgeted for a moment or two. "Well, what have we—er—arrived at?"

Franklin cleared his throat. "You'll be patient with me, and try to see my point of view?"

"Why, of course!" and he smiled.

"Well then, it's like this. In my office, Mr. Dryden, you outlined to us two problems—which may or may not be connected. The first was the most elusive I've ever been up against; I refer to what I might call the sudden falling from grace of practically all your friends in the village, so that you felt their houses to be closed to you. That problem is, frankly, beyond me, though I'd like to make certain comments if you'll give me permission."

"Do, please."

"Then I'll refer to the people concerned. Mould's peculiar conduct has, I think, been explained by Travers. He now seems ready to resume with you such a degree of friendship as you care to offer.

From what I've seen of the Rose-Blunt problem, it certainly looks to me as if those two women would come together again with a little persuading." He smiled tactfully. "The sort of persuasion I'm sure you could use. As for Mr. Parish, I've already given an opinion, that he's slowly recovering from a shock, and I'll therefore say no more about him. As for the last person—Miss Crome—there I'm quite at a loss to account for the occasional and objectionable taste she has in painting, but," he chuckled rather than smiled, "you'll be pleased to hear that Travers has purchased the chief offender among the pictures, and the only one of that particular kind that remains is fairly innocuous. In words, I say very regretfully that the first part of the problem, as far as I'm concerned, must be finished with."

"A very reasonable statement." As he tugged at his beard he was looking far happier than Travers had anticipated. He heaved a somewhat humorous sigh and lighted the inevitable cigarette. "To be perfectly serious, Mr. Franklin, I'm extraordinarily grateful to you. Few people could have exhibited the patience you did in listening to that rigmarole of mine at all, let alone coming down here and giving it so much thought and attention. There's some thing else, too. I think, perhaps, after our visits of Saturday morning I see some of those people in a different light—and myself in a different light. . . . And the other part of the problem?"

"That," said Franklin, "is very different. I may say that we have some information which at the moment we're not able to disclose. By the end of next week that information will have been examined very thoroughly and then I hope to make a statement. But I will say this. Whatever is proved from a discussion of the available information, one thing it won't do—solve the mystery of Yeoman's death."

"It might help?"

Franklin shrugged his shoulders. "Even if it gives the merest clue, which is all we can expect, your troubles will only be half begun. If I carry on from there I shall have to ask questions and make open inquiries, and your name can't be kept out of it. And it'll be a protracted inquiry and an expensive one—and I should say it'll be a hundred to one against my advising you to go with it."

Dryen nodded. "I understand. And you'll tell me what you can next week."

"Either on the Friday or the Saturday I hope to be going down to Pulvery for a week-end with Travers's people. We might call here on the way."

"Please do!" As he rose his face was beaming. "Come to tea on Friday—if you can't manage lunch. This week-end has done me an immense amount of good if it's only taught me the folly of rushing to conclusions."

He smiled as he picked up that door-knocker which was still lying on the table by the side of the carved head. He fingered it, then suddenly sniffed.

"Curious, you know. I could have sworn I smelt disinfectant of some kind!"

THE SECOND PHASE

CHAPTER VIII
BETWEEN THE LINES

IN SPITE OF the finality of Franklin's valedictory report to Dryden that Monday afternoon, there was more than one discussion in the early part of that week in Travers's flat at St. Martin's Chambers. Even that part of the problem which dealt with the backsliding of Dryden's acquaintances had been reviewed, and as for the major problem—the death of Yeoman—that had been discussed at enormous length and from every angle, though nothing remotely resembling a solution had presented itself. And when it should be discovered how the dog had died, all that was likely to happen, as Franklin put it, was merely a little more daylight to enable them to get a better view of the fog.

Travers was getting desperate. He was, in fact, only too afraid that the case was going to peter out altogether, and was, therefore, like a boy who watches the rain teeming down at two o'clock and still dares to hope the weather will clear and the pitch be fit for play at two-thirty. If he could have managed it without Franklin's knowledge he would have financed an inquiry himself, in the hope of discovering at least something exciting. After all, he had no wasteful hobbies, and far more money than he needed. In some moods he might even have financed a perfectly good murder.

On the Thursday night he was buried in his favourite chair, still casting about in his mind for something more solid than masses of forget-me-nots, devils writhing in agony, secretly buried dogs and puzzling parsons, when Franklin suddenly came in, and by the look of him, on his way to his own rooms upstairs.

"Hallo!" said Travers. "Been working late?"

"Yes," said Franklin. "Too much bother to get Palmer to order me a service dinner up here?"

Travers hopped up at once. "Of course not. Something on?"

"Got the report on the dog," said Franklin.

"Really!" He gave Palmer the order, then drew Franklin a chair alongside his own. "Something unusual was it?"

"Cyanide poisoning. Never a pellet anywhere."

Travers whistled. "Reliable man, was he?"

"Absolutely. I had a preliminary report yesterday, but I thought I'd wait for details. Now I thought we'd talk it over and decide what's to be done. Is Dryden to be told anything, for instance?"

"I see." Travers pulled a long face. "It's going to be awkward."

"Well, it depends on you," Franklin told him. "You were unofficial exhumer. Besides, if Rogers opened his mouth, the whole village may know about it now."

"Good Lord!" Travers was really alarmed. "Perhaps the police have been there and discovered half the dog's gone!"

"I don't think I'd worry," said Franklin, and sat down to his meal.

Travers got well down into the easy chair, legs stretched out. Palmer flitted in and out, noiseless and almost unnoticed.

"Now, then," Franklin began between the mouthfuls. "Who killed the dog?"

Travers's agile mind was never happier than when finding theories. Given five minutes' notice, he would have theories for the enlarged gullet of Jonah's Whale or the larynx of Balaam's ass.

"Well, I don't know who poisoned the dog, but I do know who didn't—and that's Yeoman himself. If he'd poisoned it there'd have been no reason to shift it from where Dryden found it buried. If you'd asked me how it was killed, I'd have said that the murderer had nice and handy in his pocket the usual piece of doped liver or meat."

"Which makes the murder—if it was a murder—premeditated, and I thought we agreed that couldn't possibly have happened."

Travers laughed. "Perhaps you're right. . . . And what's your own idea?"

"I'll tell you. Mind, I've had much longer than you to think things over, and even then my theory may be full of holes. All the same, I can't find a better. I say that Mould poisoned the dog so as to get his own back. He knew the route that Yeoman invariably took, so a day or so after they'd had words he left a piece of poisoned meat just off that path and behind the holly clump where the dog'd nose it. And the dog did nose it—the morning Yeoman was killed. He ate the meat and was dead before his master was—"

"Then why—"

"Let me finish. I'll answer objections later. For the moment let me assume that the dog did die before its master. Later on there was a shot—when Yeoman died, then more shots from the farmer's rabbiting party. Mould heard the shooting and after a discreet interval he came to see if the dog had taken the poison. It had, so he burned it hastily on the spot, but naturally he didn't see Yeoman lying dead on the other, and much lower, side of the stile. Later on he saw Dryden pottering about in the wood and got the wind up and moved the body to his own garden. How's that fit in the dog's death?"

"It's got one flaw," said Travers. "Why did Mould say anything to Rogers? Why did he let him know the dog was there?"

"Let me put it the way I see it," said Franklin, perfectly unperturbed. "Go back to the morning you called—the morning of the inquest on the boy Clark. Mould had to attend the inquest and he was all flurried about that and about your visit. He came out and saw Rogers just about to tackle that front bed. Rogers had been there on the Saturday and Mould had probably anticipated that he'd finish then, but the work had been too much and had had to get him the morning off. Well, Mould came out and was suddenly scared stiff. He'd forgotten all about the dog. What was he to do? Tell the man not to touch that bed after all? But that might arouse his suspicions Very well, then; on the spur of the moment he made up a yarn about the boy Clark—who was in his mind, and a convenient scapegoat—and told Rogers to re-bury the dog in the back. He also virtually told him to keep his mouth shut. Isn't that sound?"

"Yes," mumbled Travers. "I don't know that it isn't. But why didn't Mould bury the dog at the back of his house?"

Franklin smiled. "What about that mass of forget-me-nots? If he'd disturbed them, the hole would have been as conspicuous as a cemetery."

"Perhaps you're right. . . . And what was that about the dog dying first?"

Franklin's reply was so startling that Travers shot up in his seat.

"I'm going to put it to you that we know precisely how Yeoman died, and who saw him die."

Palmer moved the tripod table to the chairs. Franklin transferred his headquarters and began to pour out the coffee for them both.

"The theory," he went on, "is so absolutely simple that in my opinion it must be true. I say that Parish called at the Manor that morning full of the scheme to set Yeoman on his feet—the scheme he'd mentioned to Dryden overnight. Do you think he'd have popped his head in the door and then have gone straight home?"

"He was feeling unwell," remarked Travers.

Franklin shook his head. "Oh, no he wasn't! He was feeling perfectly well—*then* he didn't even ask the gardener if he'd seen him. He guessed that Yeoman had gone down the path through the wood, and he went that way to see. And what did he see? He arrived just in time to see Tom Yeoman kill himself by means of some simple apparatus or other, which should give the death the appearance of an accident, and which he hoped would escape detection."

"Good God!"

"What Parish thought we can hardly imagine. The shock must have been terrible. One thing that flashed through his mind was the necessity of removing that simple apparatus, in case it was discovered and the insurance company refused to pay. We've no time to go into the question of everything he thought and how he reacted, but it must have been a struggle between his own conscience and his loyalty to his friend. We must also say that the shock caused a partial recurrence of his breakdown. He hurried away from that terrible spot—past where the dog was lying dead—and out through a gap into Manor Lane. When he got home he felt ill, and no wonder. He's been a sick man ever since—and a man whose conscience carries a perpetual load. No wonder Dryden saw an immediate change in him."

"You're right," said Travers, and gave a quick nod of agreement. "I would, however, suggest one thing. You told me about the curious absent-mindedness exhibited by Parish. Why shouldn't he have some sort of aphasia. Surely he couldn't go on with his preaching and so on if he had this sin still on his mind—I mean the sin of defrauding an insurance company. A man of his type would have broken down completely. No," and he shook his head "I'd say the shock caused aphasia. Parish has forgotten what happened after he went into the garage. He's genuinely unaware of the cause of Yeoman's death—though sometimes he may be troubled by faint glimmerings coming and going from somewhere into nowhere, so to speak."

Franklin rubbed his hands. "I really think we've solved the whole thing. The trouble, of course, is Dryden. Is he to be told anything or not?"

"Heavens, no!" said Travers. "In the first place, he wouldn't believe it. Nothing would make him believe that Yeoman committed suicide, and I very much doubt if he'd believe that Parish would have done what we assume he did. Not only that, he's so very conscientious himself that there's no telling what he might do if he did believe it. One thing's a certainty. He'd be far more worried than he is at the moment."

"And what about the dog? Is he to be told anything about that?"

"I don't think so," said Travers, very quickly, "Just tell him that the information you thought you had has turned out to be of no value." Then his face suddenly changed. It was amusing to see the look of apprehension that came over it when he recognized that he was digging a pit for his own undoing. "But of course that means that the whole case is finished with!"

"That is so," agreed Franklin, and showed no particular concern. "The best thing might be to drop him a line to save going all that way round on Saturday—much as I'd like to see him again."

But Travers still had a shot in his locker. "I suppose there's no chance that that affair of Saturday could have been other than an accident?"

"Not a hope!" and Franklin laughed. "And when you mention the word chance, you're spreading too wide a net. He *might* have had his skull smashed in with a hammer and the bicycle accident might have been faked. He *might* have seen Clark put the dead dog under his window and have contrived the diabolical scheme to get his own back by sending him to South Farm after having put the only brake out of action. Fishes, in other words, might fly—"

"Beg pardon, sir, the letters!" Palmer suddenly appeared with the proceeds of the late post.

Travers ran his eye over the half-dozen or so, then made a dive. "Extraordinary! Dryden's writing, surely! Yes the Bableigh postmark. Do you mind?" He opened is glanced through it quickly, then read it aloud.

"'DEAR TRAVERS,

"'I wonder if you and Mr. Franklin would reconsider your plans for Friday. Will you both stay the night? There is ample room here, and for your man, as you know. You will wonder why I am making this request, but I have no reason I can give you—at least, which I could explain—except that I like seeing you both, and should be glad to have you.

"'I would add, principally because I would rather not refer to it again, that I am now beginning to recognize in myself two men also; one who, when you are both here, is my normal self; the other who, when he is alone, is even more gloomily pessimistic than the man you met that day in the Strand.

"'Perhaps you will let me know. There is no news from here that will not keep.

"'Yours as always,

"'HENRY DRYDEN.'"

He peered at Franklin over his glasses. "Well?"

Franklin seemed rather at a loss for words. "Extraordinary letter, don't you think?" He held his hand out for it, and read it through for himself. "There's something between the lines, if we could only get hold of it."

"You think we should go?"

"I think so," said Franklin, "That reference to two men. Very reminiscent of what he told us about Parish. . . . You going to write at once?"

"If there's time." He glanced at the clock, then halfway to the bureau he stopped. "An idea! I wonder if he would ask Parish to dinner to-morrow. In view of that overwhelming theory of yours, we might find him interesting. Besides, I haven't had a look at him yet."

"Splendid idea!" He waited till the letter was written and Palmer had been summoned, then got to his feet. "Well, I think I'll turn in early, before you begin theorizing about that letter." He frowned for a moment abstractedly, then smiled. "Oh, yes! I know what I was wanting to ask you. Why, precisely, did you buy that extraordinary picture from the Crome woman?"

"Chivalry."

"Chivalry be damned," said Franklin. "And you didn't buy it to clean her house for Dryden, though you pretended you did."

"Just a hunch," said Travers airily. "And a mania for dabbling in the unusual. . . . Like to have another look at it?"

Franklin laughed. "I'll annoy you by saying yes. . . if it's handy."

"It's handy enough." In a couple of minutes he had it on the table and was moving it about till the light made the most of it.

Franklin had a good look. "Amazing! I suppose it isn't too wild a guess to say it might be a human breast?"

Travers found it hard to be serious in the presence of that picture. "You Philistines always want something definite for your money. Photography's more in your line. This is merely the expression of an idea. Don't you remember what she told you? She said to herself, 'Aphrodite,' then let the brush have a free rein, as it were. This is the result."

"I know all that," said Franklin. "What I'd like to get at is this. Dryden said this picture gave him a feeling of repulsion. It even frightened him. Do you and I feel anything like that?"

"You're chasing rainbows," said Travers soberly. "If he said that picture frightened him, then I believe him. To you and me it's merely an abortion in paint. That means we arrive at what I said before. He's got the sort of eyes—spiritual eyes—that we haven't got." He picked up the picture. "It may be a hard thing to believe, but people do see invisible things and sense them, and you and I can't get away from it."

"Then I wish to the Lord he'd look a week or two ahead and sense something for *me*," said Franklin, smothering a yawn.

"And what's that?"

"The winner of the Derby," said Franklin. "Or isn't that what you blokes call spiritual?"

"You never know," said Travers. "If you remind me to-morrow night I'll throw out a hint or two."

CHAPTER IX
APPEARANCE OF ANGELS

IT WAS WELL after lunch on the Friday when they got away, and a dull afternoon it was. By the time they were clear of the suburbs the rain began to fall, and long before they left the main road for Bableigh it was coming down as if the heavens had opened.

"Cheerful sort of day," said Travers, with obvious irony. "Real murderers' weather."

Franklin rose to it. "Why murderers?"

"Washing out footprints—or vice versa." He waved his hand and the car skidded at the bend. Franklin started uneasily. "And talking of accidents," Travers went on, "what's the betting that Dryden wrote as he did—was anxious to see us, in other words—because there's been another accident during the week?"

Franklin grunted. "Ten to one against."

"Good enough. Taken in pennies."

He let out a series of gurgles from the horn as they approached Old House, and by the time they were ready to get out Jimson was at the gate with a couple of spare umbrellas, and Dryden was there too. Franklin's heart warmed as he saw him. Dryden shared with Travers the rare faculty of inspiring affection; he was a man, at least so Franklin felt, who could have had his choice of friends, and the affection lay in the fact that a perfectly ordinary person like himself should be so genuinely made to feel that he was one of them.

They made their way along the path to the porch, and Dryden smiled as he pointed to the knocker already installed on the front door. The room looked cheerful, with a bright fire and the table set out for tea. Travers in his breeziest mood bustled across and rubbed his cold hands.

"And how's things with you, Henry? Pretty good?"

"They might be worse," said Dryden.

Franklin might have been mistaken, but he thought he was looking less robust than his usual self. He seemed strained, and like a man who forces himself to anticipate a pleasurable time.

"Good." Travers nodded away at the fire. "I suppose you wouldn't like to settle a small bet? Any more accidents since we were here last?"

Dryden looked at him queerly. "Why do you ask?"

"I told you. Just a small bet. It was raining hard, and we wanted something to do." He rose as Jimson came in with tea. "I take it I lose. There've been none?"

Dryden caught Franklin's eye. "There has been one—and a most unusual one."

"Good Lord!" Travers stared. "Not somebody killed?"

"Come and have tea," smiled Dryden, and sat down at the table. "No, it's nobody killed. Merely that there's been an accident to Miss Faithful's wireless set. She imagines Martha did something to it. She sent for me to put it right, but none of us in this house knows anything about it, so I told her you people were coming down and you'd have things right in no time."

"I think I might reasonably claim to be paid the sum of tenpence," said Travers. "But talking about repairs, Henry, Palmer's the one. He's an unholy marvel on wireless matters. Let Jimson take him round to investigate."

"We'll all go," said Dryden. "She'd love that. I'll send Jimson round to prepare her. By the way, you'll be surprised to hear that Parish has a set now. I met him on Tuesday, and I don't know how it arose, but I found myself agreeing that a set would be company for him. Jimson tells me the man from Hastings was over to install it yesterday. It's an electric one."

"Do him all the good in the world from what I've heard of him," remarked Travers. "He's coming to-night, Henry?"

"Yes," said Dryden, and hesitated. "I'm very glad he is coming. It'll be the first time he's spent an evening out—to my knowledge— since Tom Yeoman died. . . . I wonder if you'd tell me why you wished me to ask him?"

"Just wanted to meet him," said Travers off-handedly. "Also Franklin has some theory about aphasia he wishes to work out."

"Aphasia!"

"Yes." Franklin decided to mix truth and half-truth. "We hope it won't be a shock to you, but the theory we've been discussing during the week, and which we were to put up to you, is what we consider a final one. Parish is suffering from aphasia. He has forgotten completely what happened the morning Yeoman was killed. He remembers that he went to the garage to look for him. What he has forgotten is that he went to the wood to look for him, too, and there found him dead—or actually saw him die. The shock of that brought on a recurrence of his breakdown. His mind went blank."

Dryden was staring at him, the cup held half-way to his mouth. He set it down again like a man who has had a tremendous shock, and then something that might have been relief, or shame, came over his face. He looked away as he shook his head.

"Poor old chap. . . . Terrible! Terrible!"

"Let's talk of something more cheerful," suggested Travers.

"I've only one other thing to say," said Franklin. "I'd very much like to mention Yeoman to-night, and see how Parish reacts. I'd also like you to mention certain things, no matter what, that occurred before Yeoman's death, so that we may see the extent of the aphasia. You won't mind that?"

"Not in the least. The quicker the diagnosis, the quicker the cure."

They said no more about Parish, and soon after tea set off for the scene of the latest accident. The rain looked like coming down all night, and the clouds were so low that Miss Faithful had the light on in her little sitting-room. Travers liked her at once, and it was a laughable and jolly entry when the four of them overcrowded the tiny room.

"You're looking better, you know," Franklin told her, and really meant it.

Perhaps it was the small excitement, but she seemed less fragile and her cheeks were flushed. She seemed specially anxious to put Palmer at his ease, and Travers was intensely amused at the way Palmer was taking it. Then the inquiry began. The expert ran his eye over the innards of the set, examined connections, took out the main plug, replaced it, then switched on. The valves glowed at once, and in a few seconds something could be heard. Then it roared out full—two, if not three, perfectly good programmes at the same time.

Travers caught Miss Faithful's eye and smiled. "You'd better damp it down a bit, Palmer."

"Yes, sir," said Palmer, paying more tribute to that piece of ignorance than it deserved. He twiddled the left-hand knob, but nothing happened. The noise was as raucous as ever, and through the snappy rhythm of a dance band a voice could be heard announcing names, and somewhere else a woman was singing. Palmer seemed unmoved. Miss Faithful beamed round as much as to say that people could now hear the trouble for themselves. But then Palmer swooped. The music stopped for a second, then went straight on again. It softened as if by magic. More wonderful still, there was one programme only—the dance band.

Palmer stepped back and bowed ceremoniously. "I think, ma'am, you'll now find everything in order. The plug was in the wrong socket."

She was delighted and surprised. "But how did it get there, Mr. Palmer?"

"If I might venture to suggest it, ma'am, I'd say the maid pulled it out when dusting and then replaced it wrongly." He bowed again. "It's foolproof now, ma'am. You should have no more bothers like that."

So much for that. Palmer departed amid a chorus of embarrassing applause, but the others stayed on for quite a while—Miss Faithful was so obviously delighted to have them. It was only the approach of dinner, and the vicar with it, that drove them out into the pouring rain.

"Perfectly delightful old lady!" Travers exclaimed enthusiastically. "There's a spot in your village, Henry, where you should always feel at home."

"I'm glad you liked her." The unnatural gloom of the evening, the driving rain, the shelter of the umbrella, all these gave a sort of concealment that made him reveal something intensely personal which the broad daylight might have kept him from disclosing. "It was because of something in connection with her that I wanted us all to go in to-night. I'll tell you for what it's worth; merely that I saw her the other afternoon and experienced a sense of foreboding. I can't explain it. You must take my word for it, but it was so strong that I made an excuse to see her again the same evening—and the feeling came again."

The others made no comment. As they trudged on in the dusk and the driving rain, Dryden's question seemed quite natural.

"You felt nothing of the sort to-night?"

"No," said Travers.

Franklin said nothing, and Dryden appeared to take his answer for granted. He paused for a moment at the gate.

"You'll forgive my speaking like that. It sounded foolish, perhaps, and presumptuous,"

"No, no, Henry!" Travers told him. "You'd be foolish to think that."

Dryden shook his head. "Forget I said it. . . . . Some obsession, perhaps." And he closed the gate.

The three rose as Jimson ushered the vicar in, and now it was Travers's turn to have the disconcerting experience of grasping a limp hand and listening to a voice that was directed at something behind him. It might have been the brightness of the room after that short walk through the darkness, but he blinked as he looked about him and seemed for a moment or two at a loss for what to say. Then he began to talk, and Travers and Franklin saw something of that forced geniality that had so horrified Dryden when he first had experience of it. It was not the geniality of the parvenu who chatters because he is not socially sure; it was not the garrulity of the partially intoxicated, and yet it seemed to have something of both. Perhaps Dryden's diagnosis had been correct. Parish, as he chattered and grimaced, was like a man who remembers desperately that once upon a time he could talk and laugh and set the table on a roar. Then, when Jimson came in with the beginnings of the meal, that mood passed and he became almost preoccupied with his meal, and it was hardish work to get him into the conversation.

Dryden that evening was certainly the perfect host, with a grave courtesy and a sympathy that had their origin in Franklin's revelation of the afternoon. Travers was his most entertaining and effervescent self, and Franklin was always ready at the right moment with something to keep things going—but the conversation dragged for all that. Then Dryden tried raillery.

"They tell me you've got your wireless set installed," he said. "Wonderful how you hardened old conservatives come round in time!"

Parish looked at him blankly.

"Don't you remember a year or so ago when you gave a comminatory service because you thought people stopped at home in the evening instead of coming to church?"

"Did I?" He still looked puzzled.

"Of course you did!" laughed Dryden. "Now you've become a convert. Something like Mrs. Jimson, who was horrified at bobbed hair and had her own done six months later."

Parish smiled feebly.

Travers leaned across, as if he, too, had remembered something. "Didn't you tell me, Henry, that the vicar was a poet?"

"Yes. He turns out some really admirable work."

"Have you done anything recently?" asked Franklin.

"Not recently. Nothing comes. . . . I've sat down and thought . . . and now it worries me. The inspiration's not there."

"I understand," said Travers. "You can't force that sort of thing. . . . And perhaps you won't mind my mentioning something that may be the cause of it. Losing a friend like Yeoman must have been a great shock. I met him here once and I knew what a great chap he was."

"He's dead, you know."

The remark was so startling that Travers gaped. "Yes. . . . I know. Very tragic affair."

"Mr. Dryden was telling us all about it," said Franklin. "And the whole thing seems to me to be so tragic because you might have averted it."

"I might have averted it?"

"Well, what I mean is that if you'd have guessed when he wasn't in the garage that he might have gone through the wood, you might have caught him up and the accident wouldn't have happened."

Parish made a sudden frown and his eyes wrinkled up. Then he shook his head. "I was ill, you know. . . . I don't think about it now. It always distresses me." Then he leaned across the table to Dryden. "I wonder if I might tell you something . . . something that always comes when I try to think back to that morning. . . . I see the figure of an angel, and sometimes"—his voice became an intense whisper—"it becomes a devil!"

Dryden looked enormously distressed. His own hand was shaking as he patted Parish on the arm. Travers watched quietly, and Franklin wondered if the scene would end in a breakdown. But the vicar drew his hand away, his face cleared, and he resumed his meal as if nothing had happened.

It was not until the meal was over and they had drawn up to the fire that Dryden returned to the subject of the village.

"I called on Mould yesterday," he said, and the remark was as much for the information of Travers as anybody else. "He tells me you've seen him too."

"Yes," said Parish. "I called early in the week. I don't know what made me do it, but I woke up with an overwhelming urge to go and see him. . . . He seems himself again."

"Yes. . . . And talking of Mould, I've often wondered just what you meant some months ago when you told me you had a great scheme for pulling him together. You remember? You said you were going to pry him out of his shell."

"Did I?" The words seemed a tremendous full-stop. He leaned forward, staring fixedly into the fire. He gave a sort of cackle. "Mould's a different man!"

"Yes, but why?"

"Why?" His voice acquired a tone that grated on Travers's nerves. "No need to ask why. There are things that even a man like Mould can't withstand. When it's a question of a man's soul, even the angels of God appear among men!"

Travers was startled. Dryden moved restlessly in his chair.

"You're talking metaphorically, surely."

"God's ways are not our ways," said Parish, still staring into the fire.

Franklin watched him as one watches a friend who suddenly leaves the others yards away from a precipice and walks to the very edge.

"What the Divine purpose is for Ashley Mould I can't say. For the present his feet have been snatched from the pit."

"What you mean by that I don't know," said Dryden, and again shuffled in his chair. "I do know that one or two other people might do with a change of heart too. Think of this village when you first came here—"

Parish broke in quickly: "It's patience we need . . . and faith. The powers of darkness can never resist faith." Then, all at once, he looked away from the fire and seemed to be groping back into the past. He began to smile, then turned to Dryden with a sudden surprise. "Why, that's what you and I were talking about one day! The village, you know. How people had changed." He stopped, and seemed to be groping again, then he let his head sink wearily between his hands. "It all goes so quickly. . . . My memory is not what it was."

Dryden made a gesture of hopelessness. Travers, trying to see the exact purport of the conversation, understood what he felt. He himself had been like a man groping in a fog. Just what Parish had meant was beyond him, unless his words had been fanatical vapourings, and they'd been too quietly uttered and too earnest for that. Dryden got up.

"Now what about some chess? Parish, you'll play Mr. Franklin? He'll give you a good game."

The vicar appeared not to understand for a moment, then he roused himself. "Chess, you say? I'm afraid not." Perhaps he saw something in their faces that told him he was acting strangely, because he shook his head as he rose from the chair. "I think I must have been wool-gathering. . . . But I won't play, if you don't mind. You people play and I'll watch for a bit."

"But you're in no hurry?" protested Dryden.

"I must be away by nine," said Parish resolutely. "George Finch's wife is dangerously ill, you know, and I promised to go in. . . . But I'd like to sit here for a short time. My mind isn't equal to concentration."

Travers smiled at him. "You and I will have a good gossip, vicar. These two fellows can muddle their brains if they like."

They sat chatting away by the fire while the chess-players yarned on in their corner. Travers had a tremendous surprise. Once Parish got going, he was positively fascinating. Most of the time he was talking about China and his experiences there, and Travers found him a man of subtle humour, keen perceptions and wide sympathies. Parish must have found in Travers much the same thing, for he stayed on till close on the half-hour before he became aware of the time and got to his feet.

"I'm not going to let you walk down there in the rain," said Dryden decisively. "Jimson shall get the car out."

"How far is it?" asked Travers.

"Quarter of a mile beyond Windyridge."

"I'll get the Bentley out," said Travers. "A little fresh air would do me good. You people can finish your game."

Parish protested vehemently. He was certainly not going to give all that trouble. Besides, it might not be raining. And when they looked out, the rain had actually stopped and it certainly looked not too bad a night for a walk. They saw him off from the gate.

"I'll have a look at that portrait in the morning," were Travers's last words as he shook hands. Then the vicar disappeared in the shadow of the trees and they trooped in again to the fire. It was so cosy after the damp outside that the chess was abandoned and the chairs were drawn up and the glasses replenished.

"What was that about a portrait?" Franklin asked.

"Oh, just that portrait of the poet Parnell which Dryden told us about. I happened to mention that I might be able to tell him if it were a contemporary painting."

"And how'd you find him?" asked Dryden. "You seemed to be talking very animatedly."

"How did I find him?" Travers frowned. "I won't answer that question direct, Henry. I'd rather say this. I think the aphasia idea is implicitly correct. He's forgotten everything about Yeoman and the conversations he had with you about what I may call your circle. What's more to the point, he's trying hard all the time to remember."

"What about his mannerisms?" asked Franklin.

"We all have 'em," said Travers. "I admit that queer, religious kink of his is somewhat disconcerting, but you could get used to it." He looked at the pair of them. "I expect you'll think me an eccentric, but I really like Parish. I know he's a sick man mentally, and knowing the reasons I'd say that's to his credit; I know he has some startling peculiarities, but he has an awful lot of good points." He smiled. "I never want to hear a more interesting person than he was with me. He was normal—absolutely normal. All the same, there's one question I'd like to ask."

"And what's that?"

"Well, what was the reason for all that talk of his about angels and devils and the powers of darkness? Why did he say he saw an angel whenever he went back to the day of Yeoman's death?"

"That's all the result of the breakdown," said Franklin. "It's an exceedingly mild form of mania and it'll pass."

Travers shook his head. "I think there's more in it than that. If he's got something on his mind now, what was the happening that impressed it on his mind?"

Franklin laughed. "Well, what was it? Answer a few of your own questions."

"All in good time," said Travers. "Answer me this one first. Why did he particularly refer to devils and the powers of darkness in connection with Mould, and claim that his feet were now snatched from the pit?"

"Heaven knows!" said Franklin. "Or do you know?"

Travers shook his head warily. "I can't say . . . yet. I have the glimmerings of an idea."

"Then tell us the glimmerings."

"Oh, no! If I suggested it to you, you'd say I had a kink too. To-morrow, perhaps, after we've seen that picture of Parnell."

"That reminds me." Franklin turned to Dryden. "Do you happen to have any examples of Parish's poetry? Cuttings from the papers, for instance."

"Sorry," said Dryden. "I did keep a few, but I burnt them a short time ago. They were very harmless and simple, inspired entirely by the works of his reputed ancestor." He pointed to a slim green volume on the side table. "That's the poems of Parnell, if you like to take that to bed with you. Parish's were much about the same thing—except, of course, the famous 'Hermit.' He couldn't aspire to anything like that."

"'Hermit'? The title of a poem, is it?"

"That's right, Parnell is one of the examples of a man's being remembered for one thing only. This particular poem was so famous that his contemporaries actually nicknamed him 'the hermit.'"

"I believe I remember it," said Travers. "Narrative poem, isn't it?"

Dryden smiled. "I don't write short stories, but if I did I'd be jealous of the man who first thought of that plot, Parnell hasn't that slick, modern treatment, but even he can't stop its being one of the three best stories the world has ever read,"

"Then don't tell me what it's all about," said Franklin. "If I'm going to read it in bed I'd like it to have the thrill of the unexpected."

It might have been because they sat on yarning for another hour, or it might have been the fresh air of the journey down, but whatever it was, Franklin got no farther than the first page of that poem before he felt so uncontrollably drowsy that he put the book aside and was asleep in a couple of seconds. And that was a pity. If he had read it through he might have noticed at least one thing that concerned the village of Bableigh, and if he had read it through a second time he might have saved the lives of a couple of people, But that is all problematical. The fact remains that Franklin fell asleep. Next morning Jimson saw the book at the bedside, and knowing it was often picked up and read at odd moments by his master, took it downstairs again. His wife, tired of seeing it on the table, slipped it into the bookcase. And so much for Parnell's "Hermit."

CHAPTER X
THINGS HAPPEN

IT WAS JUST before ten-thirty the following morning, and Travers was remarking for the third time that he supposed he and Franklin had better be pushing along, when Jimson appeared suddenly and announced that Parker would like to see Mr. Dryden at once on a matter of urgency.

"Show him in," said Dryden, and then to Travers and Franklin, "No need for you to move. It's probably something to do with Monday's bench."

Parker got into his stride straight away. "I've come to ask your advice about a certain matter, sir. Perhaps you've heard about it?"

"Heard about what, Parker?"

"Miss Rose's garden, sir; that rockery what she had made. She sent for me the very first thing this morning to come and see it, sir. Someone's torn all the flowers up!" "But how extraordinary!" He looked at Franklin and Travers, perfectly flabbergasted. "You mean the rockery's been destroyed?"

"That's it, sir—and, what's more, I think I know the one that did it, speaking confidentially, sir."

"And who's that?"

"Young Tanner, who drives the baker's cart from Northurst."

"But what on earth did he do it for?"

Parker explained. "It's like this, sir. He's been hanging about after that girl Dollie, the servant, and Miss Rose had occasion to speak to him about it this week, sir. She reckons she turned round quick and caught him making faces behind her back, and then she gave him a proper piece of her mind, and he was impudent—or what she called impudent. When I saw her this morning she reckoned he was the one who did it, so I went back to make a few inquiries. His brother let out he'd been out last night and didn't get home till late, and another man I spoke to, who always leaves the Roebuck just before ten, told me he saw somebody like young Tanner come out of Miss Rose's front gate."

"I see." Dryden tugged away at his beard. "Then if you know who did it, what's your problem?"

"Well sir, this witness ain't none too sure." He gave a quick look at the clock. "If Miss Rose had her way, sir, I might get myself into trouble. He'll be coming this morning about eleven with the bread, and I told her I'd have a word with him; only if she gets in her spoke, so to speak, she might say more than she ought."

Dryden blew his nose to conceal the smile. "Then why don't you see him before he gets there?"

Parker looked even more uneasy. "If I do, sir, he'll still be going there after I've finished with him."

"Hm!" said Dryden. "I see your point. But what do you want me to do?"

"Well, sir"—Parker looked down nervously—"I wondered if you'd mind having a word with her yourself? If you should happen to be there when Tanner called—" And he left the rest for Dryden to fill in.

"All right," said Dryden. "Find your way to the kitchen and tell Jimson to give you a glass of ale". He gave the pair a humorous look. "Like to go along?"

"An extraordinary piece of vandalism!" remarked Franklin, giving Travers a questioning look.

"Might as well go along, I think," said Travers. "We've got to see Parish's picture, and we can do that on the way back."

There was no excitement whatever in the village that morning, but plenty was to await them at The Pleasance. Dollie, who opened the door, showed a face that was puffed with blubbering, and at the sight of Dryden she began to cry again. Then Agnes Rose came in, accompanied by the yapping Poms. A perfectly venomous look passed over her face at the sight of the snivelling girl, and this changed as quickly to an effusive smile.

"If it isn't Mr. Dryden! And just when we're so upset," She waved a despairing hand at nothing in particular.

Dryden explained that he'd come to help. He'd seen Parker, and he hoped to see Tanner. He also introduced Travers, who sat enraptured at the story that was told them, with its delicious lack of logic and its wanderings from the point. Young Tanner was certainly due for a warm reception when he arrived with the morning loaf.

But there was nothing amusing about the garden. Whoever had set about the ruination of that rockery had made a complete success of the job, and he seemed to have worked at leisure and without any fear of interruption. Some plants had been torn up by the roots; others whose hold had been too secure, had been stripped to the soil. Quite a heap of tulips lay on the stone paths, and dwarf lavender bushes, clumps of pinks and carnations, aubretias and late wallflowers, and scores of flowers whose names none of them remembered lay strewn in all directions.

"Couldn't some of these be replanted?" asked Travers, pointing to a clump of aubretia of the most wonderful pink.

She gave a helpless look. "But I don't know where things go. And they won't grow again if they're in bloom. Look at these tulips now," and she began picking up the bedraggled blooms, only to let them fall again. Then she clicked her tongue and gave a vicious shake of the head. "I'm sick of the wretched rockery! Sick of it!"

Dryden, who thought for a moment she was going to burst into tears, looked rather helpless too. Then there was the sound of a cart, and he almost pulled her arm.

"There's Tanner. I think I'd better see him first, if you don't mind."

By the time they were at the back door Parker's voice could be heard. Dryden made no bones about scurrying off round the house, and the others followed him. Agnes Rose, who chose the route through the house, arrived at the front door in time to see the five move off in silent and solemn procession along the road towards Windyridge. Twenty yards along the road, Dryden stopped.

"Now, Tanner, what have you to say?"

He was a pert-looking youth of about nineteen, and however confident he had been in the presence of Parker, that grave procession in the presence of four six-foot men had taken most of the assurance out of him. His look was now furtive.

"What about, sir?"

"You know what I'm referring to, Tanner. Were you here last night or not?"

"No, sir. I wasn't. You ask anybody you like."

Dryden looked at Parker. The policeman took up the case with the twin facers of the brother and the other witness.

"And what's more," Parker concluded heavily, "if I was you I'd make a clean breast of it while there's a chance of keeping it out of court,"

The last attempt at bravado had gone, and Tanner was looking a badly scared criminal. Perhaps the presence of those two strangers, who looked as if they knew everything he had ever done, was the deciding factor; at any rate, he told his tale. He had been in the garden the previous night, but not in the real garden; only in the coal-shed which stood rather away from the house. He had been accustomed to spending a lot of time there on the nights when Dollie was in, and she was in the habit of slipping out of her kitchen at intervals.

"And who's to prove your story about last night?" asked Dryden.

"Dollie can prove it, sir." He looked very sheepish. "She only came out once last night, sir, and that was to say she'd had to sit with Miss Rose instead of being in the kitchen." He licked his lips nervously. "Then we said good night, sir, and she saw me start off home."

"And how'd you spend your time in the shed?" asked Franklin.

"I smoked a cigarette or two, sir . . . and I kept on waiting."

"And what was the time when you left?"

"Just before ten, sir."

They let him go after that. Parker could lay his hands on him whenever he wanted him, and there was no point in having him present when his story was inquired into. As it happened, too, the girl confirmed every word he had said. The shed floor had a good few cigarette ends, and revealed the marks of two sets of feet; but since every path of that garden, including the mazes of the rockery and the path to the front door, was stone-flagged, there was no sign of a footprint elsewhere.

"I wonder if it's any use having a word with Parish?" said Dryden. "We know he was this way at about ten."

The vicar had been a card up Parker's sleeve. "To tell you the truth, sir," he said, "I saw the reverend gentleman this morning, when he was coming from George Finch's. He told me he'd been overtook by a youth on a bicycle down the road yonder, and he thought it was Tanner."

"Mr. Parish spent the night there?"

"Oh, no, sir! He was there till after midnight, so he told me, and there was nothing stirring when he came by then. He came again this morning before breakfast, and that's when I saw him. He'd been speaking to Miss Rose."

When Parker had gone the three reported to the owner of the devastated rockery, and to Dryden fell the task of pacification and the keeping of the unfortunate Dollie out of the reach of further recriminations. Tanner, he hinted diplomatically, might not have been the vandal after all.

"Then who did do it?" she exploded indignantly.

"We can't say. Parker has just gone to make further inquiries."

"Parker!" and she snorted. "A lot he'll find out!" She gave a look that was even more vindictive. "If you ask me who's responsible for all this, it's Harriet Blunt. She put him up to it. She never did forgive me for—"

"Come, come!" Dryden spoke sharply. "You forget yourself to say absurd things like that."

She looked at him bleakly, then began a furtive dabbing at her eyes. Just when Dryden was looking as if he wished himself anywhere but where he was, there was a diversion. A quick tap at the door and it opened, and there stood the little servant, no longer weeping, but wearing an expression of fierce resolution.

"May I speak to you, miss?"

Her mistress looked at her vacantly, then pulled herself together. "Yes. What is it?"

"I'm giving in my notice now, on the spot. After the things you've said, I won't stay in the house another minute." She glared defiantly.

Agnes Rose looked as if the world was falling to pieces. Then she burst out, "You rude girl! How dare you—"

Dryden broke in frantically, "Please! please! . . . Dollie, you mustn't speak to your mistress like that. And if you leave at once you'll lose your wages."

"That you will, you impudent girl!"

"There's only one day, and that you can keep," retorted Dollie. "And your work—and your filthy temper!"

When she had flounced off, Miss Rose collapsed with a dramatic suddenness. Her lip began to tremble, then she sobbed in earnest. Franklin and Travers sidled unobtrusively to the door. There was the sound of Dryden's final attempts at consolation, then he joined them outside, his face a fiery red. It was only when they were well clear of the house that he uttered a disconsolate, "Dear! dear!"

Travers laughed, Franklin laughed, and then Dryden saw the ridiculous side and laughed too, if none too heartily.

"You're certainly a sportsman, Henry," said Travers. "It may seem very amusing now, but I've never been so thoroughly uncomfortable in my life."

"It's a most unfortunate affair," said Franklin. "If it had been my garden I'd have been infuriated. You think Tanner did it?"

"I think he must have done," said Dryden. "The evidence that he was in the shed doesn't prove that he never went out of it. The problem'll be to bring it home to him. I don't know how you people feel, but on the bench I've always stood out against convictions on circumstantial evidence." He broke off. "Hallo! What's Miss Blunt doing abroad so early?"

Harriet Blunt greeted them cheerfully. Travers liked the look of her the first moment he saw her, which was when she was almost on them, her face wearing a smile that was either demure or ironic.

"Morning, Mr. Dryden. I see you've heard the news."

"Yes," said Dryden. "How are you this morning? Mr. Franklin you know. This is Mr. Travers—Miss Blunt."

She nodded pleasantly at the pair of them. "Found anything out yet?"

Dryden was scarcely prepared for that, "You mean, who did it?"

"That's right. If you haven't, then it looks rather bad for me!"

Dryden chuckled politely. "Those guilty consciences, you know!"

She nodded, just a trifle grimly. "You see, I know Agnes Rose. The vicar gave me the tip." Dryden looked so surprised that she laughed. "Agnes buttonholed him this morning when he was coming back from George Finch's. I gathered she'd told him it was the sort of thing I might do." She nodded cheerfully. "Well, I suppose I'd better be getting along before the police return!" And off she went.

Dryden gave a prodigious sigh. "Women are amazing creatures!"

"Aren't they!" said Travers cheerfully. "And so that's Miss Blunt. Most interesting woman, I should imagine. And. here we are at the vicarage, Henry. You coming in too?"

"I'd like to, but I don't think I'd better," said Dryden. "You must definitely stay to lunch now—you can't wriggle out of it—so I'll prepare Jimson. And Parker might want to see me."

They waved him a cheery farewell as he passed round the bend, then went through the gate.

"By the way," said Travers, "don't be surprised at anything I say when we get inside. I want to make an experiment."

Before Franklin could say a word he moved on—but only for a yard or two. A long shoot from one of the climbing roses caught his hat and removed it dexterously, and before he had quite realized what had happened, an aged gardener had made an appearance.

"Hurt yourself, sir?"

"Not at all," said Travers, and retrieved his hat. "Bit dangerous these roses, aren't they?"

"I'll have 'em off at once, sir," the man assured him. "Mr. Parish started to do them himself, only that there accident happened to young Clark and stopped him afore he got as far as this. And then he went and lost the cutters."

An old woman opened the door, the housekeeper by the look of her. She was rather deaf, and the old gardener actually called over to them from the path where he was weeding, "You'll have to holler a bit more, sir!" Still, they got her to understand they were callers, and she showed them into what was evidently the study. She stopped hesitatingly at the door.

"I'll tell the vicar, sir, but he isn't very well this morning."

"Please don't," said Travers, getting up at once. "We really mustn't disturb him."

He began all over again, to make her understand, and in the middle of it the vicar appeared. He was looking very drawn, as if suffering from a sick headache.

"Awfully sorry to have disturbed you, vicar," said Travers. "We wouldn't have done it for the world, if we'd known."

Parish smiled wanly as he took Travers's arm. "Please don't go. I'm much better than I was." He drew his hand across his forehead. "The head feels numb. Some kind of neuralgia, perhaps."

"You've been overdoing it," said Franklin. "Up late last night, and then up again this morning."

"And how was your patient?" asked Travers.

"Mrs. Finch? Oh, much better. She took a turn for the better just after midnight."

He got them seated and apologized for the absence of cigarettes. "I used to be quite a heavy smoker," he said, "but somehow it doesn't appeal to me now. . . . You've been out for a walk?"

"Yes, we've been to see Miss Rose's garden. Most amazing affair, vicar, don't you think so?"

"Most amazing," the vicar agreed. "She was very distressed when I saw her this morning. Still, where your treasure is, you know," and he nodded vicarially.

"And this is the portrait?" said Travers, cutting short any further moralizing.

Franklin followed his look to the rather dingy oil-painting that hung above the mantelpiece, and rose to have a clearer view. The vicar joined them.

"Of course you realize, Mr. Travers, that I place no reliance on the story that it's either the poet Parnell or an ancestor of mine. I will say that it resembles the known prints, and we've always had the tradition in our family."

"Quite." Travers peered more closely. "It's very dirty, vicar, if you don't mind my saying so—and very heavily varnished. Why don't you have it cleaned?"

"You think it's worth it?"

Travers smiled. "Well, there's always the chance of a discovery, you know. I can say very definitely that it's a contemporary portrait, irrespective of costume."

The vicar seemed remarkably gratified. Then Franklin noticed a framed photograph of what he recognized as Naples. The vicar, it appeared, had spent some time in Italy after his illness. Franklin astonished him by revealing that his own mother had been Italian, and in a couple of seconds he and the vicar were yarning away by themselves. Travers, with his elbow touching the books on the shelf of the fireplace recess, decided to have a look at them. The first three he saw interested him, and once they had interested Parish, for though the sides were now dusty, there were certain leaves dog-eared and margins annotated. He flicked over the pages and read a line or two here and there, then looked up to find the others watching him, and their conversation at an end.

Travers smiled. "I hope I'm not being too irreverent, vicar, but your ancestor seems to have been put in very bad company." He indicated the books by way of explanation. "Here's the poems of Parnell, with a huge Voltaire on one side, and a selection from Anatole France on the other—both atheists of an ironical type."

Parish was either still feeling unwell, or he was suddenly in no jocular mood.

"Truth is put into all sorts of vessels, Mr. Travers," he said severely.

"Exactly," beamed Travers. He pulled out the ancient-looking Voltaire and exhibited it. "When I first saw this chap I thought it was the very same edition of the Cabbala which my uncle had. The binding's the same." He leaned forward ingratiatingly. "Most fascinating, all that Cabbala stuff, you know—angels, archangels, and powers of darkness." He replaced the book and appealed to Parish again. "Don't you think there are many points of resemblance to all legend, the Greek especially; I mean, where gods and spiritual powers identify themselves with the affairs of mortals?"

The vicar looked at him oddly. The stare was almost as distraught as that with which he had looked into the fire the previous night in Dryden's house.

"That would be religion, not legend."

Travers shrugged gracefully. "Perhaps you're right. You see, what I was thinking of particularly was Satanism and the Black

Mass. I know it's only one—er—connotation, but one often means that when talking of the powers of darkness, don't you think?"

Parish said nothing, but still stared queerly. Travers went airily on.

"You were mentioning something of the sort last night, you remember—at least so I gathered." He leaned forward confidentially. "Now when you referred to the angels of God appearing among men and an angel that became a devil—"

He broke off. The vicar still stared, and stared with an uncanny fixity, but his look seemed directed to behind where Travers sat. So curious was it that Travers turned his head to see what thing or person it was that was holding the vicar's gaze so unwinkingly, and then something happened. With a feeble sort of smile the vicar raised his hand. The next moment he lurched forward in the chair, and as Franklin half caught him, slid to the carpet in what looked a dead faint.

Travers was over in a flash, badly scared. "What is it? Is he all right?"

"A faint, by the look of it." He was already undoing the clerical collar and Travers found a cushion for the head.

"Find that woman!" ordered Franklin. "Get some water and see if she's any brandy!"

Travers sprinted out. Franklin pulled back the collar and undid the shirt. Round the neck beneath it was a cord, and as he loosened the shirt still farther he saw what was at the end of it—a small metal crucifix. But there seemed to be something else, tied to the crucifix itself, and with black thread. He looked more closely, then held his breath. . . . When Travers got back with the cup of water—the housekeeper fluttering at his heels—the vicar's eyelids were already quivering, and when Travers held the water to his lips he opened his eyes and stared about him.

Outside the vicarage gate Franklin stopped and patted his pockets.

"Lost something?" asked Travers.

"My gloves. Must have left them at The Pleasance. Perhaps I'd better sprint back and get them."

"I'll push on," said Travers, "and tell 'em you're coming. And I think I'll send a telegram to Pulvery to say we're on the way."

They crossed the road together. Franklin seemed very perturbed about something.

"Tell me," he suddenly said. "What was the exact meaning of all that angel and devil stuff you were talking at Parish before he went off?"

"Meaning?" He smiled. "I'm afraid it hadn't any."

"You mean to say you made it up as you went along!"

"More or less. Just highfalutin gibberish."

Franklin looked at him, made as if to say something, then mumbled, "Back in five minutes," as he strode off.

CHAPTER XI
TRAVERS WAXES ELOQUENT

FRANKLIN WAS NOT more than a quarter of an hour late for lunch after all.

"Hallo!" said Dryden when he came in. "Find your gloves?"

"Yes, thanks", said Franklin. "I mean, they never were lost. That was an excuse to go back to The Pleasance."

Travers looked pained. "Surely you know that the very first rule in bridge is not to deceive your partner."

"Deceive?" said Franklin. "I thought you knew all about it. I had the gloves in my hand when I made the remark."

Dryden smiled. "That rather alters things. But come along and have lunch."

The meal seemed to have been expressly designed for conversation, and there was no need for Jimson to officiate. Travers helped himself to cold beef from the sideboard, then resumed the attack on Franklin.

"And why did you return to The Pleasance?"

Franklin waited till they were all seated before he took out his pocket-book. He laid something on the white table-cloth.

"This is a little bunch of flowers, quite fresh, as you see. Here's a single faded one which I claim came off the same clump. Do you agree?"

Dryden got up at once and he and Travers took the specimens to the window. There seemed no doubt in the mind of either.

"I wouldn't go so far as to say the same clump," said Travers, "but they're certainly the same variety. Tell me; didn't these come from Miss Rose's rockery?"

"They did," said Franklin as he put them back in the pocket-book. "I took the fresh ones off the clump a few minutes ago. The limp specimen was tied with half a dozen others to a crucifix that Parish wears round his neck beneath his shirt. I saw it when I was attending to him. I'd fastened the shirt up again by the time you got back with the water. And you probably noticed that when he came round he didn't show any particular anxiety. I mean, his hands didn't go there to feel or anything."

"But how utterly incredible!" exclaimed Dryden, who was forgetting all about his meal. "What on earth does it all mean?"

"That's what we might reasonably discuss," Franklin told him. "We'll eat and argue. By the way, what happened in the kitchen when you went there?"

Travers looked surprised. "Nothing really. The housekeeper was there and another woman—"

"That'd be Mrs. Clark," said Dryden, "the mother of that boy who was killed. She comes in for the rough work. Parish shares her with Miss Blunt."

"Well, she was there," said Travers, "and as she wasn't deaf I talked to her instead of the housekeeper. She mentioned that the vicar had been unwell all the morning. I got the water and came along, and that's all."

Franklin nodded. "Nothing much happened at The Pleasance except that I elicited the information that Miss Rose had taken the vicar round the devastated area this morning, and that's when he took the flowers. By the way, Miss Blunt was there and the two women seemed as thick as thieves. When I'd had another look round for myself and got my own specimens I thought I'd come back across the fields if Manor Path wasn't too muddy. I discovered a perfectly clear set of footprints leading from the stile on the Northurst Road to the gate of Mould's garden, and their fellows of the other way. Please don't mistake me. The footprints were to the stile—not to the hedge of The Pleasance. Those from Mould's house to the stile were made before it stopped raining last night; those to his house were made at any time after, but probably early this morning. All that may mean anything or nothing. He may have had—indeed he probably did have—perfectly good reasons for going that way in the rain."

Dryden, who hadn't all those strings in his fingers, looked very perplexed, and just as he was about to speak Travers got in first.

"With regard to the problem of the flowers. I have a simple suggestion to offer, which may or may not cause ribald laughter. Parish is in love with Agnes Rose—that's why he wears the flowers . . . well, next his heart."

The whole thing seemed to have become distasteful to Dryden. He resumed his meal with a very straight face.

Travers tackled him point-blank. "Is it likely, Henry, or is it not? You should know."

"I do know," said Dryden rather curtly. "Parish is the last person in the world to fall in love, and Agnes Rose is the last person he'd do it with."

"I don't know." Travers wagged his head oracularly. "She's fluffy—and she may be flighty. She might have appeared quite attractive to him if she'd laid herself out to be so. Love's a damn funny thing, Henry."

Dryden gave a wry smile. "So I'm told . . . though I don't know why you should be taken as an authority, Ludo. But it'd have to be a much funnier thing before I'd believe a theory like that." He almost glared. "Why, it's positively indecent!"

"Come, come, Henry! You mustn't speak like that about the voice that breathed o'er Eden."

Franklin thought it time to pour oil on the waters. "Yours may be a capital suggestion, but the vicar's known better to Mr. Dryden than to you and me. May we leave the vicar for a moment, in any case, and go back to Mould? Another peculiar thing forced itself on my mind this morning. You know that old gardener we saw at the vicarage? I ran into him as I was leaving the churchyard and I had a word with him. He told me he puts in his time between the vicarage and Windyridge."

"You mean Smith," said Dryden. "He does as you say. The vicar doesn't want him all the time, so he fills in with Miss Crome. I borrow him occasionally to help Jimson."

"Exactly! The very point I want to make," said Franklin. "Why did Ashley Mould send for Rogers at South Farm? Rogers hadn't been near him for months. If he wanted a gardener, why didn't he walk the few yards to the vicarage and see Smith—who's always there on the Saturday and has the afternoon off? And why didn't he arrange with Marian Crome to take him from her on the Monday morning? He always goes to her then."

Dryden looked hard at him. "You mean to suggest that Mould had a very special reason for sending young Clark down that hill?"

"If you'll pardon me," said Franklin, "I suggest nothing. I mention facts and leave you to draw your own deductions. Whether or not the vicar's in love is a trifling problem. When we come to murder—or even to hint at it—that's quite a different matter."

"I don't think you've quite got the full implication, Henry," said Travers. "Don't you think we might spill all the beans about Ashley Mould—personally?"

Franklin gathered the dog was still taboo. "You remember Travers telling you he looked through the window of Mould's studio on the afternoon when we went to the wood? He then saw Mould embracing Marian Crome. He also knows that it was she who cleaned up his house and studio in preparation for Travers's visit. Now you see why I wonder why Mould didn't arrange to borrow her gardener."

Dryden looked perfectly astounded. "Embracing her, you said?"

"Embracing her," repeated Travers.

Dryden rose from the chair as if unaware of what he was doing.

"And since you may as well have it all together," added Travers, "you see why Mould's steps went last night towards Windyridge. Dinner, perhaps, but he may have stayed devilish late."

Dryden was still shaking his head perplexedly when Jimson came in with coffee. When they were all seated again, and Travers had his legs stretched well out from under him, he began that preparatory fumbling with his horn-rims that always announced an unburdening of his mind.

"As we're putting the cards on the table, there's something I'd like to put up to you both. It may appear fantastic to you, but to me it's invincibly logical. In either case it may be worth while." He looked across at Franklin. "Tell me. Why, precisely, did Parish flop this morning?"

Franklin could think of nothing but the obvious, and knew it must be wrong. "He was wretchedly tired after the strain of the night. Even the business of entertaining us two was too much for him."

"You're probably right," said Travers graciously. "But there's an alternative. It couldn't have been because of anything I deliberately said to him?"

Franklin smiled. "You told me it was bilge. Satanism and the Black Mass, wasn't it?"

"I'll explain. Henry hasn't the faintest idea what I'm talking about. You remember that same afternoon when I peeped into Mould's studio I also saw a modelled figure. It was the devil, and a terrible face it was, too. But when I called officially on the Monday, that figure wasn't on view. Still, I thought about it, and one thing led to another. I wondered about Parish, for instance, and his having been in China—a country which seems synonymous with devils, foreign and otherwise. I wondered if your peculiar and subtle aversion for Parish was because he was possessed with a devil!"

"You interest me," said Dryden, and there was nothing of the arrogant about the way he said it.

"Well, it interests *me,*" said Travers. "We can't say such things are outside personal experience. You remember some weeks ago an English jury—usually, I believe, alluded to as hard-headed—returned in the case of a vicar the verdict that he was possessed with a devil. But since I've heard more about Parish, and since I've seen him myself, I've begun to take another point of view—not that Parish has had dealings with the devil, *but that he has discovered some other people who have.*"

"What people?" asked Franklin quickly.

"I think you'll see," said Travers. "My idea, which may or may not be a far-fetched one, depends on the existence of Satanism and the cult of the Black Mass. There we are not dealing with non-existent things. You may remember the discovery last year of a considerable number of Satan worshippers at Helsingfors, when the Finnish authorities called in the help of Scotland Yard because they suspected that the chief priest was an Englishman. After that it's surely not too much to assume the possibility of there being a nest of such people here?"

"Carry on!" said Franklin.

Travers was now warming to his theory, and somehow his voice had never been so persuasive.

"I'm going to put to you both a theory which is perfectly staggering in its simplicity and completeness. On a certain afternoon in Franklin's office we discussed the possibility of a central actuating force which might have caused that sudden and curious fall from grace of most of your acquaintances in this village, Henry. I suggest we now have that motive. Let Ashley Mould be the archpriest of this horrible cult. You recall that face of his, Henry, looking at you through the window. After the death of his wife—whose influence may have acted as a deterrent—he begins this practice of Satanism and his chief convert is Marian Crome, the woman whose pictures suddenly became bestial and devilish." He caught Dryden's unuttered protest. "It may be exaggeration, a statement like that, but we must exaggerate to see clearly. The next to be roped in—or it may have been that she was the first—was Agnes Rose, a woman who is fool enough to belong to anything new. I suggest that Mould also sounded, very subtly, Harriet Blunt, and finding she wasn't the type, induced Agnes Rose to quarrel with her and get her out of her house. I further suggest that when Tom Yeoman told you what happened to his wife, he deliberately lied. His wife saw something of what was actually going on. They may even have approached her to be a convert. But Tom Yeoman knew too much about what was going on. *That's why he died.* And Parish knows why he died, and that's why he changed too. Parish knows and he's trying to remember . . . but he can't remember. All he remembers is an angel who turned to a devil, and when he gets those mystic impulses he speaks of the powers of darkness and he utters the opinion that Mould's feet have been temporarily plucked from the pit. There's the unifying motive for all your people, Henry. Am I right or wrong?"

Franklin had been nodding vigorously. "By Jove! I think you're right! There's something in it that hits true. It fits."

"Yes," said Dryden slowly. "It fits . . . and yet I feel there's something wrong with it."

"I haven't finished yet," said Travers, who was beginning to feel a tremendous surge of enthusiasm for the child of his own creating. "Take Ashley Mould. He needed a temple of sorts for his orgies. Why shouldn't he have simulated that period of the sulks so as to keep people out of the house? He hadn't the moral courage to quarrel openly with you and Parish, so he sulked instead, until he judged suspicions were allayed—or he knew that Parish, the one man who knew anything, was incapable of speaking."

"It still fits in," said Franklin.

"There's more yet," went on Travers. "Satanism has for part of its ritual, if I remember rightly, ceremonies with dead dogs and human corpses—the latter, perhaps, in the very closest and filthiest circles of the adepts, so we'll not admit that as part of the argument. But I'd like to mention Parish again, and particularly something that was seen by you two people in the church. Do you think that those agonies that Parish was undergoing before the altar were really due to his horror at the death of the boy Clark? I say they were not. In my opinion he was seen by you doing what he must often do, and that is striving to get back his memory and asking for help in the one place where he's likely to get it. And as Franklin mentioned certain suspicions of his with regard to Ashley Mould and the death of Clark, may I add something further? Why shouldn't Parish have guessed that Mould had something to do with that affair? Was that why he writhed before the altar? And even the business of this morning. Isn't it possible that Agnes Rose is wavering in her Satanic faith? Did Mould tear up the garden for her as a reminder and a sign?"

Dryden's fingers wreathed together nervously. "You terrify me, Ludo. . . . I can't believe such things . . . and yet you make me believe them."

"The truth isn't always palatable," said Travers. "Still, that's the end of the story—except for one thing—which is sheer, hard fact. In view of what Parish said last night about angels and powers of darkness, I made an excuse in his house this morning to refer to such things, and Satanism and the Black Mass. I talked at him, as Franklin said. All the time he stared—then he collapsed and flopped in a faint."

Travers regarded his cold pipe with a look of surprise, then mechanically took the matches Franklin put in his hand. Nobody seemed to know what to say, and it was Travers himself who spoke first.

"Well?"

Dryden still said nothing.

Franklin pulled a face. "Why not sound Miss Blunt about the matter?"

"We mustn't do that," said Dryden quickly.

Travers smiled. "I seem to have been doing a devilish lot of talking, but I'll make a further suggestion. You were saying, John, that you weren't any too busy, and that now the weather's better you might take a few days' holiday. You've had your own suspicions of Mould, and you've been good enough to agree with some of what I've said myself. Why not come down here for a day or two and have a further look round?"

Franklin looked rather confused. "But you can't wish me on Mr. Dryden like that!"

Dryden got up at once. "The very thing, if Mr. Franklin will come. There's nothing I'd like better. He shall make the house his own." The mere prospect seemed to be making a new man of him.

Franklin blushed, and wondered for a moment what to say. Travers glanced conspicuously at the clock, said he must see Palmer, then left them to settle things for themselves.

On the way down to Pulvery that afternoon Travers was on amazingly good terms with himself. Only twenty-four hours ago and the case had been dead as mutton; now it had all the potentialities of a first-class sensation. He made a wholly new suggestion.

"Something I'd like you to do," he said to Franklin, who had still in his ears the faint reverberations of Travers's eloquence. "As a matter of fact, I don't see that you can refuse it. Have a good man down in Bableigh next week—Potter, for preference—and put the account down to me. I like Potter, and I think he could do with a holiday, like yourself. If anything should happen to turn up, then we might see about informing Dryden."

Franklin said he thought it might be managed, and they left it for the moment at that—and they left Bableigh and the case as well, at least until after dinner that evening, when something quietly amusing happened that recalled one inhabitant of the village. Palmer always lent a hand at that one meal, and at the very end he was taking round coffee. Travers thought of something, and told his sister and the major.

"Palmer's been distinguishing himself since you last saw him."

"Really," said the major, who had a warm spot for Palmer. "And what is it this time?"

"You're making Palmer blush," protested Ursula.

"Not at all," said Travers, and clapped the old fellow on the back. "You ought to have seen him. Charming old lady—friend of Dryden's—and her wireless set went blotto, and so we took Palmer along to look at it. Do you know, he merely looked, listened, and spotted it first go. Incredible, wasn't it, John?"

Franklin agreed whole-heartedly.

Palmer coughed gently. "If I may say so, sir, I couldn't very well help finding out the trouble."

"You're much too modest, Palmer!" laughed Ursula.

Palmer stood his ground. "Pardon me, Miss Ursula, but the set is the same as my own, and the same one you have here." He bowed slightly. "You'll pardon me mentioning it, sir."

Everybody was most amused. Then Travers's eye caught the major's set.

"Come and show us just what happened, Palmer."

They gathered round while he demonstrated. The dials were set at 33-25, which meant London Regional. On the left of the set were three holes for plugs. In the farthest one went the aerial plug, and it was coloured red. The earth plug had a choice of two sockets.

"If the earth plug goes in the socket nearest us, that's its proper position," said Palmer. He switched on, made some slight adjustments, and a single programme came through. "Now," he said, "if the earth plug is put in the middle socket, we shall get greatly increased volume but little selectivity. The volume will be so great that we shall not be able to lessen it, and we shall hear every continental station that's on anything resembling 33-25."

He altered the plug. Claude Hulbert's voice was heard saying pathetically, "And what *is* the difference between an ant and an elephant?" As a background for that there seemed to be the cacophony of Europe—a band, orchestra, shrieking sopranos, voices—and Palmer hurriedly replaced the plug in the nearer socket.

"Then I take it that Miss Faithful's woman accidentally pulled out that plug and then put it back in the wrong socket?" said Franklin.

"Precisely, sir. That's what undoubtedly did happen."

"Well," said Travers, "I still think Palmer's very clever. Anybody second that?"

Everybody seconded it at once. Palmer blushed, bowed, smiled and departed.

CHAPTER XII
THE THIRD PUZZLE

IT HAS BEEN SAID that Franklin was conscientious. Ludovic Travers quoted him as the great example of a man who is too much so. Outwardly he would seem reasonably calm and collected, and he never harried his subordinates, but inside he would be all fret and worry. "Value for money," as Travers once told him, was his great obsession.

Dryden, for instance, had been most insistent on the fact that Franklin was to take a holiday. He liked him, and was looking forward to some days of his company. The position, as he understood it, was that Franklin was a guest who should nevertheless be left to his own devices. If anything could be discovered to substantiate that amazing theory which Travers had put forward, so much the better; if not, there'd be no harm done. Dryden, in fact, was not too anxious for a close inquiry, with scandal and heaven knew what in its train. What he favoured was the unobtrusive placing of Franklin in the middle of that social circle with which Travers's theory had dealt, and then leaving him to draw his own conclusions.

But that was not the position as Franklin himself understood it. He knew Dryden was a worried man, and he looked upon it as his duty to alleviate that worry. And yet, of all the cases he had undertaken, this was the most unsatisfactory, and he knew it before he arrived in Bableigh. In the three days that elapsed before his actual arrival he had cooled off to such an extent that he was almost horrified when he came to evaluate the flimsy evidence that was the cause of his visit. Travers had left for Paris on the Monday night to attend a financial conference, and without him at his elbow to ferret out new material, or cast a glamour over the old, Franklin had the feeling of being left in the lurch in a strange land with no knowledge of the inhabitants and a poor handful of mixed bank-notes that looked suspiciously like duds.

But he made his preparations for all that. Ex-sergeant Potter, the first man he had signed on all those years ago, when he had first taken over the department at Durangos Limited, was sent down to the Roebuck and booked a room for a week. Dryden was to be unaware of his existence. Somehow Franklin felt he would never stand for vulgar shadowing and peeping and eavesdropping, but every evening after dusk it was arranged that Potter should come along that back path to Dryden's gate, and there Franklin would meet him for the day's report.

Upon one thing Franklin had made up his mind. That theory of Travers's was to have a thorough try-out, and the vital spot in it was that chatty and voluble person—Agnes Rose. Parker had discovered nothing about her rockery, and young Tanner persisted in his statement, and there seemed to be some reason therefore for the visit which Dryden and Franklin paid on the Wednesday morning.

It was Harriet Blunt who opened the door to them, and she looked up to the eyes in housework. Within a minute she had left them in an atmosphere of domestic felicity. Even the Poms had become aware of the presence of a person who meant what she said. The maid had departed on the Saturday as she had threatened, and yet somehow the house had lost its overpowering fussiness.

"I'm glad she went," said Miss Rose. "I could never abide that girl, in any case. Poor Peter was always afraid of his life. Do you know, I think it was all a blessing in disguise."

Then Harriet Blunt came in from the kitchen. She smiled almost challengingly at the three of them as she took off her apron and threw it on the chesterfield. Franklin held his lighter for her cigarette.

"Agnes was telling us what a godsend you've been," Dryden told her.

"Really?" She seemed to be regarding the situation with an amused satisfaction.

"I've been telling them you ought to come here." Agnes Rose showed an enthusiasm that obliterated past records. "Don't you think so, Mr. Dryden? My dear, you can't go on down in that poky little place!"

Harriet Blunt flicked the ash dexterously into the fireplace. "You're all making rather a fuss of . . . of my not leaving you quite in the lurch."

"Well, I may be putting my foot clean in it," said Dryden, "but I must say I think it'd be the best thing in the world for the pair of you." He paused as if to screw up his courage for the question, and when it came Franklin almost shuddered at the blatancy of it. "Has the vicar been round recently?"

"Yesterday, wasn't it, Harriet?"

The reply was so natural that Franklin wondered for a moment if he could have heard aright.

"Yes—poor dear!" said Harriet Blunt. "He's not looking any too well. Do you think so, Mr. Dryden?"

"No," said Dryden reflectively. "He was preaching on Sunday, I suppose?"

He overdid it that time, and the two women looked so surprised that they were told of the fainting fit. Franklin added the moral.

"Don't you think it's a pity a man like that doesn't marry? I mean, it seems so tragic his being alone in that big house except for his housekeeper. He's not all that old, do you think?"

Miss Rose, at whom the question had been directed, showed neither embarrassment nor enthusiasm, and Franklin realized he was getting very little farther. Then his eye fell on the newspaper, and he fingered it idly.

"Most amazing case that the other day, wasn't it? All that Black Mass business."

"Black Mass?" If ever a woman was out of her depth it was Agnes Rose.

"Yes. People worshipping the devil, and so on. Perversion of the holy sacraments, and all sorts of secret abominations."

She sighed. "Oh! that's it, is it? People do such silly things, you know."

Harriet chuckled. "There's nothing like being on the safe side. Unless, of course, the devil did you a dirty trick."

"There's risks in everything," observed Franklin. "And, by the way, Miss Blunt, something's occurred to me on which I'd like to ask your opinion. It's often puzzled me, and being an artist you might help me out. Why do people represent the devil with horns and hair and all that apparatus?"

She smiled. "Do they?"

"One imagines they do. Haven't you seen busts or statues or pictures like it?"

She still seemed very amused. "I don't know that I have—I mean, not in serious art. If I ever saw one like it I'm sure I shouldn't think it was the devil."

"Then what would you think it was?"

"Oh, I don't know." She laughed. "Since I'm a diehard Tory, I'd probably think it was Lloyd George."

Dryden roared at that. He was still chuckling away when they got outside, and he nodded his head appraisingly. "A fine woman that, Mr, Franklin!"

"Yes," said Franklin, who was looking rather thoughtful. "But not a very successful beginning for us, do you think?"

Dryden sobered down at once. "No. Perhaps not." He tugged at his beard and then decided apparently the morning was far too good to waste in pessimism, and when he began to chuckle again Franklin knew he was still thinking of the miraculous change that had come over The Pleasance. Then, as they passed the gate of Windyridge, Martha Frail came out, holding a little girl by the hand. Dryden stopped at once.

"And how are you to-day, Martha?"

She bobbed slightly. "I can't grumble, sir. I had a bad night the other night, but I don't get them like I used to."

Dryden nodded, then smiled as he looked down at the little girl. She was an undersized mite, with hair of the most startling red, blue eyes, and the quaintest little features imaginable.

"And how's Fancy to-day?"

"I had to keep her at home, sir, with me. Her cold's been something shocking. Say good morning, Fancy."

The child looked down shyly. Dryden produced a handful of change, found a sixpence and put it in her hand. She looked up timidly, smiled, then looked down again.

"Say thank you," said Martha, and gave her a little shake. Then she sighed. "Never can get her to say a word, sir, when she's out. I hope she won't be like that with Mr. Mould this afternoon. He's taken a great liking to her, sir, and I'm to take her round this afternoon and he's going to do . . . one of them . . . a sort of portrait, sir."

"Really? That will be nice, won't it, Fancy? We must get him to do something for you by way of copy, Martha. . . . Miss Crome in?"

"She's gone to Hastings, sir. Was there anything you wanted?"

Dryden smiled. "Oh, no, Martha! Just wondered." He nodded and they moved off again.

"Mould ought to make something really charming of her," said Franklin. "Quite the elfin type, wasn't she?"

Dryden shook his head. "She's not very long for this world, by the look of her. . . . In some ways, perhaps, it might be better."

He stopped at the stile as if undetermined which way to go, and then who should appear but Parish, his approach hidden by the tall hedge. He looked as surprised as they.

"How are you this morning, vicar?" asked Franklin. "Quite better again?"

"Yes," said Parish, not knowing apparently to what Franklin referred. Then he suddenly simpered. "A great morning! Don't you think so, Dryden?"

"Magnificent," agreed Dryden. "And which way are you going? We were just halting to consider the matter."

"I'm seeing Mrs. Finch," said Parish, his eyes looking away beyond them. But this time it was a perfectly natural look. "Isn't that Fancy Frail with her mother? She's not at school."

"She's got a bad cold," explained Dryden. "Martha's keeping her at home. . . . I think she'll go the way of the rest, don't you?"

Parish shook his head abstractedly.

"I was just about to remark to Mr. Franklin," Dryden went on, "that in some ways it might be better. If she were to marry some day and perpetuate that terrible thing . . ." He broke off. "What about Northurst, Mr. Franklin? Suit you? Come along, then, Parish. We'll have your company as far as Finch's cottage."

On the Thursday afternoon they spent an hour or two looking over the countryside in Dryden's car. Coming back by Northurst they saw a thick-set man with dark jacket and sombrero hat striding along ahead of them.

"Mould!" said Dryden, and drew the car up alongside. "May we give you a lift?"

Mould stared, then recognized Dryden. "That's very good of you. I can't say I'm over partial to exercise."

"Hop in then," said Dryden.

Franklin introduced himself, and moved his own quarters to the back for company. He also explained that he was staying with Dryden, that he had once thought of taking the Manor, and that if the gentleman was the famous sculptor, then it was indeed a stroke of luck to run across him even like that.

Dryden was letting the car dawdle, and he leaned back to make his own contribution to the conversation. "Met Martha Frail yesterday. She told us you were using Fancy as a model."

"Yes," admitted Mould, and seemed quite pleased that they knew it. "I've had my eye on her for some time. Very difficult to get models in a place like this, Dryden."

"I expect it is. Country types pall, I expect."

Mould made a wry face. "They wear too many clothes, blast them! You know"—this to Franklin—"all that humbug about the Greeks is merely sneaking admiration for what we consider lack of modesty."

Before he could expand that thesis, Dryden was drawing up at the stile. Half out of the door, Mould stopped.

"Like to come to the studio and see what there is?"

"Delighted to," said Franklin. "I think we might drive you right home, then Mr. Dryden can come in too."

Since hearing the Saturday revelations of Travers, Dryden had felt a furious anger against Mould, though since that anger had its origin principally in the liaison with Marian Crome, he knew it to be bigoted, if not absurd. But in Mould's studio it was impossible to feel anything but admiration, and the sculptor became merely the background of his own work. The clay figure of Fancy Frail they liked enormously.

"You'll hardly believe it," said Mould, "but it took me an awful long while to induce Martha to take her clothes off. She had the child all dressed up in what I imagine was her Sunday best. Enough to make one retch."

"And what are you ultimately making of it?" asked Dryden.

"A lead figure, I think. Not Peter-Pannish in the least; just the sort of thing that might stand at the end of a cypress walk." He surveyed the clay model again for himself. "I'll do a couple more, probably, before I'm satisfied."

"I wonder if a perfectly low-brow amateur might make a suggestion," said Franklin. "It's a difficult thing to do—really. I'll never forget how furious a friend of mine was when a well-meaning busybody like myself hinted he might find a certain piece of landscape a good subject."

Mould smiled. "I had the same experience some days ago. There was a disgusting blue tetter of some filthy weeds all over that garden outside there, and it was seriously suggested to me that they'd make a good picture." He stopped suddenly. "Sorry! I'm afraid I'm rather putting you off. What were you going to propose?"

"Well, I'm afraid I'm a bit of a fool," said Franklin, "but when you were mentioning the difficulty of getting local models I couldn't help thinking at once of Miss Faithful. I think her face is one of the most striking I've ever seen."

"Miss Faithful," said Mould, and seemed to be thinking back. "I don't think I've seen her for some time." He nodded. "Yes. She was a very distinctive type. . . ."

Dryden broke in there. "Well, we're very grateful to you, Mould, for showing us all these lovely things, but we really must be going."

From the quietness of his manner on the short run to Old House, Franklin knew there had been something in that coupling of Mould and Miss Faithful that had irritated Dryden enormously—and yet he hardly knew how to apologize. But the mood passed as quickly as it came, and Franklin took care to keep that afternoon's encounter out of the conversation.

That same night Potter made his first report, and it included the news about Fancy Frail. The landlord of the Roebuck had a daughter of the same age, and the two children were accustomed to play together. Martha Frail had taken her daughter to Mould that afternoon for the second time, and was going again the next day for the last sitting. Mould had given her five shillings a visit.

The rest of the report was far more intriguing. At about nine-thirty the previous night he had strolled through the church walk and along Manor Path, and just short of Mould's studio had seen the light from the opening of the door. Thereupon he had backed into the hedge and immediately afterwards a woman came out of the gate and passed within a yard of him. It was Harriet Blunt.

But when Potter had seen the light he had also become aware of the presence of at least two other people in that studio, and making up his mind to take a chance, he got through the hedge and wormed his way to the actual fence that faced the studio door, only the width of the path away. He then heard the voice of Mould at the gate, and a lady's voice in return, though he had no idea what they were saying. The thing that interested him most was what he could see on the table just inside the half-opened door— that figure of the devil which Franklin had described to him.

"Quite small, was it? About a foot high?"

"That's it, sir," said Potter. "And coloured a sort of red. Only all this happened very quick, sir. He was back in the studio and had the door shut again before you could say knife. Then he put the light out, locked up, and went indoors."

Franklin nodded away at the darkness. "Any chance of getting inside that studio to have a good look?"

"I doubt it, sir. I might look through some night if I got on the roof . . . but I doubt if my fourteen stone'd agree with it."

Franklin grunted. "And what about your landlady? She a good gossiper?"

"None better, sir. She's told me already all about Mould and that Miss Crome. She's been seen going there at all sorts of times." Potter did a chuckle. "If you believe half you hear, sir, she ought to have worn out a couple of perambulators by now."

In bed that night Franklin thought things over. Travers's theory had received its first confirmation . . . and yet he wasn't sure. Agnes Rose had shown such a natural ignorance of Satanism and similar practices that it was only too obvious that she was a member of no such secret body of worshippers. And Agnes Rose was a woman incapable of dissimulation; if ever a person was visible and on the surface it was she. Then had it been Harriet Blunt who had deliberately made the quarrel which was to get her away from the woman who was too chattering and uncertain to be admitted to the abominable circle which she herself had just joined? When he had mentioned such things on the Wednesday morning, her attitude had been one of calculated and cynical indifference. And yet somehow Franklin felt that Harriet Blunt was not the type to be dragged into any close association with Mould or Marian Crome. It was all very puzzling . . . perhaps Potter would discover something more vital . . . or Travers, perhaps, might see the real inwardness of it . . . and with that Franklin went off to sleep.

On the Saturday morning a letter came from Travers. He hoped to be in Pulvery that week-end, and would call at Bableigh on the Monday morning. Dryden was out that afternoon, attending some sort of function at Hastings, and with the thoughtfulness which always characterized him, had gone by bus, leaving the car at Franklin's disposal should he be inclined to use it. But Franklin preferred to remain indoors that afternoon and lounge in comfort, and but for the disquietude about the stagnation that seemed to have fallen over the case, he might have been drowsily content. As he lay back in the chair his eyes fell on the ancient rafters; all about him were the evidences of a perfect taste that knew how to include comfort. If he looked through the leaded window he could see the distant line of hills, warm with sun. If he stretched his arm to the bell, Jimson would be in with tea. There was the thought of Dryden, too, who had been such a wonderful person to live with; always charmingly attentive, comforting in himself, always interesting and often unusual.

That was Franklin's worry. Somehow he wanted, with all the urgency in the world, to find out something to satisfy Dryden, who had been so amazingly decent about the whole affair. But the farther Franklin cast his net, the less he caught, and as he read over and over again his own notes on the week's happenings, he found them a meagre assortment. They represented the disappearance of that ephemeral theory of some sort of attachment between Agnes Rose and the vicar. They eliminated Agnes Rose from any part in the practice of Satanism, if such indeed existed, and substituted possibly the name of Harriet Blunt for that of her effervescent and newly reconciled friend.

As for the existence of those abominable practices on which Travers's theory had depended, nothing further had come to light, unless—and Franklin frowned—there was something peculiarly devilish and subtle about Mould and that small child whom he had taken such a sudden desire to model. He thought about that for a moment or two, then left it. Travers might know the connection, perhaps, and in any case it was far too risky a matter even to hint at in Dryden's hearing.

As far, then, as Franklin could see, there would be nothing whatever that Dryden could be told, and he himself looked like cutting a remarkably poor figure. Something desperate would have to be done, and half a dozen schemes forthwith went through his mind, only to be discarded. Even if Mould could be lured away and his house ransacked, and the presence of heaven knew what abominations discovered, then he doubted if that would constitute a definitely criminal offence. And then something came as an inspiration. Why not take the example of certain Chancellors of the Exchequer and raid hen-roosts? There *was* a certain piece of information that might be imparted to Dryden; a piece of information that had been deliberately set aside—and that was the dog. Dryden might not like it, and Franklin himself hated the idea of deceiving a client, and yet the scheme seemed good.

So good did it seem that Franklin drafted out the letter during tea. It was to be of the clumsily anonymous type, addressed to the police at Northurst and giving the information that the dog which had disappeared after the death of Yeoman had been buried in Mould's back garden. That letter would reach the police on the Monday morning when Dryden would be sitting on the bench. In accordance with custom, the matter as affecting his own village would be reported to him, and unless Franklin was much mistaken, it would be decided to send a detective officer to Mould to make inquiries. Mould would have to do quite a lot of explaining. The matter would, moreover, become public property, and people would begin to open their mouths. Some stone or other might be dislodged which would end in a positive avalanche.

Then came another brain-wave. Why not drop a line to Travers asking him to come over early so that they could have a chat while Dryden was away? And it might even be arranged that Travers should be present at Mould's house when the detective called. Franklin smiled to himself and set about both letters, using his rough paper for the anonymous one. Then he strolled along to the post office and posted them in case he should change his mind.

It would be about half-past five when he became aware of some sort of excitement in the direction of the kitchen, then there was a quick tap at the door and a very flurried Jimson entered.

"Beg pardon, sir, but can you tell me exactly where to get hold of the master?"

"I can't tell you exactly," said Franklin. "He said he might be late. . . . Is anything the matter?"

"Miss Faithful's dead, sir. Martha just found her."

"Dead! . . . You mean, she's died?"

"That's right, sir. Lying dead in the chair."

Franklin went through to the kitchen, where Martha Frail was crying away, with Mrs. Jimson telling her not to take on. There was a sudden silence as Franklin entered.

"Anybody in the house, Mrs. Frail?"

Martha sobbed that there wasn't.

Franklin thought for a moment, then made up his mind. "I'll go round to the house, and you'd better come too, Mrs. Jimson. Jimson, you take the car and fetch Doctor Sawyer at once."

They went round by the back, the way that Martha had come. Inside the sitting-room everything was unnaturally normal. Miss Faithful, lying back in the chair, might have been asleep, her eyes closed and her head nestling in the angle. Franklin touched the cheek. It was warm; so was the hand, though the pulse had stopped.

He stood there, still feeling the unnatural peacefulness of it all. Death, as he had usually met it, had been in no such placid form. The sun was shining through the open window and a bumble bee was buzzing, and but for the quiet sobbing of the women there was no other noise. He took Martha's arm.

"Go and wait in the kitchen. There's nothing we can do here."

"Can't we lay her out, poor dear?" asked Mrs. Jimson.

"Not till the doctor's seen her."

He went to the front door and opened it ready for Sawyer's arrival, and when he got to the kitchen, found that Martha had pulled herself together. In a couple of minutes she was actually voluble.

Correctly sorted out, her story became this. She had worked in the cottage all the morning and had left just after noon. Miss Faithful had been none too well, and had spent the time in the chair, doing some sewing, and her work-basket was still there, as Mr. Franklin had probably seen for himself. The afternoon Martha had spent with Miss Crome, and had happened to mention that Miss Faithful was none too well, whereupon Miss Crome had sent Martha round at once with some special cake she had made, and a message to say Miss Crome would call in on the Sunday.

It was three-thirty when Martha delivered the message, and she took advantage of the opportunity to listen for a minute or two to the wireless, which Miss Faithful had switched on. "A violin was playing something lovely!" At just before half-past five Martha had called in again to bring the groceries, and had then found the old lady dead. As Martha proved by a wave at the sink, she had had her tea and had washed up.

"The wireless was going when you got here?"

"Oh, no, sir!" said Martha. "She must have turned it off."

There was a knock at the front door and the doctor was in the room by the time they got there themselves. He muttered something to the women, gave a nod at Franklin as he went straight across to the body, then stooped down and examined the face and moved the head gently. After he had taken out his watch and shaken his head solemnly, he turned round.

"What time'd you find her, Martha?"

"Exactly twenty-five past five by that clock it was, sir."

He grunted. "Five minutes sooner and she'd have been alive," He turned to Franklin. "I know you, don't I?"

Franklin explained things, and the pair of them carried the body upstairs and laid it on the bed, and left the women to see to things. Sawyer announced that he'd have to be off.

"Dryden in?" he asked. "He's not? Then perhaps you'll tell him to get into communication with her nephew. He has the address." He held out his hand. "Martha's sleeping here to-night."

He was gone so quickly that Franklin had to chase him down the path.

"Anything to tell Dryden about an inquest?"

"Inquest?" Sawyer glared. "There's no inquest."

"Heart, was it?"

"Of course it was. The woman ought to have been dead long ago!" and off he went.

Franklin went back to the room again and prepared to wait till the women should come down. A lovely little room, he thought, and so different from what it had been when all of them had crowded in that night . . . the night when Dryden made that curious mention of foreboding. Then he smiled to himself. Whatever there had been in Dryden's other prophecies, there was nothing psychic about that one. Even he himself had seen that a breath of wind might carry her off. And that was where she had been sitting. There was the *Radio Times,* from which she chose her programmes. There was her work-stand which Martha had moved over to the corner for her—its scissors still projecting as if carelessly thrown in. There was the set she had turned off for herself . . . and then he made a quick move forward. Surely not! And yet it was so. Those plugs were again out of place. They were where Palmer had found them that night—and he claimed to have left the set foolproof! Then who in heaven's name had moved the plugs again?

The answer suggested itself and he went quickly to the foot of the stairs. Martha put her head over the banisters.

"Yes, sir?"

"Are you absolutely sure you didn't touch the wireless when you came in just now?"

"No, sir. I didn't even go near it. I didn't even think about it—I was too upset."

Franklin frowned. Extraordinarily curious thing! He heard Martha's voice again, talking back into the bedroom, then she leaned over again. "Would you mind coming up a minute, sir? That's something we think you ought to see."

What the two women showed him was even more peculiar. When doing the dead woman's hair they had discovered that someone had cut off a lock. Franklin could see the severed ends.

"She must have cut it off to send to somebody!"

Martha smiled, caught Mrs. Jimson's eye, and both of them smiled.

"She wouldn't cut it off from there if she did, sir," said Mrs. Jimson. "This has been cut off recent." She had an idea. "Somebody must have come in while you were running round, Martha! That's what it was, sir, and a pretty piece of cheek it was, too. They saw the poor dear laying there and took a piece of her hair for a keepsake like."

Franklin looked at the pair of them and wagged a finger. "Nothing's to be said about it, you understand? Nothing—even to Mr. Dryden. It's impossible that anybody should have had the impudence to do what you suggested, Mrs. Jimson, and what people will say is that Martha took the lock of hair herself—which is equally absurd and might make more trouble."

He listened to Martha's indignant assurances, then made his way downstairs. Martha was right. It was not herself who had taken that lock of hair. It was that other caller of the afternoon, who for some inexplicable reason had tampered with the wireless set. And who had it been? Parish, who had called to see if the set was like his own? Mould, who had come to have a look at the face of the woman he had not seen for some time?

Franklin shook his head. The death had undoubtedly been a natural one, and Sawyer's brusqueness at the inane question had been justified. And yet . . . curious, wasn't it? Yeoman died, and there was something strange about it. Clark died, and even the manner of his dying left doubts in a thinking mind. Now the soul had flickered from that fragile body upstairs and . . . He stopped short. The lock of hair. Who might have taken it?

Before he knew it his mind had turned on Dryden himself—the man who had loved her like a son. But Dryden had been away at Hastings. But had he? The thoughts flashed on. Dryden, the friend of Yeoman; the one who had befriended Clark. Dryden, who had himself first drawn attention to the village of Bableigh . . . . Then Franklin stopped short again, and for a moment felt desperately ashamed. That was what came of letting one's thoughts run on. He would think no more about it. Doubtless there was some natural explanation for everything and he would wait till it presented itself. And as he replaced the plug in its correct socket he determined to say no word to Dryden of either the altered set or the missing lock of hair.

And when Franklin himself broke the news to Dryden later that evening, and saw the shock and the distress, he was more ashamed than ever. He went round at once and found Parish there. The vicar had just heard about it, and he, too, was most upset. He proposed, he said, to make an allusion to the dead woman at the evening service. Dryden and Franklin said they would certainly be there.

WHEN POTTER CAME ALONG that night, Franklin would have been perfectly content if he had had nothing to report. As it was, Potter had a staggering piece of news.

"Miss Crome's sold her house, sir."

"Good Lord!" said Franklin. "How'd you find that out? Village gossip?"

There was far more than that to it. Potter had become rather restless at having nothing definite to do and had made up his mind to spend an hour or two at Hastings. In front of him on the way to the main road and the bus had been Miss Crome, and when they alighted at the other end he strolled casually behind her, and on the spur of the moment entered close behind her the house-agents' for which she had made a bee-line.

"Order & Hunt was the firm," said Potter, "and it must have been Order behind the sort of counter they had in the office. He says, 'Good morning, Miss Crome. Afraid we haven't got any news for you yet.' 'That's all right,' she says. 'I've sold it privately. I hope you don't mind.' 'Not at all,' he says. 'I'm very glad for your sake. I'm rather afraid we shouldn't have been able to do much ourselves. It's awkward to sell a property when you're not allowed to advertise it. Make a good price?' 'Yes,' she says, quite pleased. 'I'm getting six hundred down, the balance as soon as the purchaser's bank have arranged a mortgage for the rest. You'll still keep the matter confidential, won't you?' she says. And then a clerk caught sight of me and it took me five minutes to get out of the place, and where she'd gone then I hadn't any idea."

"Amazing bit of luck!" said Franklin. "Wonder why she's selling it? You any ideas?"

"What I thought, sir, was that she might be going to marry that Mould sort of sudden like; kind of spring it as a surprise on the village, and if so, she wouldn't like people to know she was selling her own house."

"Maybe," said Franklin. "But what beats me is why they don't live at *her* house if they're going to get married. His lease expires very soon and he won't get it renewed—that is, if they sell the Manor."

"I know, sir. That's what beat me when I began to think it over. Unless, of course, sir, they're both going away then."

There was no point in argument and Potter left with instructions to keep his ears open. Franklin was extraordinarily pleased. At last he had something definite to tell Dryden. Then when he returned to the house he felt that Dryden was in no mood for news of any kind that night, and it was not till the following morning, after breakfast, that he thought the moment had arrived. Dryden was staggered.

"You're quite sure?"

"Dead plumb sure," Franklin told him. "How the information reached me I'm not at liberty to say, and I must add that it's implicitly confidential."

"Amazing!" said Dryden. "And, as you say, if she's marrying Mould, why don't they want her house?" He shook his head. "I wonder if you'd mind my putting out a feeler or two—very tactfully, of course."

"Why not? You might ask her if she'd ever thought of selling, as you've a friend who took a great fancy to the house."

"A friend?"

Franklin smiled. "The ubiquitous Travers."

Dryden sighed. "A most mendacious sort of business, all this. I had no idea I could develop into such a thorough-paced liar."

They went to church that evening and sat well to the front in the Dryden pew, with Agnes Rose and Harriet Blunt just behind them. It was a simple service with well-chosen hymns and Parish at his best, and if there was one thing Franklin was to remember it was the last few words of the sermon.

Parish made an impressive figure as he leaned forward between the candlesticks of the pulpit, and there was an earnestness of conviction about his words that must have come from some very deep feeling.

"Let me die the death of the righteous and let my last end be like hers." He paused at that first deliberate misquotation. "We read that on at least one of the tombstones in this churchyard, but are we sure that all those hundreds about whom it has been written and spoken did really die as we imagine the righteous should die? I, for one, would hesitate before I pronounced such a verdict too universally. But this evening, this peaceful summer evening, in this peaceful and ancient building, the words seem to come naturally when we remember Elizabeth Faithful and her example and her life and her end. I am certain"—the voice was raised and he smote the desk of the pulpit—"certain beyond any human contradiction, that among those who have left us and are now gathered round the throne of the Eternal, there is to be found at this very moment the soul of our sister who yesterday sank into sleep. . . ."

Dryden strode home at such a pace that Franklin wondered what was pricking him till the conversation brought it out.

"What did you think of the sermon?" he asked.

"I thought it was splendid," said Franklin. "He was so obviously feeling all he said." He hesitated for a moment. "I know it was perfectly unpardonable of me to think such a thing at such a time, but I couldn't help wondering whose tombstone the words were written on, and what the relatives would think of Parish's disclaimer."

"That was old Jacob Clark's stone," said Dryden. "He died before I was born, so Parish was perfectly safe." He shook his head fiercely. "What always irritates me is the assumption of the clergy that they are in the special confidences of God." He stopped with such abruptness that Franklin overshot the mark. "Didn't you get the impression that Parish was guaranteeing the presence of Elizabeth Faithful in heaven?"

"I don't know." Franklin was rather disconcerted. "If he conveyed that impression I don't think he intended to."

"Perhaps you're right." He moved on again with the same suddenness. "Curious, you know, how, in spite of what I do, I remain out of sympathy with Parish. Somehow I can't help thinking that the fault must be on both sides." He shook his head again. "I wonder."

Somehow Franklin wondered too.

Travers turned up early on the Monday morning, full of excitement and curiosity. He was quite upset about Miss Faithful's death and announced his intention of having some flowers sent down from town at once, but when it came to the twin mysteries of the lock of hair and the altered plugs of the wireless set, he was perfectly at a loss.

As to there being any ulterior motive in Mould's sudden craze for the modelling of Fancy Frail, that was a matter on which he refused to commit himself, though he nodded away with an air of preternatural wisdom and hinted at strange possibilities. That Agnes Rose had no idea whatever of the vicar's supposed infatuation caused him little perturbation, and the only real enthusiasm he manifested was at Potter's discovery of the visit of Harriet Blunt to Mould's studio by night.

"We're coming along," he said. "And you'll pardon my saying so, but I thought you and Dryden had a rather exaggerated idea of the virtues of Miss Blunt when you took her side over the Rose quarrel. And what's the particular line of action now?"

Franklin told him about the dog. Travers hailed the scheme as one after his own heart.

"Don't you worry about Dryden," he said. "I'll manage him. You own up and I'll do the rest."

As it happened, everything went with a smoothness that exceeded the most optimistic of anticipations. Dryden, who seemed delighted to see Travers again, set the ball rolling with his own question.

"You're not going to be in a hurry to get away?"

"Must get back to-night," Travers told him. "You forget I've got a living to earn. Also I must see Mould this afternoon. Want a present for somebody and I think he's got the very thing I have in mind."

"Mould!" said Dryden, and told them the amazing thing that had happened.

Franklin assumed his best professional manner. "I ought to say at once that I was behind that letter."

"Really?" It was difficult to say if he were shocked or surprised. "You mean . . . the dog is really in his garden?"

"Yes," said Franklin. "It's where the letter said it was. That kind of letter carries no stigma with it. Scotland Yard get them by the hundred."

"I think the idea's perfectly splendid," said Travers. "The beauty of it is, as no doubt you've seen, Henry, that the police get the information without Franklin being concerned at all—which means that you won't be brought in either, and that's the very thing you wanted. And what are the police going to do?"

"Frost, the detective sergeant, is coming to see me after lunch. I thought if I saw him here in the presence of Mr. Franklin, it might be a way of knowing what line to take. That was before I was aware that you knew all about it."

The tone of the last remark was distinctly rueful. As Travers knew, his nature was so frank and open that he had a horror of the furtive or secretive, and if he had had his way, Franklin would have been shackled and hampered by such quixotic conditions that his stay in Bableigh would have been purely a rest cure.

"I'll tell you what we might do." He included both Franklin and Dryden in the offer. "I'm seeing Mould this afternoon. Let me leave just as this sergeant of yours arrives here. Give me time to get to Manor Cottage, then let the sergeant follow me up. I shall then see how Mould takes the visit, and with luck I might represent the Home Office at the exhumation."

Franklin accepted with such keenness that Dryden was carried off his feet. Travers was looking that afternoon as if he were bound for the duchess's garden-party. His suit was a warm brown, and the soft hat a lighter shade, and there was certainly an air of suave exclusiveness about him. Mould looked decidedly gratified at the call, and by contrast looked remarkably grubby.

"You've just come from Pulvery?" he asked.

"Yes. I spend most week-ends there. I believe I told you." He relaxed to the extent of a deprecatory smile. "We're all apt to get a little garrulous at times. However, have you anything that would suit me?"

"At that price I'm afraid not," said Mould. "Still, come along to the studio."

On the way Travers paused to survey the garden. "I see you've got some more plants in. . . . No more forget-me-nots turn up?"

Mould wasn't interested. He had moved on and was waiting at the door, and inside he was much more himself as he exhibited this and that. The only new things seemed to be those clay models of a child. Travers talked discursively with his ear inclined for the sergeant's step on the path. It came, in the middle of Mould's opening gambit on lead figures. There was a knock at the studio door and Mould looked up to see a tallish man who might have been anything from insurance agent to general canvasser.

"Yes?" said Mould, with more than a touch of aggression.

"You're Mr. Ashley Mould, sir?"

"Yes. What is it you want?"

The sergeant explained courteously and apologetically. At the first mention of his calling, Travers, who had retired discreetly into the background, saw on Mould's face such a fiery flush of red that he edged nearer again. Then his face went white and he began to bluster.

"You can't come here, you know, making suggestions like that. I've told you I found it, and Rogers will bear me out. If it's buried, what do you want to disturb it for?"

"Well, sir," said the sergeant mysteriously, "that, in a manner of speaking, is our business. The thing is, sir, do you give me permission to remove the dog?"

"Do what you damn well like," exploded Mould. "Take the dog and get to hell out of it—and the quicker the better."

Frost knew his job, and he decided not to get annoyed. Mould looked round for some moral support and Travers came forward solicitously. The two went along to the place of disinterment, and when Mould had most ungraciously lent his spade, the exhumation began. A couple of spits of soil were removed, and then the spade struck something. It was uncovered with as much care as if it had been the Portland Vase. Travers, craning shamelessly over to look, ventured on a comment of polite surprise at the sight of the black, stringy, repulsive fragment.

"But I say, that isn't a dog, surely!"

"No, sir," said the sergeant, and nodded obscurely. Then he gave Mould a look. "This is a curious thing, sir, if you don't mind me saying so. You've claimed to bury a dog, and all that's here is a head and front legs. Where's the rest?"

Mould was as surprised as anyone. All he could suggest was that Rogers must have tampered with the animal for some obscure reasons of his own. The sergeant inquired after Rogers's whereabouts, then produced a tin of lime and packed up the poor remains amid a silence that hinted at unutterable things. As soon as he had gone, Travers, who had remained aloofly sympathetic, put his sympathy into words.

"Pretty rotten for you, all this. What's the idea, do you think?"

"Idea!" He spat the word out. "Damned interference and nothing else."

"Yes, but how did he know you'd buried the dog?" Before the answer could come he appeared to be in the throes of some tremendous brain-wave. "I say! I think I know why the police consider this dog so important. Somebody was telling me—Dryden, I think it was—that somebody in the village was shot or something and his dog disappeared. They rather had the idea that it had been poisoned." He nodded suddenly at Mould with a fatuous directness. "I'll wager that detective fellow had orders to take it away so that they could analyse the remains!"

Mould stared and caught his breath. His face flushed with such a wave of colour that Travers looked away.

Mould stuttered, "Poison it? . . . But who should . . . I mean . . ."

Travers smiled discreetly as he took the other's arm. "I don't think I'd worry if I were you. After all, there's no particular harm in poisoning a dog—if it's dangerous. Mind you, speaking as one man to another, if you did do it, I'd keep my mouth very tight. They'll never prove anything."

The arm was snatched away. If Travers was looking like a soulful secretary-bird, Mould was an infuriated bantam.

"Look here! What are you getting at? Are you suggesting—"

"My dear Mould!" He waved his hand airily. "I'm suggesting nothing—except that there's no need for you to worry."

"Worry!" A curious look came into his eyes. "You seem very interested in this blasted dog. Very interested!" He glared with a ferocity that made Travers draw back. "You were here that morning when Rogers buried it. Dryden sent that man here. That's it—Dryden!" He shouted the words. "You came here too. You came from Dryden!"

"Aren't you talking rather noisy nonsense?" Travers was immensely on his dignity.

Mould's face purpled as he seized his arm and began to hustle him away.

"Get out of this quick, and don't come here again. Tell that bloody poet Dryden I said so!"

Travers thrust himself clear and made his final protest. "I think perhaps you're going to be very sorry for this ridiculous conduct."

Mould took a step forward, then as he read into the words something that Travers had never intended, a look of what could only have been fear came over his face. Travers turned his back abruptly and made his way through the side gate and out to the road. A few yards along the lane he looked back, but there was nothing of apprehension in it; the only disquiet he was feeling was for Dryden, and that Mould should go out of his way to cause him some petty annoyances. Nor was Travers discomposed; he had enjoyed that rencontre with Mould far too much, and at one moment, when he had taken his arm and looked down at the pinky island of skull in the sea of frizzy hair, he had been nearer laughter than anything else.

But he was not laughing now. That look back had been instinctive; something arising out of the fact that he was seeing Mould in an entirely new light. Then, all at once, he checked his long stride, and for a moment or two he must have looked rather ridiculous standing there in the lane and polishing away at his glasses. This time there could surely be no mistake about the theory. A new theory, was it, or merely part of the old? Travers shook his head and hooked the glasses on again. Whatever it was it was far too tremendous a thing to be even whispered before it had ceased to be theory and had become irrefutable fact. There was a question here of a man's life or death, and a false or premature step might ruin everything.

Then what was the best thing to do? Certainly nothing must be said to either Franklin or Dryden. No, the theory hinged on one thing. Would Mould see that he had made a false move, and would he therefore try to obscure the whole issue by apologizing? That was it—and Travers smiled as he moved slowly on; once let Mould apologize and the theory would have a foundation of fact. After that—well, all sorts of things might happen.

As he lifted his head contemplatively, there was a movement of something black on his right, and he turned to see the figure of Parish disappearing behind the hedge of Manor Path in the direction of Windyridge. The vicar was evidently going visiting, and with the thought Travers had another idea. Something had worried away like a gnawing tooth whenever he thought of the strange juxtaposition of those three books on the shelf in Parish's study. Parnell, the preacher poet, between two giants of the calibre of Voltaire and Anatole France; something like Christian crushed between anti-Christ and Pagan. . . .

It was Mrs. Clark who opened the door. The vicar, she said, was out, and she didn't know where.

"I think perhaps I ought to come in and wait," Travers told her. "I'm staying with Mr. Dryden, you know, and there was a picture I was examining for Mr. Parish. If he isn't back in a minute or two, tell him I called to see the picture again."

He took the picture down and laid it on the table, then put those three books behind the head for support. When the woman was well clear he took out the Parnell and turned each leaf methodically. Out of the hundreds of pencil annotations and underlined phrases or passages he found nothing into which he could read the slightest ulterior meaning; it was in the Introduction only that he discovered something that made things more clear. The reference was to Parnell's "Hermit."

"Whether or not there was a common source for this story, and both authors made use of it, is unknown to me. I prefer to think that during his stay in England Voltaire read, and was struck by, the story of the hermit as told by Parnell, and afterwards incorporated it, with certain alterations of his own, in his 'Zadig,' that Oriental romance for the original idea of which he is certainly indebted to 'Rasselas.'"

So much for the editor of the edition of Parnell's works which Travers was holding in his hand, and so much for the presence of Voltaire cheek by jowl with a seventeenth-century divine. And when he came to look into the Voltaire again, there was the confirmation—the leaf turned down at "Zadig." Travers smiled excitedly as he replaced the two beneath the head of the portrait and took out the Anatole France.

This time he drew blank. One leaf was turned down and one only, and that from what he could see of it had nothing to do with either Voltaire or Parnell. It was a story, as far as he could judge by a rapid glance through, about a holy man who was tempted of the devil, and at the end—there were only three pages of it—was a curious mark in what might or might not have been Parish's own pencilling—

(M ?)

and what it meant Travers hadn't the faintest idea. And he had no time to find out. Mrs. Clark, who was either suspicious or restless, tapped at the door and looked inside.

"Anything I can get for you, sir?"

"Thanks, no," said Travers. "I just happened to have finished. Tell Mr. Parish, will you, that I'll look in again if I have time," and he replaced the picture and departed.

Franklin and Dryden were at their ease in deck-chairs in the shade of the front lawn, and Sergeant Frost had already left a report. Travers rather gathered that Franklin had been skating over remarkably thin ice.

"Incredible!" was all that Dryden seemed capable of. "One might understand the burying of a corpse, but to bury half of it and leave the rest! Can *you* explain it for us?"

Travers nodded mysteriously. "I can't, Henry. I mean, if I had a dog to bury I'd make a job of it at one go. Mind you, there's just this. The part that's now in the hands of the police may have no value at all."

"You mean Mould deliberately removed the body part for that reason?"

Travers smiled suggestively. "That'll be for the authorities to say. The great thing is that Mould's now in the open."

As they strolled over to the house he began to tell them of his own experiences, then broke off suddenly to wave his hand at the bronze knocker on the door. So tremendous were the implications of that additional theory that had come to him that afternoon, that he was forced to give it some expression.

"Look at that now! Not the product of a guilty conscience, do you think?" And then before they could debate the point, "I suppose you haven't got ideas on the subject of lead figures, Henry? Do you prefer animals, for instance, or humans?"

CHAPTER XIV
THE TELEPHONE RINGS

TRAVERS WAS on quite good terms with himself when he arrived back in town that Monday night. Things, from his point of view, were going much better at Bableigh. Dryden was being educated up to the fact that however much of a nabob he might be in his own territory, investigations can never be conducted without investigating. Moreover, things were happening. The dry bones were beginning to stir, and stir to such purpose that, Dryden or no Dryden, the case must now go on. And if the bones moved too sluggishly Travers was prepared to do some stirring for himself—always provided that Mould stirred first.

That was why he was in a state of considerable excitement when the post brought a letter the very next morning.

"DEAR MR. TRAVERS,

"May I apologize unreservedly for the gross way I insulted you yesterday. I can say no more than that, except that it was as inexplicable to myself as it must have been to you. I would like you to know, however, that I have been worried lately by interfering busybodies and village gossip, and I can only think I must have suddenly been driven frantic by what seemed at the time a further unnecessary interference.

"If you should have mentioned the deplorable business to Mr. Dryden, for whom I assure you I have the profoundest respect, I beg that you will convey the same apologies to him. I hope that you will then wash the whole unfortunate affair from your mind, and I trust that at some time in the near future I may again have the pleasure of seeing you at Bableigh.

"Yours sincerely,
"ASHLEY MOULD."

Travers nodded over that letter with immense satisfaction. The coast was now clear. Mould had been so scared that he had neglected to withdraw himself into his natural shelter—a fit of the sulks. At once, then, Travers wrote him a letter, which Mould probably considered charming, and which most people would have known to be fulsome. Later in the morning he strolled along to the Conard Gallery and asked to see somebody responsible. Maurice Conard happened to be there himself and at once took him to the office.

"Something particularly confidential I wanted to ask you," said Travers, accepting the offer of a cigarette. "It's about a client of yours."

"Depends on who the client is," said Conard. "Still, go ahead."

"Her name is Marian Crome."

Travers received a look that began as the professional and ended in the roguish.

"Yes. . . . You a friend of the lady's?"

"My dear Maurice!" protested Travers. "Surely . . . but still, if you must know, I'm not. Say what you like."

"I don't know that there's anything I can say," and he obviously wasn't hedging. "We received a letter from her asking for terms and so on, and she sent us two canvases. We showed both for the specified time, and one had sufficient publicity value to be put in the window. We charged a pretty stiff figure and she paid up without question. A few days ago we reminded her that the contract had expired, and she wrote that we were to hang on to them for a bit as she wasn't sure of her movements. And that's the lot. . . . And what's the trouble?"

"There isn't any," said Travers. "If there should be, I'll see that you know as soon as anyone. The real point is this. May I borrow those two pictures, taking all risks and returning this afternoon?"

"You may not," Conard told him bluntly. "What you may do is take them away on approval to show a friend. . . . Want 'em packed, or will you take 'em as they are?"

When Travers left the Conard Gallery the two pictures accompanied him in the taxi, carefully shielded from ribald view. In the dining-room he removed the wrappings, propped the pictures against a couple of distant chairs, and lay back in his chair regarding them contemplatively. Palmer, entering with lunch, was for once moved from his wonted stoicism, and gave a start that almost amounted to a shy.

"They're visitors, not permanent," came Travers's voice from the chair.

"Indeed, sir!" He cast an official glance. "You'll pardon the question, sir, but might I ask what they are?"

"Certainly, Palmer, certainly! The larger is a lady in her bath, and the—"

"In a bath, sir?"

"That's right. The other is a reminiscence."

"I see, sir," Palmer observed politely, then with his usual jerk of a bow, "I'm afraid I'm not up to this modern art business, sir."

"Some people don't know when they're lucky," said Travers facetiously, and turned their faces to the wall. "Now get hold of Sir Charles Lambry and tell him I must see him for half an hour this afternoon. Time to suit him."

At half-past three Palmer carried the pictures down again, and with them the "Aphrodite" that was Travers's own property. The taxi-driver carried them to the Harley Street door and then prepared to wait as requested. A politely surprised man-servant admitted Travers and his pictures to the waiting-room and then helped to transport them to the consulting-room.

However great a man Sir Charles had become, he neither anticipated respect from Travers nor got it. What he had been at school he continued to remain, and the last time Travers had seen him, and that on the Friday, he had cursed the head off him for opening with two spades, although, as Travers remarked, he had only made a fourth to oblige.

"Here we are then," Travers now remarked amiably as he held out his hand. "And how are we to-day, Charles? The liver better?"

"Much better," he was assured. "And what are all the packages?"

Travers took a seat on Sir Charles's side of the table before replying. His face lost its flippancy. "I'll tell you straight away, Charles, that I'm here on a mighty ticklish business. Implicitly confidential isn't a strong enough description of what we're going to talk about."

"Not yourself!" He looked most concerned. "I thought your man spoke very lugubriously."

Travers permitted a smile to flicker across his face. "Not at the moment, Charles. No, what I want is your opinion on something inanimate; your opinion as alienist or psychiatrist, or whatever the latest term is. Do you mind?" and he began to untie the wrappings.

Sir Charles, who knew Travers as well as most people, watched the preparations for the miniature exhibition, then put on his special glasses and had a look, arms well under his coat-tails. He looked puzzled at first, then smiled; then frowned when he caught sight of Travers's unusually serious expression.

"I know it is rather funny," Travers remarked, "but I'd like you to be as serious as you can about this little show. It may mean the difference between hanging a man—or not."

"You'd like me to certify—"

"No, no!" broke in Travers. "Nothing to do with insanity. What I want to do, if you'll be good enough to listen, is to tell you all I know about the woman who painted those three atrocities; and about her friends and her environment." He permitted another smile to flicker. "The text will be, 'I was not ever thus!'—and if you weren't a better art expert than myself, as well as what you are when you're in this room, you'd never have been told a word."

In five minutes Sir Charles had heard all Travers had to tell. He rubbed his chin.

"Hm! Neo-Cubist, was she? and suddenly switched over to this stuff. Hm!" and he tucked his arms well under his tails again as he rose for another look.

"Make it simple, Charles," Travers asked plaintively. "None of your Jungian prose or Freudenese."

The other removed his glasses. "One question first. Were the other pictures that you saw of this type made up largely of rotund masses of paint? What we might call circular shapes?"

"That's right," said Travers.

Sir Charles appeared not to hear the answer. "Under certain conditions they might be phallic—"

"Surely not!" protested Travers. "I mean, that'd be crude reproduction of sex—"

It was the other's turn to interrupt. "I was going on to add that such conditions were not present in this particular case. They're more in the nature of adolescent dream shapes, which, as you know, have their origin in sex." He nodded at the pictures, then took his seat at the desk. "I can solve your riddle without much difficulty, I think. The change which this particular person was driven to make was due to an overwhelming sex-experience. If I could spend a short time with the person concerned, I'd perhaps be more sure."

Travers clapped the two Conard pictures together and began to tie them up again. "That's all I want to know, Charles. And would you be prepared to take your stand in the box and repeat that opinion if it were a question of hanging a man on it?"

The other smiled dryly. "You won't frighten me by threats like that, my dear fellow. I say the problem's an elementary one. How it can mean the Old Bailey I'm damned if I know."

"No doubt you're right, Charles." He fastened the straps and tested them, then held out his hand. "Very grateful to you, my dear chap."

"You're not going already?" Sir Charles had only just begun to get into his stride.

"Must," smiled Travers. "Can't trespass on your time, you know." He picked up the "Aphrodite." "Something I was forgetting. Keep this and have a look at it sometimes. If you change the opinion you've given me this afternoon, let me know at once." Then, as the man left with the bulky package, he gave a last, confidential whisper. "When you send the bill, don't forget that frame's worth a couple of guineas!"

And as the taxi took him back to the Conard Gallery he was still on excellent terms with himself. Everything was now ready for the first inquiries at the Bableigh end.

Franklin stayed on for the funeral on the Wednesday afternoon and returned to town the same evening, though Potter had been left for a few more days at Travers's special request. Like Travers, Franklin was on quite good terms with himself. The holiday side of that week in Bableigh had been a wonderful one; and as for the business side and the final interview with Dryden—which latter he had been rather dreading—there had, after all, been nothing to worry about.

"I'm afraid I haven't been of much use to you," he had said diffidently when the good-byes were being said.

"Use?" smiled Dryden. "You've done me the kindness to be the most excellent company for a week. The nurse is going, if I may say so, and leaving a night-light. You've turned my own village inside out for me and shown me things I never suspected. If that isn't use, what is?"

Franklin began to put his own thanks into words, but the other wouldn't hear a word of it. The debt was all on his side. "You shall hear about the dog as soon as I know myself," he said, "and perhaps you'll run down or allow me to see you in town to decide then how to proceed further."

"You'll always get me at Durango House," Franklin told him, and that was how things were left.

It was after dinner on the Thursday that Franklin had caught up sufficiently with his work to afford an hour or two with Travers. His reception was an enthusiastic one.

"Curious you should drop in just when I was thinking about you. And how'd you leave Dryden?"

Franklin picked out what he had come to regard as his own chair. Travers hastened to pour out drinks.

"Dryden was in great fettle. I don't know that I ever met a man who pays more for the knowing." He shook his head at some amusing recollection, then gave a queer look. "I'll tell you something I'd never tell to any other living soul. There was a second or so last week when I allowed myself to think something of which I'm desperately ashamed. All sorts of things flashed through my mind about Dryden . . . that lock of hair that was taken was the thing that set me off."

"Funny, isn't it?" said Travers. "Still, I don't think I'd go on reproaching myself about that. It's your job of work to suspect all mankind. Anything new turned up since I left?"

"Not a thing. Miss Blunt paid another nocturnal visit to Mould's studio, which may interest you. Unless Potter discovers something sensational there's nothing for it but to see what the police make of the dog—and Mould."

"But you've plenty to go on?" said Travers.

"Depends on what you mean by 'plenty.' I know a river where there's plenty of fish. The trouble is getting 'em out."

"Always ways and means," said Travers cheerfully. "This case was nebulous from the first. When you come to consider what's been done, I think you'll admit the progress has been perfectly staggering. Don't you admit it?"

"I'm not so easily staggered," Franklin told him. "All the facts that I'm sure of in my own mind are what other people might call fancies. I know that Yeoman died under suspicious circumstances; I know the same about Clark, and I suspect the same about Miss Faithful. And what can I do about it?"

"Sit tight and call them coincidences. Something definite's bound to happen before long."

"If by definite you mean another pseudo-accident," said Franklin, "then I hope you're wrong. Another billion-to-one chance and I'll be in an asylum." He had been looking at odd papers in his pocket-book, and suddenly sat up. "I knew there was something I wanted to discuss with you. You remember that theory of ours which seemed to account satisfactorily for the loss of memory or aphasia we assume Parish has got? You agreed with that theory; then, before we could do anything much on it, you produced that wholly new theory—the Satanism one. Tell me: how do you fit Parish, and Yeoman, and the wood, into that?"

"I don't know that I can. Parish might have gone to the wood as you suggested. There he might have seen Mould kill Yeoman—"

"With what weapon?"

Travers shrugged his shoulders. "Does that matter? The fact that Dryden said there were only two other guns in the village has nothing to do with it. It might have been with Yeoman's own gun. All I suggest is that the shock of what he saw gave Parish a breakdown from which he is slowly recovering. He's forgotten, as we said, all that happened from the time he entered the garage till the time he returned home. If Mould killed Yeoman, it fits in with the Satanism theory. Your theory, that Parish saw Yeoman kill himself, doesn't fit in with it. It leaves it wholly out of account."

"I know," said Franklin, and shuffled restlessly. "I'll tell you to your face that your Satanism theory is the maddest and most fantastic thing a sane man like myself ever relied on. The only reason I abandoned my own in its favour is that it fits everything in so beautifully."

"I know that myself and that's why I propounded it," smiled Travers. "In your office that afternoon, Dryden wondered if there was any unifying force that had actuated the village. Was what we called the problem of the back-sliding community one problem and Yeoman's death another, or were they one and the same thing? What's more; were all the problems inside the backsliding community connected with one another or independent occurrences? I know my Satanism theory is fantastic—but it does connect and unify everything in the most uncanny way."

"Exactly. That's what I like about it. Even then, as far as Yeoman's concerned, it's only a motive for his death. It isn't helping to prove to the satisfaction of a British jury the precise manner of that death."

"Plenty of time yet. Wait till the Northurst police have finished with Mould." Franklin was too preoccupied to notice it, but the subject was changed far too suddenly. "What about an hour's chess? Seems months since we had a game."

Franklin hailed the idea and hopped up at once. "I'll get the apparatus if you'll fetch the table. . . . Only an hour, mind you. None of your midnight orgies."

"An hour it is," began Travers—and then the telephone bell rang at his elbow. He took off the receiver.

"Yes. . . . Mr. Franklin? Yes, he's here! . . . Hold on a moment, will you?"

He smiled over at Franklin. "Durango House chasing you. . . . Drains probably wrong at Buckingham Palace."

Franklin gave a grunt of annoyance as he took over the receiver. His tone was quite snappy.

"Hallo! . . . Yes, speaking. . . . Oh, one moment and I'll take it down."

He felt for his pencil and gave Travers a meaning look.

"Yes. All ready. . . . From Potter. . . . Bableigh. . . . Fancy—Frail—missing—since—afternoon—stop. Last—seen—in—mother's—garden—stop. Search—continuing—stop. . . . Yes, thanks. I shall be here. . . . Good-bye."

He hung up and looked round to find Travers regarding him steadily.

"What do you think of it? . . . You heard it all?"

"Yes, I heard it," said Travers. "You're going down there again?"

"First thing in the morning . . . or at once." He seemed too restless to sit or speak. "You know Fancy Frail? The child who sat for those models you saw in Mould's studio?"

Travers looked at him with what was intended for humorous exasperation. "My dear fellow, you really mustn't begin to discourse on that! Potter must have phoned from Northurst, and heaven knows how long ago that was. For all we know, she's probably tucked up in her cot by this time."

"I know," said Franklin, and began taking the pieces out of the box. "As you say, we'll wait a bit. There may be another message." He looked up again. "Damn funny, you know! That garden's only a stone's-throw from Mould's!" He caught Travers's look of whimsical reproach. "Right oh! I'll say no more. But it's damn funny, all the same."

THE FINAL PHASE

CHAPTER XV
FRANKLIN IS FRIGHTENED

FRANKLIN LEFT TOWN very early the next morning, driving one of the service cars, and as he came to the tiny village of Bableigh he saw that something serious had happened. The scene, in fact, was rather like that of the morning when young Clark had been killed, with little groups of people standing in the street, and then the car swung round the bend to Old House.

Jimson had the door open before Franklin had finished knocking. He seemed perfectly prepared for the visit as he picked up the suit-case and Franklin stepped inside.

"Very glad to see you again, sir, if I may say so."

"I'm glad to see you, Jimson," said Franklin. "You weren't expecting me, were you?"

Jimson halted. "Didn't you get our telegram, sir? It was sent off last night."

Franklin clicked his tongue. "And Mr. Dryden? Is he in?"

"He's at the cottage, sir. He left word that he'd been in before twelve, and you were to wait."

"Look here, Jimson," said Franklin, "I'm in the dark about all this. What's happened exactly?"

"You knew about Martha Frail's little girl, sir?"

"I knew she was missing last night."

Jimson nodded solemnly. "She was found this morning, sir. In the well. Drowned."

"Good God!" For a moment or two he could only stare.

Jimson shook his head. "It's a bad business, sir. Nice tidy little body, too, and all she had left."

Franklin sorted out that confusion of mother and child. "And how'd the child get in the well, Jimson? Somebody leave the top open?"

Jimson took the hat and coat. "Well, sir, from what the master told me, I gathered that Martha left the little girl playing in the garden just after tea, and went over to the shop. When she came out, sir, she met a neighbour and had what she called a few words. When she got home she missed the little girl, but she didn't think much about it till it was time for the child to go to bed, and then she went round to the Roebuck, where she thought she was playing. To cut a long story short, sir, she got alarmed, and people started looking for her, and when it got dark we all got a bit scared, and Mr. Dryden himself lent a hand—up most of the night, as a matter of fact—going through the woods and everywhere. Then this morning one of the men had the idea of looking in the well, and there she was, sir. They got the poor little mite out, and that'd be about eleven o'clock."

Franklin was very upset, and he couldn't help making the remark, "This is a very unlucky village nowadays, Jimson; don't you think so?"

"You're right there, sir!" said Jimson wholeheartedly. "I heard one or two say the same thing last night, sir. First there was Mr. Yeoman they had an inquest on, the only one I ever knew in this village, sir. Then there was young Clark, and now there's this." He broke off suddenly. "Here's the master, sir, and Doctor Sawyer."

He went out to the hall and Franklin heard his, "Mr. Franklin is here, sir," and Dryden's, "Thank you. The doctor won't be staying to lunch."

Dryden seemed absolutely washed out—the strain, perhaps, of being up all night. He gave Franklin a tremendous grip as he shook hands.

"I'm very glad you've come down. You know Sawyer, don't you?"

The doctor had recognized him first time. "You're the unlucky star of this village, Mr. Franklin. First you arrive for a bicycle accident, then I find you with Miss Faithful, and now this."

"A terrible business," said Franklin.

"Well," and he looked round belligerently, "if fools of women will leave the wells open—"

"Don't say that!" cut in Dryden quickly. "She's paid for it heavily enough if she did leave the lid open." He smiled nervously. "Sorry! I'm a bit out of sorts this morning. You'll have a drink, the pair of you?"

The doctor had whisky and Franklin beer. The conversation was resumed from over the top of the doctor's glass.

"You said if she left the lid open. That child couldn't have opened it." He turned to Franklin. "For years I've been hammering away. When there's no more children left to drown, it'll be made compulsory to have the tops crowned in and pumps in the kitchens."

Dryden, with the hope of changing the topic, got him to sit down. Franklin turned a blind eye.

"I suppose, by the way, the child did die by drowning?"

Sawyer looked at him in astonishment, then saw the humour of it. "It's the usual thing, you know, when you drag people from the bottoms of wells."

"Not so fast," said Franklin. "I know I'm a layman, but people have been poisoned and strangled and then thrown into wells. Still, being serious for once, she did die of suffocation from drowning, if that's how you people phrase it?"

From his seventy years Sawyer regarded Franklin with polite toleration. "Yes . . . that's what she died of."

Dryden was recognizing there was more in Franklin artless chatter than the doctor saw. Franklin included him in his next pronouncement.

"Did you see that atrocious case in the paper the other day, where some sexual maniac attacked a small child and then threw the body in a well? Curious, you know, doctor, the ideas that come into one's head. As soon as Jimson told me this morning what had happened, that was the first thing my mind flew back to."

Sawyer nodded, then finished his tot. "Nothing of that sort here. Everything's as plain as the nose on your face." He picked up his hat. "The mother says she was playing with a ball when she last saw her. The ball was found in the well. That's plain enough, isn't it?"

He strode off to the door without waiting for anything further from Franklin. He did nod back from the hall door, and that was the last of Sawyer for that morning.

Dryden came back, and it was not hard to see that he wished to avoid any mention of the tragedy. They talked about the ride down, the wonderful weather they were having, everything, in fact, but the drowning of Fancy Frail. Then after lunch Dryden seemed more spiritually fortified.

"Well," he said, "this thing has got to be faced, and the sooner we face it the better. Sergeant Frost is coming this afternoon, and I'm meeting him. You'd like to see the well and talk things over?"

"I would," said Franklin. "About the cause of death? You agree with Sawyer?"

"Oh, yes! I saw your point, of course, in putting forward all those suggestions, but there's no doubt. Not a bruise on the body or mark of a struggle."

Franklin turned aside to pleasanter paths. "It's a strange thing, you know, but Travers and I were saying the other day that if a professional murderer were set adrift in a village he could have the time of his life if his methods were reasonably subtle."

"You mean Sawyer?" said Dryden quickly.

"Not necessarily Sawyer alone. I mean, there's no real need for the country practitioner to keep himself plumb up to date. I very much doubt if he could. Sawyer's an extreme example, because he's an autocrat of the old school. . . . By the way, I left town before delivery of your telegram this morning."

"You came by chance!"

Franklin temporized. "I suppose that's what it amounts to in the end. . . . You sent for me because of this dreadful business?"

Dryden nodded. "I grew very alarmed. Panic perhaps would be nearer." He turned and put the question with a passionate directness. "Can all these things be accidents? I ask you, is it credible?"

Franklin shook his head. "They are credible—individually. It's this repetition that's incredible. But let me ask you a question. When you heard the child was drowned, and saw the spot and visualized the circumstances, did you think it was an accident?"

"What else could I think?"

Franklin had never seen him so strongly moved.

"It was natural. It isn't that that disturbs me. What is so terrifying is the something inside me that insists on being heard, something that says these things can't be accidents." He made a gesture of helplessness. "Is there some malignant force at work in this village? Has it eaten of the insane root?" He shook his head wearily. "What does Sawyer know in spite of his assurance? Martha herself told me this morning that she had never left that well lid open in her life."

"She made the one mistake," said Franklin. "Still, we'll know more when we see the ground."

They went out by the back path. Everything was peaceful, and the village now seemed to be sleeping drowsily in the sun. A drone of voices, like the hum of sleepy bees, was coming from the little school as they passed it. Across the road at the very last cottage the gate was open, and they went round the corner of the house by the cindered path.

"I'll have a word with her first," Dryden said quietly. "Then perhaps you'll say something. She'd think a lot of that."

At the back door, its tiled step still muddy from the work of the morning, Dryden stopped short. The door was open, and Franklin could see the kitchen table and then a door beyond which was open too. There was the sound of a voice, and Dryden held his breath and turned his head quickly. Franklin heard the voice too, a solemnly intoned voice—the voice of Parish.

". . . And teach Thy handmaid that Thy ways are not our ways. Thy ways are inscrutable. . . ."

Dryden turned abruptly, and with a quick shake of the head moved back to the corner of the cottage. Franklin, running an eye down the garden, saw Frost standing by the gate that led to the meadows and Manor Path.

"There's Frost," he said. "We might see Martha later . . . if you think best."

That cindered path from the front gate now led them down the garden to the well, which stood some fifteen yards from the kitchen door. It circled the well, then ran on to the gate from which Frost was now coming to meet them. Franklin liked that detective sergeant, with his quiet manner and pleasant voice and unobtrusive shrewdness.

"A bad business this, Frost," was Dryden's reply to the detective's salute.

Franklin nodded friendlily.

"As you say, sir." He cast his eye round. "And this is the well where it happened?"

There were several things that became apparent when the well itself and its surroundings had their first real inspection. The meadows, it is true, were open, but the backs of the cottages on the Northurst Road were so hidden in ancient fruit trees that the walk from Windyridge to the church seemed never overlooked. From Mould's house one could slip in a matter of seconds into Martha's garden, and run no risk of being seen—unless a pedestrian was using Manor Path. The hedge of the garden was so tall and overgrown, and its trees so straggly, that once inside the garden a surreptitious caller was unseen from outside—and, still more to the point, the bedroom windows of the neighbouring cottage were invisible, at least from the well.

Round the well the suckers of plums and lilacs had made a dense screen, then towards the cottage there was a patch of weedy grass on which the child had played. The well itself had the usual brick surround, eighteen inches in height, in which was the hinged lid beneath the windlass. Frost stooped to lift it, and found it opened easily enough. He set it back against the wooden framework, then moved it to and fro with his finger to see what force would bring it down again. Then he stood back and looked.

"You knew the child?" asked Dryden.

"Oh, yes, sir!" Frost knew at what he was driving. "What I suggest is this, gentlemen, and I'd like you to test it for yourselves. I think you'll agree we shan't find a child to test it with, because we'll never know how strong the dead child was—or wasn't." He lifted the lid with one finger. "If you test that, you'll agree that, easy as it goes for us, no child was tall enough or strong enough to get the leverage. But once the child climbed on the surround it had the leverage. I suggest the child had the idea of looking down the well—she was a queer little soul, as we know, and only the other night she and the youngster at the Roebuck were reading about a fairy in a well. I say, then, that she tried to open the lid from the ground, then she got on here and it opened. In her hand she held the ball she'd been playing with. But when the lid was open and she leaned forward to look, she put her hand on top to steady herself, like this. The lid came forward and in she went."

Dryden sighed with what was certainly relief when he had tested that out for himself.

Franklin was disposed to agree. "There's only one thing I would say, sergeant," and he looked him clean in the eye, "and it's the comment of a comparative outsider. This is an accident—obviously. But what has happened to the laws of chance? Here's a village—a hamlet, perhaps, would be nearer the mark—that has three fatal accidents in three months." He shrugged the question.

Frost shook his head. "I know all that, sir. The chief constable was mentioning the matter only an hour ago. Still, you can't get away from what's under your nose. We're not dealing with figures put on a sheet of paper where you've got some idea what sort of answer you ought to get. I haven't got the education of you gentlemen, but when I was thinking this matter over just now, I couldn't get away from the idea we let ourselves go too much by averages and all that sort of thing. When anything unusual happens we try to find an unusual explanation, and the more I know of my job, the more I find there's precious little that's unusual at all."

Dryden nodded. "There's a lot in what you say. And now about the inquest . . ."

Franklin left them to it and moved on towards the cottage, and waited by the side path. Then voices were heard and the vicar emerged from the back door, Martha at his heels, her face thin to emaciation and her eyes rubbed to a vivid red. At the sight of Franklin she looked frightened and stepped back to the door again. The vicar came on.

"Ah! Mr. Franklin, isn't it?" and he held out his hand.

Franklin took it, then let it fall. So steady was the vicar's gaze beyond him that he turned too to see what it was that caused the stare, but he saw nothing.

"A very bad business, this."

Parish came back to earth, and he seemed to see the other for the first time.

"Yes, a very bad business." He nodded, as if to himself. "And yet, you know, there must be some purpose behind all these things, if only we could see it."

Franklin was vaguely irritated. "Philosophy's all very well in its place, vicar. It won't fill the gap in Martha's life."

Parish spoke almost grievingly. "Patience, Mr. Franklin; that's the lesson we're here to learn."

"Damn patience!" exploded Franklin, and then was sorry for the outbreak. "I beg your pardon, vicar. I think I was rather upset."

Parish nodded heavily, and somehow the action irritated even more. Then he held out the same limp hand.

"I'll bid you good afternoon, Mr. Franklin," and he moved off with a vacant kind of nod.

As he disappeared round the front of the cottage, Dryden's voice was heard, and Franklin turned to see him enter the back door. In a couple of minutes he was out again.

"Frost gone?"

"Yes," said Dryden. "He went by the meadows. Better not to be too conspicuous. It only leads to gossip. . . . I suppose Parish couldn't wait."

"Apparently not," said Franklin. "At least he's gone on."

Dryden saw that something had ruffled the usually placid Franklin rather badly. He gave him a quick look. "Well, we'll go on too, I think," and he slipped his arm inside Franklin's. "Poor Martha's in a bad way. . . . Parish's kindness upset her very much. He gave her five pounds. Made her take it."

Franklin felt rather ashamed of himself for a moment or two, and Dryden must have gathered what he was thinking.

"He's a strange mixture. . . . Even now a lovable man at times. Just now I'm reproaching myself for not remembering it oftener."

Potter was standing at the gate of the inn garden, smoking his pipe. He gave them a courteous good afternoon as they passed.

Dryden stopped for a moment. "You helped us with the search last night, didn't you?"

"Well, sir, I did lend a hand."

"Very good of you. . . . The fine weather's going to last, don't you think?" and he moved on again.

"Quite a superior-looking man, that," he said to Franklin. "Jimson tells me he's looking for a house in this district." Just short of the church gate he stopped, looked away over the south valley, then up at the tower. "The very day to see the view from up there. What do you say? Shall we let the four winds blow on us?"

Franklin smiled as he mopped his forehead. "One wind wouldn't be a bad idea. . . . You can get to the top?"

"Oh, yes!" said Dryden. "There's a stone stairway going right up."

The church was delightfully cool, though rather musty. The tiny door in the wall beneath the tower was a problem for Dryden's huge frame, and the stairway darkness itself except for the light of one unglazed opening, and the worn stones made treacherous going. At the top Dryden reached up and pushed back a wooden cover and in a moment they were out in what seemed overpowering light.

Franklin took off his hat and let the light breeze play round him. Across to the south was what was clearly sea, and he could discern the smoke of a boat in the Channel. As his eyes swept round he could see the tiny spires of churches peeping from belts of green; farms, the valley by the woods where Yeoman used to shoot, and nearer still the far side of Martha Frail's garden and the top of the well. As he set his hand on the coping, Dryden took his arm.

"I don't think I'd risk it if I were you. Those stones are none too secure. . . . Wonderful view, isn't it?"

They stood there for some minutes while Dryden pointed out this and that, then made a move down again. Franklin went first and waited at the bottom till Dryden should negotiate the narrow door. He squeezed through laughingly.

"Well, that's done it. Must do something about this fat." His voice lowered. "A look round the church now, do you think?"

"I think so," said Franklin, and turned towards the aisle. He stopped and held Dryden with him. The sun sent beams of light across the nave, and through the strange pattern of light and shade something black could be seen crumpled up against the velvet of the altar.

"What is it? . . . Parish?"

Franklin mumbled something as he moved forward to the matting. Then he ran, and by the time Dryden was at the end of the aisle, he had the vicar's head in his arms. Dryden knelt too.

"Is he . . . all right?"

"A faint, probably. . . . The vestry, quick! See if there's any water!"

Parish's face was bloodless and his lips a bluish streak, and yet it seemed to Franklin that this was no ordinary faint. The lips were together and the breathing was too regular. There was nothing of that stertorous snorting that often goes with epilepsy. Then, as he loosened the collar, Dryden came back.

"No water there. . . . His hat's there. That's all there is."

"Try the vicarage then."

He heard the scurry of Dryden's feet, then listened again for the heart beat. It still seemed regular enough. Then he let the head down gently to the crook of his knee and took off his coat for a cushion. As he raised the head again he saw the thin neck and the cord that held the crucifix, at the end of which had been tied those pinkish flowers. With finger and thumb he drew the cord up till the crucifix was clear of the shirt. To the middle was fastened a tiny curl of vivid red hair!

For a moment his own heart must have stood still, then he thrust the crucifix down again. What, in the name of sanity, did it all mean? Had Mould killed that child? Did Parish know it, and had he brought the lock of hair to spread out before the altar as he prayed? Or was it that Parish had loved the child and had identified himself with it by the lock of hair that touched his bare skin? Was this some ritual of love that he—Franklin—had stumbled clumsily across and spoiled of all its beauty? And why those flowers where the curl of red hair now was? And—most staggering of all—it must have been Parish who had taken the lock of white hair from the head of the old lady whom Martha had found dead in the chair.

Franklin roused himself and then looked down again at the white face of Parish—a face that at that moment was that of some ivory saint. He laid the head with infinite care on the folded coat and drew his arm away. All at once the unconscious man began to stir. His body moved as if he were trying to escape from something that was holding him down. His arms began to weave the air, as if freeing the head from a net that enveloped and smothered it. The lips began to murmur. Words came clear and startling as the eyes opened and stared through the light to the shadows by the far door.

"The angel!"

The stare was more fixed. The lips shaped themselves again, then there was a moan and a look of horror. The hand went before the eyes as if to shut off the awful thing. The moan became a ghastly whimper, and Franklin for a moment felt afraid. What it was that frightened him he had no idea, but his arm tightened and he found himself clutching the body of the whimpering man as a nurse might clutch a child.

The feeling was gone in a flash as the whimpering ceased. The eyes lost their stare. He looked at Franklin like a man bemused, and then collapsed as if all his strength had gone.

"Where am I? . . . What is it?"

"It's all right," said Franklin soothingly. "You must have fainted here. Mr. Dryden and I found you."

He nodded feebly and made as if to rise. Then Dryden was heard coming down the aisle and the old housekeeper with him. They made him drink some of the water, and bathed his face and temples, and between them got him through the churchyard and across to his own house. Just short of the porch he shook them off almost irritably, and the colour was already coming back to his cheeks. Dryden offered to send Jimson at once for the doctor, but he wouldn't hear of it. He would be better, he said, in a few minutes. Mrs. Hopper made signs to them behind his back that they'd better go and she could manage him.

Outside the vicarage gate Dryden stopped and shook his head determinedly. "I'm going to insist on someone seeing him. If he won't have Sawyer he shall have another doctor. He must go away for a holiday; don't you think so?"

Franklin grunted something and Dryden moved off again. Franklin held his arm. "Would you mind going round the back way? There's something I'd like to say."

Dryden flashed a look at him and they turned towards the back path. Franklin said nothing till they were level with the hedge of Miss Faithful's garden, then something seemed to come into his mind. It was to cover his nervousness that he pulled out his pipe and began to fill it.

"I don't know what you'll think of me, Mr. Dryden, but I want to tell you that I'm sorry I failed to see your point of view when you spoke of . . . well, of sensing things." He spoke with such an intensity that Dryden for a moment was disconcerted. "You're right! There's something devilish going on in this village. I knew it in that church. What's more, if it takes me years I'm going to find out what it is."

Dryden nodded gravely. "What was it you felt in the church?"

Franklin turned away. "I don't know. Don't ask me what it was. It came in a flash and it went in a flash, but, by God! I never want to feel it again. It was as though I was in a tomb—icy cold and something terrible looking at me."

He moistened his lips nervously while Dryden watched him. Then he put the pipe back in his pocket and moved on.

"Perhaps you can help me," he said. "I'll try to tell you just what happened after you left."

CHAPTER XVI
TRAVERS CARRIES ON

ON THE FRIDAY evening the papers told Travers just what had happened at Bableigh. Whoever was responsible for reporting local news had become struck by the curious coincidences that were affecting the remote Sussex hamlet, and had communicated his ideas to a news agency. There was a photograph of Bableigh church, but it was the headings that showed what news-interest lay in the story itself:

UNLUCKY SUSSEX VILLAGE
THREE FATAL ACCIDENTS IN THREE MONTHS
CHILD DROWNED IN WELL

The story was a re-hash of the Yeoman and Clark affairs, with a rather more detailed account of the drowning of Fancy Frail. Travers himself pondered a long while over that latest tragedy, and was no wiser than before he had read. Then he wrote a note to Franklin, who, if he read between the lines, would let Dryden go alone to the inquest.

What Travers now intended was to pursue to some very definite conclusion that new theory of his which had been temporarily laid aside with the return of Marian Crome's pictures to the Conard Gallery. The inquest was to be in the village school at eleven in the morning. The doctor would be there, and the rest, he thought, might be left to chance.

But Travers was to have an extraordinary piece of luck. It was fortunate that he should have come through Northurst at all—merely the desire for a change of route at the expense of a few extra miles. It was by chance that just when things happened, he should have been crawling round a dangerous bend. As it was, he saw a car drawn in at the side of the road and a chauffeur with his head inside the bonnet, with an elderly, grey-whiskered man hovering anxiously at his elbow. Travers drew his own car in just round the corner.

"I believe that's the Bableigh doctor," he remarked to Palmer, and hopped out at once.

Sawyer saw approaching him a man of obvious breeding and the owner of a very expensive car, and his manner was vastly different from what it might have been.

"Morning," said Travers politely. "Can I be of any help to you?"

"That's very kind of you," said Sawyer. "I'm afraid my man can't make it out at all." He hesitated before saying what was plainly in his mind. "I suppose you're not going near Bableigh?"

Travers smiled. "But I am! Hop in and I'll give you a lift."

They drove off with Palmer at the wheel, and Sawyer explained matters.

"My name's Sawyer and I'm a doctor. There's an inquest on at Bableigh and I've got to give evidence."

"I've heard Henry Dryden mention you," said Travers. "I'm due at Old House for lunch, as a matter of fact."

"You know him?"

"Oh, rather! I was at school with him." His face assumed its original gravity. "I'm fond of Bableigh, you know. I'd like to live there."

Sawyer looked surprised. "Why don't you buy the Manor?"

"Too big for me. No, what I'd like is a week-end place; something of the style of Manor Cottage. By the way, isn't the lease of that due to expire soon?"

"I believe it is," said Sawyer.

Travers sighed. "Yet I don't know. My aunt's perfectly terrified of T.B."

"T.B.?"

"Yes. Consumption. The present tenant's wife died of it, didn't she?"

Sawyer guffawed. "I don't know where you got hold of that, but I attended her and I ought to know. Her lungs were as sound as yours or mine. Her trouble was gastric."

Travers clicked his tongue. "How absurd of me! But she was an invalid, wasn't she?"

"She was," said Sawyer. "I don't mind saying she was in a bad way when she came here. . . . If you don't mind dropping me here, at the school."

The car slowed down at the little schoolhouse, before which quite a crowd of people were assembled. Travers, in the act of telling Sawyer that the pleasure had been his own, noticed three cars drawn up and wondered whose they were. Then as he settled again in his corner he caught sight of Spence of the Evening Record, who was button-holing the doctor. And that, as Travers recognized, was another stroke of luck.

Franklin, who must have been watching from the window, came down the path as the car stopped. "Hallo! Going to leave the car there? Dryden made me swear to make you stay to lunch at the least."

"Splendid," said Travers. "Perhaps it might be better to take her round."

Palmer was already fussing round with a duster.

"Take the car to the garage," Travers told him quietly. "Then go to the corner and let me know when people begin coming out of the school."

Travers loved little stratagems like that. He appeared to be on such good terms with himself that Franklin saw nothing unusual in the suggestion that they might as well sit outside on such a morning, and the dust of the road might well be washed away in a tankard of Dryden's beer. But after his very first swig, Travers saw there was something one-sided about the gaiety of the summer morning. Franklin was a long way from his usual quietly communicative self. When he had heard the happenings of the previous day he knew something of the reason.

"And you're going to stay on?"

"Yes," said Franklin, "I don't know what I'm going to do, but here I am and here I stop till Dryden kicks me out."

Travers nodded. Then he frowned to himself as he sat there twiddling his fingers unconsciously. "This angel business of Parish's—what is it? Hallucinations?"

"Maybe," said Franklin. "But there was more to it than angels. If there was any truth in what we heard him say that night when he came to dinner, he saw a devil too."

Travers grunted. "Dryden's right. He's heading for a bad breakdown, that chap. He ought to have a holiday. He's far too good a sort to kill himself as he's doing at present. . . . And the curl on the crucifix; what did you make of that?"

"Dryden and I talked it over for quite a long while. If we settled on anything, it's this, though I'd rather Dryden put it into words than me. That crucifix chafes his skin like a hair shirt. It's his reminder of personal worship; his connection with God, if you like. He put the hair on the crucifix to identify the child with himself and God. He brought the child, as it were, with him into the presence of God. Perhaps he imagined Miss Rose was very upset about her garden and put the flowers there for the same reason. He also took a lock of Miss Faithful's hair, and then, perhaps, forgot that he did it."

Travers nodded again. "And what about Mould in all this?"

"Nothing at all. Potter says he refused to help with the search and said it was all moonshine." The first smile stole over Franklin's face. "By the way, the county people made nothing out of the dog. Your own exhumation was a bit too thorough. Frost saw Mould again and Mould practically told him to get on with it."

"Don't blame him," said Travers, who rose to his feet as Palmer made a sudden appearance at the gate and then disappeared. Franklin rose too. "I'd rather like to stroll down the village. You coming too?"

If Franklin had been in his best form he would have known that something was in the wind; as it was he showed no particular enthusiasm. Travers chose the front way, guessing that Dryden might take the back; then, as they drew near the school and the crowd, which had hardly begun to disperse, Franklin was very astonished.

"Good Lord! Where do they all come from?"

"Heaven knows!" said Travers. "Just shows what a little publicity can do."

He had been watching the crowd as they approached and was wondering if he had cut things too fine, then all at once a reporter of the Globe who knew Franklin well, made a bee-line for him and put the question point-blank.

"If you don't mind my asking, Mr. Franklin, are you down here on business?"

No sooner was Franklin engaged than Travers retired well into the background, with an alacrity that had nothing to do with good manners. Two other reporters were making their way across, but the man Travers was looking for was Spence, the special crime-reporter of the Evening Record. But Spence had seen Travers first, and was making for him with a grin that might have been broad or ironical. Travers countered with another, and got in his question.

"Morning, Spence! And what was the verdict?"

"The same old dope," said Spence. "But it's nice to see you and Mr. Franklin at a rustic inquest. Where the carcass is, I take it?"

"There's nothing of the eagle about me," said Travers, and drew him on one side. "You can keep a secret?"

Spence looked most indignant.

"All right then. Put into your copy the statement that you saw Mr. Franklin and myself down here. Make it perfectly clear who Franklin is, and hint at something in his line."

Spence looked at him. "What's on?"

"I can't tell you." He put on a mighty serious face. "What I will do is give you my word that if a rabbit bolts you shall know where the hole is before anyone else. That good enough for you?"

"Perfectly, thanks." He coughed tentatively. "There was something, then, behind these accidents?"

Travers smiled. "That's not in the bond!" He held out his hand. "Good-bye. I'll rely on you and you can rely on me."

After that flagrant selling of the pass he moved on to the rescue of Franklin. The whole affair had not taken more than a couple of minutes, and when he caught up with him, Franklin was clear of his interceptors and laughing and waving his hand. Then, as if sent by a punctual providence, who should be coming from the direction of Windyridge but Harriet Blunt.

"Come on!" said Franklin. "I've got a scheme to get rid of those fellows," and he hailed her at once. Travers, he said, was most anxious to see some of her work, and under the shelter of her wing the pair passed through the outskirts of the crowd and into the house.

Travers pulled his weight by making conversation. "So Miss Rose has a cold, has she?"

"Oh, she's much better," she told them. "She was actually able to discuss who was going to have the next accident!" Her laugh seemed none too sincere.

Franklin took up the running. "I know. Extraordinary series of coincidences, isn't it?"

"They're not getting on your nerves, I hope?" Travers inquired solicitously.

"Oh, no! But it's disconcerting, you'll admit. Still, let's talk shop. It's so much more interesting—for me."

She set out quite a number of pieces, few of which Franklin had seen before. Travers admired them all, but what he fell in love with at once was the figure of a man leaning on a spade, a countryman in shirt sleeves and wearing corduroys tied in at the knees. Something in the face struck him as familiar.

"I suppose you'll laugh at me, but isn't that Rogers?"

She laughed. "It is! How'd you know him?"

"Oh, merely spoken to him once or twice." He picked up the figure again. "A fine piece of work, Miss Blunt. You ought to get quite a good cheque for it."

"As a matter of fact, I don't know that I ought to sell it," she said. "You see, I'm not responsible for all of it. Mr. Mould did the modelling, and the rest was mine. You'll see both our initials on the base."

"So there are!" He showed them to Franklin. "Wonderful idea for two artists like yourselves to collaborate."

She had a look at it herself. "It is rather jolly, isn't it? That was our dress rehearsal for something much more ambitious." She paused. "Now I've committed a real indiscretion. I wonder. . . . You'll promise not to say a word to a soul?"

"Finger wet, finger dry," said Travers solemnly.

She went to another room and came back with something carried with infinite care in the crook of her arm. Whatever it was it was to have every chance, for she pulled up a display table and posed the object on it.

"There! What do you think of that?"

As Travers looked he felt the blood rush over his face, and groping for his handkerchief blew his nose with protracted violence. There, coloured and glazed, was the great clue that had suggested the presence in Bableigh of the worship of evil. Then, once the first surprise was over, he saw no reason to change his opinion as to what it represented. The devil it certainly was, with little horns sprouting from the temples, and hairy chest at which thin, hairy hands were clutching, and a face convulsed with heart-rending agony.

"Amazing!" He rubbed his chin contemplatively. "Wonderful Whieldon colouring. Modelling masterly. . . . And what do you call it, exactly?"

"The dying faun."

He felt another suffusion of red, and blew his nose again. Franklin, who had been standing by, flushed also, and turned away.

"The dying faun," repeated Travers. "Hm! It's quite a good title."

"Mr. Mould would have liked the broken arrow in the chest and the hands clutching it," she explained. "His theory is that you can't have this sort of thing too realistic. I didn't agree."

"Quite right," said Travers hastily. "A dramatic reticence, if I may say so. . . . And is one permitted to ask the price?"

She shook her head. "It isn't decided yet . . . but it'll be an awful lot of money. We may place it privately."

Franklin, in spite of his singular preoccupation that morning, could not forbear a malicious contribution. "We're certainly very grateful to you for showing it. It's been most interesting, even for me."

Travers bought the figure of the gardener, and they said good-bye. The village street was almost clear, though quite a crowd was by the Roebuck. Travers, stealing a look at Franklin's face, saw his lips puckering ironically, then caught his eye. Franklin laughed. Travers laughed too.

"I must say," he said, "that it was jolly decent of you to take it like that. Mind you, heaven forbid that I should shelter behind the skirts of Potter, but you'll admit that he also took it to be the devil."

"It was," said Franklin. "It was the very devil!"

Travers shook his head. "That's not worthy of you. Still, the original theory's not absolutely to be discarded, do you think?"

Franklin said he didn't know, and was so obviously thinking about something else that Travers began to be anxious. Since he had last been down something seemed to have happened to Franklin. It wasn't like him to abandon gratuitously the chance of a lifetime in leg-pulling, such as the dying faun had offered, Travers frowned slightly, then prepared to write his own epitaph for the episode.

"In any case, you know, I'd virtually decided to discard that theory as a proper basis for investigation."

Franklin looked round quickly. "Don't say you've got another!"

"If you ask me on Tuesday morning, I'll tell you more about it," said Travers.

The announcement fell flat. "Tuesday," repeated Franklin, almost mechanically, then seemed to take no further interest.

Travers sat on yarning so long after lunch that Dryden pointed out the absurdity of leaving before tea. It had been Dryden himself and Travers who had done most of the talking; Franklin had gradually dropped out, and had finally disappeared somewhere upstairs. He reappeared with tea, carrying that volume of the poems of Parnell. As he laid it on the table he looked much more cheerful.

Travers pulled him in a chair. Since Dryden had given him his own version of what had happened the previous day, he was beginning to understand what was on Franklin's mind.

"Been improving your literary education?"

Franklin smiled, "I don't think I'd go so far as that." As he looked up at them it was obvious that he was trying in his own way to explain. "The truth is, I couldn't sleep very well last night, and I came down and hunted for a book. I had another shot at what you told us was Parnell's great poem."

Dryden looked quite interested. "You liked it?"

"I did. It's just about the kind of thing I'm capable of understanding. Plenty of jam round the pill."

"Let me see," said Travers reflectively. "I'm a bit hazy about that poem. What is the story exactly?"

Franklin looked to see if he were serious, then shook his head. "Mr. Dryden will tell you. He'll do it better than I."

Dryden nodded at Travers. "I wish you would have a word with him. For the hundredth time I'll tell him that I hate a formal style of address, devised for no other purpose than to keep people at arm's length. . . . And I won't say what the poem is about. For one thing, I'd probably get it wrong, and for another I've done too much talking already."

"Right oh!" said Franklin. "I'll do my best. By the way, I want to put two propositions up to you after I've given my version. And you did say, didn't you, that Parish's—er—infatuation for Parnell and his poetry amounted to almost a mania?"

"That's right."

"I see," said Franklin lamely. "Well, this poem, 'The Hermit.' It says a hermit once began to wonder why vice should prosper in the world and virtue suffer. He doubted what the poet calls providence's sway. That's the first proposition I want to put to you. The whole of this poem is an attempt to prove that the ways of providence are inscrutable, and I seriously ask you if that's the origin of the phrase that Parish's mind seems obsessed with on certain occasions."

Dryden put down his toast and stared. He looked at Travers. "He's right! And I know that poem almost by heart, and it never occurred to me!"

Travers sat up. "This is getting quite exciting. And what did the hermit do?"

"He went out into the world to see things for himself," said Franklin, "and the first person he met was a young man, who joined him on his walk. The first night they were entertained very well at a house, the master of which was very proud of a golden goblet in which he gave them their wine. Next morning when they left, the hermit discovered that his companion had stolen the cup, and what was funnier, the following morning, after they'd been entertained shockingly badly at the house of a miser, the thief presented the miser with this goblet and said how grateful they were for his magnificent hospitality!"

"I remember it now!" said Travers. "I remember reading it in another version. Voltaire used it in 'Zadig,' you know, Henry. Didn't the youth strangle somebody, and didn't the hermit suddenly curse him and say he'd stay no longer in his company?"

Franklin nodded. "You've got it. And then under his very eyes this youth disappeared, and in his place stood an angel."

Travers thought it was curious how he said those last words.

Dryden repeated them. "An angel. . . . Yes. . . . And that was your second proposition?"

"It was," said Franklin, surprised at the quickness with which Dryden had seen it. "I do ask very seriously whether that has anything to do with those hallucinations from which Parish appears to suffer at times. Has his admiration for this particular poem of the man he claims as an ancestor now become a sort of harmless mania?"

"I think he's right, Henry," said Travers. "It's a form of obsession that's perfectly common. And didn't this angel justify his actions to the hermit, if I remember rightly?"

"He did. He showed the hermit that the loss of the goblet saved the first man from the sin of pride, whereas the unexpected gift to the miser made him wonder, and finally be more hospitable in the future. The angel said the very one he'd strangled would have led his own father into sin. I'm afraid that's a bit muddled, but the great thing is the hermit saw that things weren't all they seemed."

"Quite. He learned, in fact, that the ways of providence are inscrutable." Travers seemed as pleased as if he had made that discovery for himself. "That's really a capital piece of work; don't you think so, Henry? And it shows what a ticklish piece of mechanism a man's mind is."

They went on talking about Parish and Franklin's discovery, and then there seemed to be other things that had to be talked about, and it was only when dinner was mentioned that Travers reluctantly rose to go. The two saw him off from the gate, bound, as they supposed, for Pulvery, but at the main road Travers turned north and cut back to Westinghurst, where he and Palmer had a meal. Just before dark Travers returned to Bableigh, via Northurst, coming no nearer to the actual village than just short of Windyridge.

At that particular time, as he judged, Franklin would be meeting Potter, and both would be out of the way, but he made his way across Manor Path most carefully for all that. There was no light in Mould's studio, but a faint glimmer was coming from the kitchen, as if a door was open to the front of the house. In a moment he was through the gate and behind the studio, from the shelter of which he emerged on the flower-bed that fronted it, and there he trod about till the place was deep with footmarks. That done, he made his way with the same circumspection back to the car.

It was nearly midnight when he arrived back in town. The three evening papers he always took were lying on the kitchen mat, and he looked at the Record first. Spence had certainly lived up to his promise. After a short account of the inquest there was a lot of circumlocutory chatter, and then the hint that if Bableigh had any more accidents something ought to be done about it. Then, as a tail-piece, was something that went beyond innuendo.

"Coincidences, we all know, are strange things. There was the gentleman, for instance, who held four aces three times running at poker, and whose widow was allowed to collect the proceeds.

And since we seem to have got into a less serious vein, we might mention yet another curious coincidence at Bableigh this morning—the presence there of John Franklin, the head of the detective bureau of Durangos Limited, and Mr. Ludovic Travers, one of the firm's directors. It should, however, be admitted that both gentlemen denied that they were investigating—as has been not unusual with them in the past—anything of a criminal or suspicious nature. They were merely lunching with a friend. All of which shows the respect which should really be given to coincidences—especially in a village so coincidentally unfortunate as Bableigh."

Travers smiled to himself as he read that. Spence had done him proud. Next he marked the paragraph heavily with red pencil, and set about the concoction of an anonymous letter to Ashley Mould. When it was finished Palmer copied it on his own notepaper, after which Travers went to bed.

Next morning he returned to Northurst, or near enough to it for Palmer to post letter and paper in a pillar-box. Then he pushed on to Pulvery and got there in time for lunch. The same afternoon he wrote a letter in his own handwriting to Ashley Mould saying he would be in Bableigh on the Tuesday and hoped to have the pleasure of calling. All of which done, Travers, with the sigh of a man who knows when a job's well and truly finished with, proceeded to dismiss the village of Bableigh from his mind.

CHAPTER XVII
THE FOG THICKENS

NEITHER OLD HOUSE nor Bableigh itself had any premonition that Monday morning of the events that culminating day was to produce. One man only—Ashley Mould—knew as soon as the post arrived that the day was the most vital in his life. At first he panicked badly, then when he had got over that, found himself confronted with a choice of actions on which his life might depend. It was nearly ten o'clock by the time he had made up his mind—as sooner or later it would have had to be made up, whatever the post had brought.

Dryden was at Northurst and Franklin had the house to himself. Half an hour of that and he made up his mind the morning was too good to spend indoors. Just through the churchyard he overtook Parish on Manor Path, and the vicar, who was in one of his breezy moods, hailed him gratefully.

"You're coming my way, are you?"

"Depends where you're going," said Franklin.

"Well, I want to see Finch's wife—she's only just out of danger, you know—and I wanted a word with Martha Frail."

"Martha Frail?" He smiled. "Sorry! I forgot she might be working at Windyridge."

"All the better for her, poor soul," said Parish. "It takes her mind off things." He shook his head. "A sad life, Mr. Franklin. A sad life."

"Yes," said Franklin. "She's all alone now. A pity, you know, that she and that other poor woman, Mrs. Clark, can't live together now for company."

Parish stopped dead. "Now that's a capital suggestion! A capital suggestion!" He moved on again, nodding away with satisfaction, then began to discuss pros and cons. One of the women would have to give up her home, and that might be a difficulty. What did Mr. Franklin think?

Franklin, at the moment, was thinking about something else. Mould was shutting the gate of Windyridge behind him, and that had meant a visit at a remarkably early hour. And as Franklin set his foot to the ground he saw Potter striding on well ahead in the direction of Northurst, and by the time he had turned to see how Parish was faring over the stile, Mould came abreast of them.

Franklin gave the usual polite smile. "You're abroad early, Mr. Mould."

Parish chimed in with, "Good morning, Mould. A capital day!"

Mould gave the pair of them a look that was perfectly malignant, and went by at such a pace that he looked like overtaking Potter. Franklin was so taken aback that he watched the sombrero disappear over the top of the hedge round the bend before he turned to Parish. The vicar was looking nowhere in particular and seemed quite unperturbed.

"A curious man, Mr. Franklin," was all he said.

Franklin grunted. "You saw his look, vicar? What I've done to him I don't know. He was all right when I saw him last."

But Parish was crossing the road. He opened the gate and courteously waved Franklin through. Round at the back, through the open door of the outhouse, Martha Frail seemed to be scrubbing something and there was a strong smell of petrol. By the time he had reached the scene of the operation he knew what it was—dry-cleaning. At the same moment Marian Crome appeared at the back door.

"This is a surprise!" She seemed quite delighted as she came over, and she smiled at Martha. "As you see, we're having a real spring-clean. Loose covers and everything."

"If you don't mind my saying so," said Franklin, "aren't you taking a bit of a risk? I mean that stuff is awfully dangerous."

She laughed. "Oh, it's all right. We've got the windows open, and the door. So long as nobody smokes, you know."

Franklin stooped down. "Well, we might as well put the stopper back on the tin." Then he had to laugh. "Good Lord! Why, you've got enough petrol here to spring-clean Bableigh!"

She looked surprised. "Is there a lot?"

"A lot! Why, there must be the best part of two gallons!"

"It looks something like a spare tin from a car," said Parish, who'd been looking about him with quick motions of the head, like a sparrow.

"Do you know," she said, "I thought it was a lot when I paid the boy for it. I told him to bring me a tin of petrol and this is what he brought."

"Use what you want and make him take back the rest," He caught Martha's eye. "How are you this morning Mrs. Frail?"

"Not so bad, sir, thank you."

The sight of her was so distressing that he turned away and left Parish by the door. Marian Crome went with him to the house.

"You'll come in and wait for a bit?"

"Thanks, but I won't," said Franklin. "I'm not really with the vicar, you see. Just out for exercise—and you're frightfully busy. Perhaps you'll let me come to tea sometime."

"Do, please." She saw him off at the front gate and he turned left for the village. Somehow he felt out of tune with Parish that morning and ran no risk of his company A long pipe under the tree at the back of Dryden's garden—the spot where he and Potter met at night—and he went back to the house again.

Dryden was in rather early that morning and he had a surprising bit of news. Travers had rung him up at Northurst police station, knowing that it was bench day, and all the request he had to make was for the whereabouts of the last maid that had been in the Mould household, if Dryden happened to know it.

"What on earth's he doing?" said Franklin. "Setting up an establishment?"

"Between ourselves," said Dryden, "I rather gathered that it's his sister who wants a maid. You know what Travers is!" and he smiled. "As it happened, I knew the girl. I may say I helped her to get her present post at Lewes."

"Did he say what time he'd be here to-morrow?"

"I'm afraid he didn't," said Dryden ruefully. "He clothes his most innocent queries in such a series of mysterious wrappings that I'm perfectly bewildered. I always have to wonder if he's pulling my leg."

After tea that afternoon Franklin made a request. Would Dryden like to run down to Hastings in the car? He had hazy recollections of having been taken there when in petticoats by his mother, and had never seen the place since. He had always meant to go back one day, but somehow the opportunity had never come.

"Splendid!" said Dryden. "We'll go to Hastings and you shall recover your youth. You'll find the place altered."

It had so altered that Franklin was bewildered. The only thing he remembered, and that very dimly, was the cliff that rose sheer from the sea at the east. Still, they walked as far as the sea road took them, then turned back to the front again.

"Across the road by that red car!" said Franklin suddenly. "Isn't that Miss Crome?"

Miss Crome it was, so Dryden said, and as Franklin saw for himself at a second look. What had put him off was the fact that she was sauntering along by the shops as if to kill time, and that was rather different from the striding, energetic manner that seemed part of her. Then, half-way along the front, Dryden suggested taking a seat.

They sat there for quite an hour. The time went extraordinarily quickly and it was fascinating to watch the various types that passed, though the season had hardly begun. It was just as they were moving off again that Dryden saw Marian Crome approaching and got to his feet. The three chatted for a moment or two, then Dryden made a suggestion.

"If you should happen to be going back now, why not let us give you a lift?"

She blushed slightly. "That's very good of you, only, you see, I have to meet somebody—a friend. If they weren't here at three o'clock I was to wait till eight and no longer." She changed the subject. "I met the vicar just now. Perhaps he'd like a lift."

They strolled along to where she had last seen him, but Parish had disappeared, so they got out the car and set off again.

"Curious her being here," said Franklin. "She said nothing about it this morning. And did you notice she was having trouble with her pronouns? It's a man she's meeting, or she'd have referred to a 'she.'"

Dryden must have thought of Mould, for he frowned slightly. Then he smiled. "Well, we mustn't talk scandal. And honi soit, you know!"

The next piece of news for that day was contributed by Jimson when he brought in the after-dinner coffee, and an astounding piece of news it was.

"There's been great excitement in the village this evening, sir. They say Mr. Mould's gone away."

"Gone away!" said Dryden, and glared at him, "Who says he's gone away?"

"Well, sir, all I know is there was a furniture-van there all this afternoon taking things out, because I saw it myself. Then they say there was a big car there, too, and Mr. Mould got in it with a lot of luggage and went off at about five o'clock."

What the reason for that could be, neither could fathom. If Mould and Marian Crome were getting married, why was he removing his furniture? If he was going away to live, one would have supposed that her furniture would have gone rather than his, and in view of the fact that the morning's spring-cleaning of loose covers and oddments pointed to changes of some sort or other. Or was the solution that he was going away and she was not—that the marriage was, in other words, off? And why had he abandoned the considerable portion of his lease? And why that perfectly damnable look with which he had passed Franklin and the vicar in the morning? And why—as Franklin suddenly recalled—had Travers hinted at certain happenings on the Tuesday morning?

Franklin was grateful that Dryden had never made a comment when he rose of an evening with the formula, "Well, I think, if you'll excuse me, I'll get a breath of fresh air." That evening Franklin was tremendously anxious to hear if Potter had additional news. He had, and some of it was utterly bewildering.

When Franklin had caught sight of him that morning he was following up Harriet Blunt, whom he had seen set off from the schoolhouse attired as if for a journey. Hastings, he had imagined, and he had been right. Shortly before he reached the main road he was overtaken by Mould, to whom he courteously gave the seal of the morning. All he received in return was a ferocious scowl, a return so strange that when Mould alighted at Hastings, Potter determined to keep an eye on him. Using a window as a mirror, he watched his progress till he was almost out of sight and then set off in pursuit. Then, turning the first corner, there was Mould waiting for him.

"Just like a turkey-cock, he was, sir. He said, 'What are you following me about for?' I said, 'You'll pardon me, sir, but I'm not following you about. The street is perfectly free.' 'You let me see you again,' he says, 'and I'll call the police. And tell that to them that sent you.'"

"Them?" said Franklin, suddenly alarmed. "What'd he mean by that, Potter?"

"Well, sir, he must have meant the firm. What else could he have meant? Though, mind you, sir, I'm dead sure there's no soul in this village has the slightest idea why I'm down here."

Franklin shook his head. "There's something wrong somewhere. And what happened then?"

"Well, sir, I thought I'd let him alone and see if I could pick up that Miss Blunt, and then blowed if I didn't see Mould going into a bank. What's more, sir, when I got back and had my dinner it was just by luck I happened to stroll to the end of the garden and what should I see but a car drive away from his house, and what looked like a furniture-van drawn up, so I nipped off down Farm Lane and through the wood and out just in front of the house behind a clump of holly. A furniture-van it was, sir, and a couple of men taking things out of the house and putting 'em in. They went off about four-thirty, but I got the name of the firm—a Hastings firm—and then a largish car comes up, and after a bit a lot of luggage comes out, heavy stuff, some of it, and finally Mould comes out and is driven off. As soon as they'd gone, sir, and the children who'd been watching, I had a good look round. You can take it from me, sir," Potter concluded impressively, "that that house is as empty as a hollow nut, and that studio too."

"Any gossip in the pub?"

"None that I didn't know for myself, sir. Some reckoned he'd bolted because he'd put that Miss Crome in the family way. What you think about that, sir, I don't know."

Franklin thought for a moment. "Go back to the pub at once and see if you can find out whose the second car was. Somebody may have recognized the driver. First thing in the morning, go to Hastings, to the firm who owns the van, and find out all you can. If there's anything very urgent, make no bones about sending a note round to me."

It was unfortunate that that should be the first night on which Potter was the first to leave, but Franklin sat on under the tree trying to think things out and feeling extraordinarily perturbed. That Mould had had Durangos Limited in his mind when he made that allusion to Potter's employers, Franklin was inclined to disbelieve. It must have been Travers and Dryden he was alluding to, and the angry gibe had been a throw-back to the afternoon when Travers had been present at the exhumation of the dog. But what disturbed Franklin most was that Mould had gone at all. A hurried departure might mean escape—and escape from what? And above all, where had he escaped to?

Then he had an idea, that Marian Crome knew all about it and at a pinch might be made to disclose in some way, if not what had been happening, at least where Mould was. Potter, too, might get hold of something at Hastings—and as Franklin remembered that he also was sure of something else. That noise he had heard the last few moments had been coming from the garage. There was the sound of gears changing, then the lights of the car in front of the house. Curious, the car going out at that time of night! Then, as he opened the back gate, there was Dryden's voice calling to the house and the grind of gears as the car was shot off.

The moon was well up and as he stepped through the side gate he saw someone standing in the porch, head inclined as if listening. It was Mrs. Jimson.

"Here you are then, sir." She was a plump, contented soul whom nothing could surely disturb. "The master said if you came, sir, you was to go to Windyridge."

"Windyridge? . . . What's the matter?"

"Only another one o' them accidents, sir. Miss Crome this time."

He stood there for a moment, then turned on his heel and ran down the path. It was almost ten o'clock and the village was quiet except for two men who were outside the inn and shouting something about buckets. It was a hot night and the clothes began to stick as he ran on across Manor Path to where a glare lighted up the roof of Windyridge like a crimson halo. As he slowed at the stile he saw lights in The Pleasance, and then the lights of Dryden's car. From the darkness beyond the house voices were buzzing, and before he could enter the gate something was seen coming down the path. It was Dryden and Jimson and two other men carrying what looked like a body. Two other men, and Potter came behind.

"What is it? . . . Is she dead?"

"Badly shocked," said Dryden. "Would you mind opening the car door?"

Franklin almost jumped as Agnes Rose's voice sounded in his ear. "Shall I sit with you or in front?"

"With me, I think," said Dryden quickly. He leaned out to Franklin. "We're taking her to Northurst Hospital. See what you can do."

The car moved slowly off and Franklin watched it till its tail-light disappeared. As he turned, Potter was standing alongside him.

"Would you like to go round the back, sir? The fire's practically out now."

He felt the heat as soon as he turned the corner. From what the men told him and what he could see, there had been an explosion in the shed and Miss Crome had been hurt. The roof had gone, or fallen in, the window had been blown out, and all that was left was the four walls. The smoke was still rising; everywhere was splashed with water and the air reeked of charred wood.

"How'd you men come to see it?" Franklin asked.

"I was going home from the Roebuck and Miss Rose hollered to me," one of the men told him. "I ran off back and fetched these others."

"How did Miss Rose know about it?"

"She reckoned she heard an explosion, sir, and then saw the flames."

"I see." He nodded at the ruins of the shed. "There doesn't seem any more you people can do at the moment. I'll stay here myself till Mr. Dryden gets back, and I'd rather like to have a word with you, sir," indicating Potter. "Good night, everybody, and thank you very much."

There was a mumble and the small crowd, rather amazingly, began to shuffle off. Before Franklin could say a word, there was a patter of steps and Martha Frail came puffing round the corner of the house. She had a bout of coughing and they had to get her into the kitchen and make her drink some water before she could speak, and then all she could tell them was that she had heard Miss Crome had been killed, so she slipped on her things and ran all the way. Then she began coughing again.

"I'm sorry, sir," she managed to splutter, "but that petrol must have got into my chest."

"Well, take your time, Martha," said Franklin. "And what time was it when you finished using the petrol?"

"About three o'clock, sir."

"Three o'clock!" He looked at Potter. "But there couldn't have been any fumes there this evening to cause an explosion!"

She shook her head. "There weren't any fumes, or whatever you call 'em, there. The place smelt as sweet as a nut, sir. I had the door and window open to let the air through, and nobody would have known there'd been any petrol at all."

"Miss Crome knew that?"

"She wasn't here, not when I finished," said Martha. "One of the village boys brought a note for her just before two, and she came out and said she had to go to Hastings in a hurry. She said I wasn't to stay late, sir, so I just did a bit about the house and went off about five. Oh! and I know who it was brought the note, sir. It was young Walter Fitch who's just left school."

"Good! And what about the shed door. Was it kept locked or not?"

"It wasn't locked, not that I know of, sir. Nobody ever takes anything about here."

"It was shut when you left?"

"Yes, sir; I shut the door and the window both."

He caught Potter's nod back towards the table. On it was a metal candlestick of the dish type, trodden badly out of shape.

"Well, Mrs. Frail," he said, "you've been very helpful. Mr. Potter here will see you safely home. You can't do any more good here, and you ought to be in bed." He helped her to her feet.

"And what about locking up, sir?"

"I'll see to that if you tell me where the key's kept."

"Why! it's in the door, sir."

"So it is!" He laughed. "Of course, she opened the door as soon as she got back from Hastings. And where's it kept when she's out, Mrs. Frail?"

"I'll show you, sir."

She pointed out a brick in the doorstep with a hollow beneath it, then he went with them to the gate. He held out his hand.

"Good night, and don't go worrying about Miss Crome. She'll be all right. Get off to sleep quick."

She shook her head. "There won't be much sleep for me to-night, sir."

As he went slowly back to the kitchen he knew what she meant. The afternoon was the funeral of the little girl. All at once he felt a blind anger come over him as he thought of things—inexplicable, maddening, damnable things, and then as he bit savagely on his pipe he suddenly laughed as if he had gone mad. And mad he must have looked standing there in the moonlight against the smoking background of the blackened shed. One tremendous thought had come to him. This time the murderer had gone too far. His planning had gone wrong. What should have been plain to all the world as an accident—as another amazing coincidence, if one so preferred it—stood out clearer than that moonlight as nothing of the sort. Marian Crome should have been killed in that shed, but something had gone wrong. If she recovered she would talk; if she died the case would still be there to work on. And there should be no more hesitation on the part of Dryden. The policy should be the free hand and everything in the open air.

He found himself chewing on the cold pipe, and moved on to the kitchen. The fire was laid in the grate and he put a match to it, then looked about him. In the cupboard was what he expected—a packet of candles. He fitted one to the battered candlestick and went out to the back again, but five minutes' search failed to find the one that had originally been in it. As for the shed, nothing could be done there. The roof had fallen in and the floor was strewn with tiles and rubbish. Then Potter's steps were heard coming round the back way.

"Had a stroke of luck, sir," he said. "One of those men was the father of the boy who brought that note. Mould sent it. He gave the boy sixpence to bring it."

Franklin nodded. "It fits like a glove. Know any more about all this?"

"Not a thing, sir. I'd just got back to the pub when we were all fetched up here. I helped put the fire out, and that's all."

"Did you see Miss Crome?"

"Not really, sir. That Miss Rose was looking after her, and she kept moaning away something terrible. I did notice she had a coat of some sort on, as if she went straight to that shed as soon as she got in. I mean, that's what I've been thinking since I've known more than I did then."

"Right!" said Franklin. "Now listen to this. Go back to the pub and say you've got to stay here all night by Mr. Dryden's orders. Bring back some food for yourself, and get the key from under the brick and make yourself comfortable. I'll explain to Mr. Dryden. If anybody should come poking about in the night, detain him or make sure who he is. If it's Mould, hold him and I'll take the responsibility. First thing in the morning I'll be here again and you can go to Hastings."

"And any orders about going back to town, sir? I ought to say something at the pub."

"Back to town!" said Franklin, and looked at him in amazement. "There'll be no town for us for a bit. Here we are and here we stay till this thing's settled one way or the other."

CHAPTER XVIII
DOUBLE DAYLIGHT

FRANKLIN WAS UP at five o'clock the following morning, and when he got to Windyridge found Potter making a cup of tea. Nothing had happened during the night.

"What's the news about the lady?" he asked.

"Not so bad as they thought," said Franklin. "From what I could gather, she was blown back against the house and burnt one hand pretty badly. If she hadn't had her hat on she might have had her hair alight. The trouble is, from our point of view, that she had a bad shock, and they won't have her questioned for a bit."

"Well, it might have been worse, sir," said Potter philosophically. "And there's one thing I'd like to put up to you, sir, if you don't mind. I assumed last night that because the lady was still dressed she'd gone to the shed as soon as she got home. Why shouldn't she have been home and then gone out somewhere again—to see what had happened to that Mould, for instance?"

"Yes," said Franklin slowly. "That'd fit in too. But why did she go to the shed at all? And what's far more to the point, how did the one who staged the accident know she was going to the shed? Everything depended on that." His face lighted up. "I know, Potter. The cat! You seen a cat about here?"

Potter shook his head, but Franklin was already making for the shed. They got to work removing tiles and plaster, and in less than a minute found the partly burnt body of the cat. Then came a broken saucer. Two minutes later they uncovered a charred basket and the bodies of four kittens.

"Put 'em all back," said Franklin. "That detective sergeant's due from Northurst at what Mr. Dryden described as an early hour. That may be now, and it may be after breakfast."

"You think I'd better be going?" asked Potter.

"Oh, no!" said Franklin, and rubbed his hands. "We're finished with all that sort of thing, and Mr. Dryden admits it. I don't mean we're to spread abroad who we are, but the police must know who we are and what we know. Have a hunt round now and see if you can find a candle—the one she was carrying in the stick."

Potter found it almost at once, trodden underfoot by the path. As Franklin guessed, it was a new one, with the top cone hardly burnt down. Had it been old, the socket of the candlestick would have been tallowed, and the candle might not have parted company with the stick. And while Franklin was demonstrating that, the sergeant appeared at the door, with a "Hallo! What's this?" His eyes nearly popped out of his head when he saw Franklin.

The situation was explained, Potter was suitably introduced, and departed in search of a square meal before his trip to Hastings. Frost nodded back at him.

"One of the old hands, sir?"

"That's right," said Franklin. "An old C.I.D. man."

Frost nodded again. "And if I might say so, I had an idea when I saw you, sir, that you weren't all you were supposed to be. Not that there's any point in mentioning that now. . . . May I have a look at these kittens?"

They went over to the shed.

"If I hadn't been too flurried last night I could have known that in two minutes when Mrs. Frail was here," Franklin told him. "I think perhaps you'd better ask her to make sure. Go easy with her. That child of hers is being buried to-day."

"I know, sir. Twelve o'clock this morning. . . . And what's your idea of what happened last night?"

"This," said Franklin. "Some time after the departure of Martha Frail, and not too long before the return of Miss Crome—in other words, about half-past eight to nine o'clock—some person who was perfectly aware of what had been going on in the shed during the day, and who was also aware of the existence of the kittens, and that Miss Crome was at Hastings, walked calmly into this shed and scattered petrol everywhere. It was a hot night and the stuff vaporized at once. Martha will tell you how much she left in the tin, but I'd say it was well over a gallon. Miss Crome wanted to see if the kittens were all right, and took the candle to the door here. She held it in her right hand and undid the door with her left, stooping forward as she did so. The door was only partially open when the explosion took place, and that's why she wasn't badly burnt."

"You think it's as easy as that, sir? I mean, there can't be many people slip through a mesh as small as you've drawn."

"I think it's even easier than that," said Franklin. "You know anything about the gossip in this village? Miss Crome and Mould in particular?"

"Months ago," said Frost laconically.

"Right. Then take the facts of yesterday. Facts, mind you, and draw your own conclusions. Mould went to Hastings first thing, after calling in here to see Miss Crome. He returned in a private car with a man—probably the owner of a furniture-van which drew up later. This man departed, and so did Mould's furniture, in the van. Later, another car took Mould away and all his personal luggage. Mould, in short, left the village lock, stock and barrel. But, he didn't want Miss Crome to know this. It was her he was running away from, and it was her money he was running away with. That's a guess, but I think it's a good one. What I do know is that after he called to see her yesterday morning, he went straight to a Hastings bank. However, what we know is that as soon as he got back from Hastings in that private car, he sent her a note which told her to go at once to Hastings on urgent and secret business. He mentioned a rendezvous and said she was to call there every hour and not to wait later than eight. That meant she'd miss the eight bus and couldn't return till the half-past eight. Ostensibly he'd gone away, establishing some kind of alibi, I'd imagine, but he doubled back here in time to lay the trap for another perfect accident. And that's your case as I see it."

Frost already had his note-book out. "You're right, sir. Get Mould and you get the man."

"I hope you're a good prophet," said Franklin, afraid as ever of his own optimism. "Now may I suggest something? Come and see Mrs. Frail at once. Then see Potter and arrange to go to Hastings with him, to pick up Mould's trail. In the meanwhile come back here and write up your case."

Frost locked up and pocketed the key. Franklin waited outside while he interviewed Martha Frail, and it took only five minutes for the evidence to be complete. The cat had had kittens, and they were housed in the shed. During the cleaning operations cat and kittens had been removed to the kitchen, and when she left at five o'clock Martha had put them back again with a large saucer of milk, and had shut door and window so that nothing could get in to hurt the kittens. As for the candlestick, Martha had cleaned it that same morning, since Miss Crome had used it the previous night just before going to bed.

There was some subtle difference about Old House that morning at breakfast. While there was nothing of the "I told you so" about Dryden, it was easy to see that he was at least not displeased that wisdom had in his case been justified of her children. The intangible that he had felt and the invisible that he had seen had now become things that Franklin could see and feel. Moreover, Franklin had promised results. The evidence at Windyridge stood out as plain as the pot of marmalade on the table, and unless Marian Crome died of her injuries—and that seemed very unlikely—then the virtual murderer should be known before the week was out.

Dryden was wearing a dark suit in the place of his usual grey tweeds. He proposed to go to the funeral, if only as a mark of respect to poor Martha, and Franklin, on the spur of the moment, said he'd like to put in an appearance too. They were talking about it when Jimson came in rather perturbed.

"Mrs. Clark would like to see you, sir. . . . Something to do with the funeral."

Mrs. Clark looked rather flustered at appearing in that room in her working clothes and apron. She had come round, it seemed, on her own initiative, after a short argument with Mrs. Hopper. She herself had arrived at eight o'clock, as usual on a Tuesday, and had been scrubbing the passage to the study when the vicar came along. He said Mrs. Hopper had just told him about the accident to Miss Crome, and did she know any more news about how the injured lady was getting on?

Mrs. Clark understood how difficult it was for the vicar to understand the housekeeper, and gave him the news as she had heard it—the same, in fact, as she had already told Mrs. Hopper. The vicar appeared most distressed. He said he had been speaking to Miss Crome in Hastings that very evening. He had come by the house and across Manor Path a few minutes before the accident had happened. Mrs. Clark had then rounded off the conversation by remarking that it was a mercy the poor lady hadn't been killed, or at the least been blinded, and that might have been worse. No sooner had she made that remark than the vicar stared at her.

"He began that muttering of his, sir"—so Mrs. Clark described it—"and then he went pale as a ghost, and I knew what that meant—one of them fits of his—so I helped him through the door and into a chair, and then I got Mrs. Hopper. We got him round all right, sir, after a bit, only he would keep on muttering to himself about the lady's eyes." She shook her head. "It was all my fault, sir, telling him about her being blinded and putting ideas into his head."

"What do you think causes these fits?" Franklin asked her.

"Worry, sir, that's what it is. He's one of the tender-hearted sort, and these things keep happening and drive the poor gentleman till he's half off his head. He was the same worrying over my poor boy, sir. You'd have thought it'd have been his own."

Dryden coughed. "And your idea is that he's not well enough to conduct the funeral."

"No, sir, he's not, and that's the truth. Mrs. Hopper got him to go and lie down again, and he hasn't done that before."

Dryden got up at once. "I'm much obliged to you, Mrs. Clark. I'll have a word with Mr. Parish myself." He was still shaking his head over the matter when she'd gone.

"You're worried about him," said Franklin.

"I am," said Dryden. "What's more, I'm going to talk to him very seriously. Whether he likes it or not, he's going away for a holiday. Jimson shall take a note to Squires of Northurst to ask him to officiate."

The upshot of it all was that Squires did take the service. Parish had been like a man very tired of everything, and to Dryden's amazement had agreed with all he had said. He would take a holiday in a few days, as soon as he felt well enough to make the arrangements. Harriet Blunt was at the funeral, and it was when Dryden and Franklin were standing by, watching the first shovelfuls of earth being thrown into the grave, that Dryden noticed her close by, and walked over.

"I've been wanting to see you about something," he said. "Two things, in fact. First, I'd like you to do me a favour. Tell Martha I'd like her to come regularly and help Mrs. Jimson."

She beamed at him. "That's perfectly splendid of you! She's been so worried about things since Miss Faithful died. She'd love to come to you."

"You'll do it then." He nodded. "The second is rather harder to put. Miss Faithful's cottage is empty and I've deliberately had nothing done about it. I'd like to offer it to you."

Her smile suddenly froze—then she blushed. Something was worrying her.

"Promise me you'll not tell a soul if I let you into a secret?"

Dryden nodded gravely.

"Well, I'd have loved to have the cottage—only something happened before Miss Faithful actually died. You see . . . well, I've bought Windyridge; that is, I've paid down all I have and got a mortgage for the rest." She looked up at them. "You will keep it very secret, won't you? Miss Crome is going away—where and why I don't know—by the middle of the month and I'm moving in then. Taking over the furniture and everything."

Dryden hardly knew what to say, then said the graceful thing. "Well, I call that wonderful news. . . . I mean, that you're going to be permanent."

"Wonderful," added Franklin. "And aren't you all excited about having a house to yourself?"

Now it was all out, she laughed and looked as pleased as anything at the anticipation of it all. "Maggie Clark's going to make her home with me—sleep there and everything." She laughed again. "We're going to keep an eye on Agnes, just across the road!"

Franklin, catching sight of Frost by the church gate, left them talking and moved quietly off. The sergeant caught him up round the corner and they walked on to Old House. His news was a facer for Franklin. Mould had bolted. Got clean away, in fact.

"Bolted!" repeated Franklin. "Where to?"

"London—unless that was all bluff."

"Then where's his furniture gone?"

"Gone nowhere, sir. It's on sale at Hastings at this very moment! Some of it's in the shop window."

That Hastings firm had turned out to be furniture dealers rather than removers. Potter had recognized in the yard behind the shop one of the men who had been at Bableigh, and according to him the boss had gone to inspect the contents of the house and had bought the lot. Frost had thereupon seen the proprietor for himself. The story was true. When Mould first came to Sussex he bought most of his things from that firm, and that was why the proprietor had had no hesitation in driving Mould out to Bableigh, inspecting the things and paying for them in cash. Mould, it appeared, had had a sudden call to go abroad for some time, and being uncertain of the duration of his absence, had preferred to sell rather than store.

As for the bolting to London, that had been easy. The landlord of the Roebuck had noticed the driver of the car that had taken Mould away. He was a Northurst man and Frost had known him and the garage he came from and had got the information that Mould had been driven to Northurst station. There he had taken a ticket for London, and his luggage and himself had left by the five-twenty.

"And what's your line of action now?" Franklin asked.

"Well, sir, I just came to report to you, as we'd agreed. My orders will have to come from those above me. There's no charge against him, you know, whatever we suspect."

"I know," said Franklin. "That's the devil of it. What's more, I'm open to lay ten to one that when Miss Crome gets well enough she won't lay information—whatever she may think." He held out his hand. "Let me know what happens. I'll let my firm know about Mould. I don't think we ought to let him get too far away, do you?"

The sergeant mounted his bicycle and rode off. Franklin opened the gate and there was Travers installed comfortably under the tree, with Jimson standing at ease but laying down the law about something or other for all he was worth. Travers kept nodding away like a mandarin. Then Jimson saw Franklin approaching, made his final point and scurried off. Franklin took the deck-chair that was vacant.

"The very man I've been waiting to see. What was the idea of that remark of yours about things happening on a Tuesday—to-day, that is?"

Travers looked pained. "A curt greeting to one who's been absent so long! And about Tuesday—which, as you remark, is to-day—I remember saying no such thing."

"But surely! . . . After the episode of the dying faun."

"So you're bringing that up, are you?" said Travers. "Merited, perhaps, but not wholly necessary. Still, I do recall the occasion to which you refer. My remark was that if you mentioned the matter to-day I might give you some information about something that was on my mind."

"And what was on your mind?"

"Well, I wondered if Mould would decamp."

"Good God!" said Franklin. "Why'd you wonder that?"

Travers shrugged his shoulders. "Brain-wave, you know. It seemed to me the place was getting too hot to hold him."

"I see."

Travers's face was still a courteous blank and there was nothing to be read there.

"You knew he had gone?"

"Oh, yes! Jimson told me. He didn't tell me where,"

Franklin remedied the deficiency. Travers was looking quite serious by the time the recital was over.

"You must get hold of Mould," he said. "Go into Northurst first thing after lunch and get the office. Find out if he did go to town last night. That artistic get-up of his ought to have been remembered at Victoria."

"I will," said Franklin, then rose.

Dryden was coming across the lawn. "Sorry I'm late," boomed Dryden. "And how are you, Ludo? Heard all the news?"

"Yes," said Travers. "Troubles are nearly over now, Henry, what?"

Jimson's voice came from somewhere close at hand. "Lunch is ready now, sir."

"Right!" said Dryden, and looked at them. "Shall we go and have it?"

Long before Homer it must have been a theme of poets that tremendous results spring from trifling causes. The history books are sprinkled with the preparatory remarks that this great man and that could never have known at a certain trivial moment that something of incredible importance was about to take place. This was another such moment. As the three stood there and then turned slowly to make their way to the porch and lunch, Travers, who topped the pair of them, extended his long arms over their shoulders with a boyish gesture, and they moved across the lawn like that.

"The three fates!" he said flippantly, then pulled the others to a standstill before the newly planted border which they had to cross. "Surely you've not been planting out mignonette, Henry!"

Dryden stooped down and looked. "Mignonette it should be. And why the surprise?"

"No surprise, Henry. Only that I like old-fashioned flowers. We had a ground-floor nursery, as you may or may not remember, and there was always a bed of mignonette beneath it."

Dryden nodded benevolently. "I always have mignonette because it reminds me of that delightful story by Anatole France."

Travers pricked an ear. "And what story's that?"

"Surely you know it! But perhaps Franklin doesn't. It's about a holy man whom the devil wanted to get at. Unfortunately for him he never had a chance. Whenever this holy man left his cell and wandered round the bare ground outside for the sake of exercise, he always had his eyes glued to some sacred book or other. The devil tried every dodge he could to make the old gentleman think of something secular or profane. Once he did that, you see, the devil would have something to work on. Then at last he had a great scheme. He sowed mignonette in the garden. When it bloomed, the holy man sniffed and wondered what it was. Then he had a look at it. Then he took a fancy to it and began to water it and—well, there you are. The devil had him!"

Franklin laughed. Travers half raised his hand to his glasses, then let it fall again.

"Charming story, isn't it?" said Dryden. "Ruined, I fear, by the telling. . . . Come along and let's see what's happened to this lunch."

Travers lagged behind for a moment and Dryden waited for him.

"You're staying overnight?" he said.

Travers shook his head. "Sorry, Henry. Must get back this afternoon. Frightfully important business."

Dryden was very concerned. "Then I shan't see anything of you at all. I promised Squires I'd see him at Northurst this afternoon to call at the hospital. Miss Crome, you know. . . . Perhaps I oughtn't to go."

Travers clapped him on the back. "Nonsense, Henry! I'll be down again in no time." He thought for a moment. "Thursday, as a matter of fact. Got to come this way on business."

There was no more reference to that till Dryden was actually leaving for Northurst after lunch. He still seemed most reluctant to leave a couple of guests to their own devices.

Travers had a last word with him at the car. "Should I come along on Thursday, Henry, would you mind if I brought a guest to lunch? No! tea'd be better. Quite a delightful person. You knew him at school. Lambry."

"Lambry? Not Tubby Lambry?"

"That's right," said Travers, and they both smiled. "You haven't seen him for years. He's a frightfully important person nowadays, you know."

"Tell him I'll be delighted." His hand moved to the gear-lever.

"Oh! and one last thing, Henry. You needn't mention it to Franklin, but there aren't going to be any more accidents!"

Dryden stared. "No more accidents?"

"That's right," repeated Travers. "No more accidents, Henry."

He stepped back and watched Dryden slowly move the car off. Franklin, who'd been watching by the gate, buttonholed him at once.

"What was that about coming down on Thursday?"

"Come and sit down," said Travers, "and I'll tell you."

He took Franklin's arm and marched him over to the deck-chair. He seemed rather hesitating himself for a bit, as he hooked off his glasses, then hooked them on again. Then he made a curious sort of grunting noise as he pulled out of his pocket that volume of Parnell's poems that had been lying on Dryden's table.

"I think you and I know what all this business in Bableigh is about. I mean, we know all about the accidents . . . and things."

Franklin stared at him. "How do you mean?"

"Well, let's suppose they weren't accidents. Suppose they were murders, done by one and the same person. What, then, is the motive behind the lot?"

"The motive?" He shook his head. "I don't get you."

"Why was Yeoman killed?"

"Don't know," said Franklin, "unless there was something in your Satanism theory after all."

"And Clark?"

"Don't know again—unless Mould had a grudge against him."

"And Miss Faithful?"

Franklin stared again. "She wasn't killed. She died in her chair."

"Oh, no! She was killed—at least I believe so. So was Fancy Frail. And why?"

Franklin shook his head. "The only thing I can think of is that some mischievous boy or some maniac saw the child looking into the well and tipped her in on the spur of the moment."

"That may have happened," said Travers quietly. "It probably did happen. And then there's what should have been the murder of Miss Crome, which was obviously arranged, you'll say, by Mould." He hesitated again. "I know you won't laugh at me, because the whole thing's too desperately serious, but I'd like to tell you where we can find the answer to all those silly questions I've been asking."

"And where's that?"

Travers tapped the thin green volume gently with his finger. "Here, in this book. It's been under our noses since the very beginning."

Half an hour later the Bentley was drawn up outside the gate and the two were having a final word.

"You go to Hastings yourself," Travers was saying. "There can't be so many florists there. It's the likeliest spot."

"And what about Potter?"

"My God! you mustn't shift Potter!" Travers had never been so in earnest. "He'll have to stick it, whether he likes it or not."

"And you'll get hold of the office?"

"I will." He took his seat at the wheel. "And I'll get hold of the Yard."

"The Yard?" said Franklin. "Aren't you going a bit too far?"

Travers smiled enigmatically. "There's more in this than meets the eye." He let out the clutch. "See you on Thursday afternoon. And don't forget to wangle the business of Parish."

CHAPTER XIX
THE DECKS ARE CLEARED

WHEN LUDOVIC TRAVERS left Bableigh that afternoon he began what was probably the most hectic twenty-four hours of his life. He pulled up first at Tonbridge and called up Scotland Yard. Superintendent Wharton was not in at the moment, though expected again during the afternoon.

"Inspector Norris in?" asked Travers.

"Yes, sir. If you hold the line we'll have him here in a couple of minutes."

"Never mind," said Travers. "Take a message for him. At six o'clock I must see either him or Superintendent Wharton. Most urgent. I'm speaking from Tonbridge and am coming straight up now."

That call over, he got Durango House and his secretary. Two things were to be done most urgently. The names of the three likeliest booksellers were given, and they were to be asked for a copy of Voltaire's "Zadig," translated or in the original, and it was immaterial whether the story was by itself or in a volume of collected works. The book should, in any case, be in Mr. Travers's room that evening. Secondly, Sir Charles Lambry was to be rung up and requested to see Mr. Travers at ten o'clock the following morning on a matter of great importance. Sir Charles was to be requested to let nothing interfere with the engagement.

Travers drove on towards London, crossed the river at Vauxhall, and headed north for Hyde Park and Bond Street. He drew the car up outside Altemayer's shop and entered. Claude Altemayer happened to be there. Travers took him confidentially by the arm.

"I see you have a piece or two of Mould's in the window?"

"Yes," said Altemayer. "You want to purchase?"

Travers shook his head. "I've seen 'em already—at his studio. But tell me, Claude, did he bring them along last night or this morning?"

The other looked surprised.

"It's all right," said Travers. "It shan't go any farther than our two selves, if you wish it. This morning, wasn't it?"

"I don't know what you're getting at," said Altemayer, "but it was this morning, about ten o'clock. Three large pieces and one unfinished. Said he'd got to go away for a bit and didn't know when he'd be back."

"Didn't know where he was going, I suppose?"

"I didn't ask him."

Travers smiled. "I don't expect you did. He's a good feeder for you people, you know, Claude. His work's likely to appreciate and I'd hold on to some of it if I were you—not that you want my advice. . . . You don't know if he was in town last night?"

"He rang me up at my house at about seven. Said he was at some hotel near Victoria. Name something like Cavendish."

Travers held out his hand. "Very much obliged. I'll drop in next week and see if I can relieve you of one of those pieces." He turned back at the door. "Sorry to be so pertinacious, but was he wearing that war-paint of his?"

Altemayer smiled. "To tell the truth, I hardly recognized him. He had on an overcoat and a bowler."

Travers laughed. A hundred yards farther on he stopped at a telephone box and looked for the Cavendish Hotel. The four he found were far from Victoria; on the other hand, there was a Caversham Hotel on the spot. He rang up on chance and drew a runner. Mr. Mould had stayed there the previous night and had left just before midday.

At Trafalgar Square he got out of the car and walked to New Scotland Yard. Superintendent Wharton's grizzled face wreathed in smiles as he was shown in. Travers smiled too at the sight of the general's twinkling eyes and weeping-willow of a moustache, and he had, in any case, a tremendous admiration for George Wharton.

"What's the idea of pinning me down here? Making sure of me for dinner?"

Travers simulated amazement. "How you do it beats me, George. The human mind holds no secrets from you! . . . And in the meanwhile, how long will it take you to get hold of Paris to find out if a certain chap's arriving there at seven-thirty?"

That led to half an hour's talk. Wharton promised something by the following evening, and that was the best he could do. If it was true that this man Mould would visit Meister's with the smaller and more easily portable pieces, then his trail might be picked up there. In the meanwhile, the Caversham Hotel part could be verified, and it might be ascertained if he had really left on the boat-train. As for the main part of the proposition that Travers had put up, Wharton was far too wise a bird to make a risky move.

"Right oh!" said Travers, as if the loss were Wharton's. "Dinner's at eight to-night, George. I'll see you again to-morrow, and in the meantime, chew this fact over. Mould's taken years to acquire a certain reputation. If you find out that he definitely has bolted, and bolted under another name, then it means he's got to begin life all over again, or else his bolting is absurd. Ask yourself whether he'd do all that if it weren't a matter of life or death."

It was nearly seven o'clock when he arrived at Durango House, to find a copy of "Zadig" lying on his table. Even more important was a message from Franklin.

"Purchase verified at Hastings. Clerk remembered unusual order of dozen packets. Details available this end."

It looked for a moment as if he were going to rub his hands over that message, but he pushed the bell instead. For the next few minutes he was dictating a précis of an extract from Voltaire, and when he had run his eye over it, and polished it up, asked for six copies to be run off and sent round to his flat. Then all at once he realized he was feeling uncommonly hungry, and remembered that he'd had no tea. And he'd forgotten to warn Palmer that Wharton was coming. And what about that message to Lambry? He found it on the desk. Ten o'clock would be definitely reserved. Travers nodded and made a note in his small book. Breakfast would have to be early and Palissier & Crewe seen at nine. As he walked along to St. Martin's Chambers he smiled as he thought of Franklin, who had doubtless just finished his meal and had stoked up in readiness for an all-night watch.

Travers was so well known to the firm of Palissier & Crewe that a request so out of the ordinary caused much excitement in the private office. Had they any reproduction pre-Reformation plate, and something in the nature of a chalice if possible?

Then when he had chosen a two-handled bowl from the only two specimens that were available, he proceeded to amaze William Palissier still further.

"Now," he said, "I want you people to get to work on this at once. Dull it down and give it the appearance of a genuine old piece." He smiled at Palissier's look of horror. "You needn't worry. The bloke who's seeing it isn't an expert, and he won't know it isn't silver. Batter it about artistically—and I must have it round at my place some time to-night."

A quarter of an hour later he was being shown into the Harley Street consulting-room, and it was quite a solemn Travers who took his seat on the consultant's side of Sir Charles's table. It had been with a very fleeting smile that he had received the greeting, "Well, I suppose you've come to take away that damn picture!"

"Nothing about pictures this time, Charles. Unless, of course, you've changed your opinion about its—er—origin."

"If the facts were correct on which I based the opinion, there's not much hope of that."

"Good!" He nodded with, what was for him, a remarkably serious face. "The fact is, Charles, I want you to recognize that I'm most frightfully in earnest. Have you read about that strange series of accidents that took place in a Sussex village called Bableigh?"

"Hm! Yes. I don't mind saying I was rather interested."

"Well, Henry Dryden lives at Bableigh, Charles. I want you to go down there with me to-morrow, and stay for about two hours."

Lambry's face was a mixture of all sorts of emotions. Travers drew his chair in closer before a word could be said.

"I know just what you're going to say, Charles, but just you listen to me. I've got two things in my pocket that are going to make you cancel anything you've got on for to-morrow afternoon, and it's on those two things that I want your opinion."

"What two things?"

Travers fumbled in his breast pocket and produced a copy of that message he had received from Franklin, and the précis of the "Zadig" extract. It was an hour later when he rose to go, and Lambry went with him to the very door.

"You're sure Dryden has no idea of the particular work I'm doing?"

"I know he hasn't," said Travers. "He knew about your knighthood, of course, and he knows you're here in Harley Street. . . . Two o'clock to-morrow, then."

"That's right. And your man will bring me back."

Perhaps for the first time in his Harley Street career he stood at the door and watched the taxi drive away, and he kept a patient waiting ten minutes while he read over again the three typewritten sheets.

Travers went straight back to Durango House and rang up the Conard Gallery from there. The manager informed him that Mr. Conard was away, but as far as he knew they had had no further instructions with regard to the two Marian Crome pictures.

Next he called up Wharton and received an interim report. Mould had arrived at the Caversham Hotel at seven o'clock on the Monday night, and had certainly crossed to France, via Dover, on the Tuesday afternoon. A further report should be in by six o'clock. Travers promptly sent a preliminary wire to Franklin, treated himself to a special lunch, and then, to allay his rapidly increasing excitement, spent the afternoon at the latest big thing in the talkies.

After tea he decided to wait no longer, and made his way to the Yard again. Wharton announced that he had been in the very act of ringing him up at Durango House. Mould had been picked up at Meister's in the rue St. Honoré at ten o'clock that morning. He had disposed of a quantity of small works—details would follow later—and immediately on leaving the Gallery had booked a passage to America on the Prince Igor, which was sailing from Cherbourg that night. How he had managed the business of the passport was not at the moment known, but he had booked under the name of Martin Ashford. Further, he had left Paris by the midday train, and was being followed to Cherbourg. A report from there would arrive early the next morning, and in the meanwhile further instructions were requested.

"And what instructions are you sending?" asked Travers.

"If he sails, to keep an eye on him," said Wharton. "If we want to hold him at the other end we can always question his papers. And you might like to know that Norris went down to Lewes this morning to see that little servant-girl you unearthed."

Travers seemed very amused. "And you let me leave this room last night, George, with the idea that I was a sensation-monger!"

"Perhaps you are," said Wharton. "The trouble is, we fellows can't take risks. . . . And, by the way, if this goes any further who's going to lay information?"

"I've got him all ready for you," Travers assured him. "A funny little schoolmaster who lives at Hampstead. Only I don't think I'd mention hanging to him—at least not for the moment. It mightn't do his school any good. Parents are curious people, you know, George."

One more telegram to Franklin and Travers's tour of duty had come to an end. And when he got to his rooms and saw the really fine job that Palissier had turned out, he was so delighted that he treated himself out again, to the latest thing in musical comedies.

It had been with the connivance of Jimson, and quite unknown to Dryden, that Franklin had spent the early hours of the Thursday morning in the open air. Potter relieved him just before breakfast, and then at about eleven Franklin strolled round again to see if Potter had anything to report.

"Nothing doing at all, sir," said Potter. "Only one thing I've just heard, sir, though I didn't believe it. That Miss Crome's back home again."

"You mean out of the hospital?"

"That's what they say, sir. Mind you, I haven't been along to see."

Franklin nodded. "I'll see to it myself. And don't forget you're off duty at four."

It took him a good time to make up his mind. Potter's information was most likely true since Dryden had reported overnight that Marian Crome was doing splendidly and could certainly be questioned almost at once. But what was worrying him was the actual excuses he could make and the method of attack. Perhaps a little exaggeration—even a lie or two—would bring out the truth. In any case, there'd be no harm in strolling round by Windyridge to see if anything was happening.

As he arrived at Mould's back gate he gave a little jump. Marian Crome was in the act of opening it, and he had almost touched her as he passed. Her arm was bandaged, and as she glanced at him and then hurriedly lowered her eyes, he knew she had been crying. He turned back.

"And how are you feeling now, Miss Crome? You remember me, don't you? Franklin, you know. I'm staying with Henry Dryden."

She gave a feeble sort of nod and began biting her lip.

Franklin opened the gate and stepped inside the garden. "Miss Crome, I want to speak to you as a friend. Nobody shall know what we're going to talk about—that is, if you'll let me talk to you. Will you come inside the studio?"

She bit her lip again. "But it's locked!"

"I have the key," said Franklin quietly. "I have the key to all sorts of things, Miss Crome. I'm not what you thought I was. I was brought down here specially to make inquiries into all sorts of things." He opened the door and drew back for her to pass through. The room was empty except for a couple of unwanted packing-cases, and he made her sit down.

He had seen a good many women cry in the course of his life, and yet he had never felt so utterly uncomfortable as he was at that moment. She was the last woman in the world with whom one could associate tears—a fine, strapping figure of a woman who ought by rights to have been a man; a woman, nevertheless, who had arranged even the bandage artistically, and had set the tiny curls protruding round the corners of the tweed hat, and had put on her beads and used that same attractive scent—and all in the hope of seeing a sensual little beast of a man with soggy face and frizzy hair.

Perhaps she realized something of the same incongruity as she suddenly put the handkerchief away and looked up at him defiantly. "Why did you make me come in here?"

"For your own good," said Franklin quietly. He drew up the other box and sat down facing her. "I'm your friend, Miss Crome; you've got to believe that. I know you came here this morning hoping to see Mould." He shook his head. "I don't think you'll ever want to see him again."

"What right have you got to talk to me like that?"

He stopped fingering the papers he had taken out of his pocket and looked at her. "You don't think I'm your friend? That Dryden's your friend? . . . You don't say anything to that. But wouldn't you rather talk to me here than talk to the police?"

"The police!" She stared.

"Yes," said Franklin. "The police. You had a strange accident the other night, Miss Crome; an accident that ought to have ended fatally. Somebody was anxious for you to disappear. . . . I see you've been thinking that too. You've been wondering why Mould never turned up that evening at Hastings; why he never saw you in hospital, or sent a word, and why this place is all empty. Perhaps you know."

She drew back with a quick, nervous movement of what might have been shame, then her fingers went to her mouth and her eyes opened in horror. "You mean the police have . . . have taken him away?"

Franklin smiled. "Not yet—"

"Oh! but they can't. I mean, it was an accident! It was all my fault." She leaned forward confidingly.

"You see . . . I was stooping down inside the shed—"

Franklin laid his hand on her arm. "Miss Crome, why tell me all that when I know what happened? And you know what happened." He shook his head as one would at a naughty child. "Let me tell you what I know. You sold your house confidentially some days ago to Miss Blunt, though the information didn't reach me through her but through yourself. You had made certain arrangements with Ashley Mould. Last Monday morning he saw you and got your cheque and cashed it at Hastings. It was for quite a large sum. Then he lured you away to Hastings, while he was removing every stick of furniture from the house. He'd sold the lot to a dealer, whose name you can have. He then went ostensibly to the station and took a ticket for London, though it was not till the following morning that he went to Bond Street and sold some of his things to a firm. He might easily have doubled back here again and have arranged that accident which was to have removed yourself and left him free . . . with that very useful cheque."

She shook her head vehemently. "It isn't true! He couldn't do a thing like that!"

"Miss Crome, what I'm telling you are facts that can be proved to the hilt. I know, with no possibility of doubt, that Ashley Mould went to Paris to dispose of the rest of his things, and that he's now on a liner bound for New York, and he's under a different name. If you could have looked out of your window last night you might have seen the smoke of the boat that took him away."

That broke her down. Franklin moved over to the window and waited, then put the key in her lap.

"I think I'll go now, Miss Crome. You stay here as long as you wish, and when you go lock up and send the key back to me at Old

House." Try how he might he could summon up no sympathy, and as he reached the door he turned and looked at her, sitting with her back towards him. "You know that what I've told you is true? Nod if you know it."

She nodded.

"And did Mould's wife know what was going on?"

She shook her head.

Franklin nodded. "You were going away, Miss Crome, before all this happened. Let me advise you now—as a friend. Get away at once. Go so far that you'll never hear of Ashley Mould again. . . . He hasn't taken all you have? I mean, you've still got enough to live on?"

She nodded as she groped for the handkerchief.

Franklin shut the door quickly and made his way towards the church. On a sudden impulse he turned right and crossed the road to the school-house. Harriet Blunt gave a little gasp of surprise as she opened the door.

"Not an official visit," said Franklin, "but something desperately urgent. You knew Marian Crome was out of hospital?"

She shook her head. Franklin told her quite a lot of things in very few seconds. Perhaps she'd see her at the studio. And she ought to be got away as soon as possible. The place was bound to be alive with gossip.

Harriet Blunt pushed him aside and shut the door behind them. "I'll go at once."

"But your hat . . ." began Franklin, but she was already across the road and running towards Manor Path.

It was a quarter to four that afternoon when the Bentley drew up outside Old House. Dryden, who had been in a state of extreme perturbation those last few days, was waiting on the lawn. At the first sight of Lambry his face broke into a smile, and he went across with hand thrust out.

"Well! well! well! This is a pleasure."

Travers, who had had a quick word with Franklin, broke up the reunion at once. He hustled the three of them into the house. "No idea it was so late. And Parish is coming to tea they tell me."

"Yes," said Dryden, and looked rather bewildered at being kept from conversation in his own house.

Travers took him by the arm. "Then we haven't a minute to lose. Come upstairs for a minute and have a rehearsal. Charles will excuse you. He knows all about it. Or he can come too. Franklin can stay and welcome the parson."

And before he was properly aware of it, Dryden found himself mounting the stairs. Travers stopped for just sufficient time to give Franklin the parcel.

"Untie that and put it on the table there. Tell you about it later. And for the love of heaven don't let Jimson take it away to polish it!"

CHAPTER XX
IN THE MOONLIGHT

PARISH WAS LOOKING quite different from what Travers had anticipated. Try how he might he could see no difference from Parish at his best. There was a fair amount of colour in his cheeks and his manner was assured. The old tricks were there, but it would have been an abnormality if they had been missing.

When Charles Lambry was introduced his name seemed to convey nothing.

Dryden confided in the company, "Parish hasn't been very well, I'm sorry to say. Been working much too hard. Still, he's promised me that he's really going to take a holiday."

"I'm very sorry to hear that," said Lambry, and at once took a seat by the vicar's side. But Jimson came to see where tea was to be, and the lawn was decided on.

Parish was made much of for the next hour, and he must have been talking most of the time; then Travers asked to be excused for a minute or two and took Dryden with him. Franklin had disappeared somewhere a few moments before, and Parish rose to his feet at once. Really, he said, he'd have to be going. Dryden wouldn't hear of it.

"You stay and talk to Lambry," he said. "We'll be back before you know it."

But in the dining-room Dryden was far less philosophical: All this mystery and scheming was beyond him.

"What is all this that's going on, Ludo?" he said, and Travers thought for a moment he was going to be angry.

"Perfectly simple," said Travers. "Charles is a doctor, and a famous one. We've all wondered what the precise nature of Parish's illness was, and whether there's anything in that aphasia theory. Charles will tell us."

"Yes, but this ridiculous figure you're making me cut over the bowl!" and he waved his hand contemptuously at the two-handled piece of pre-Reformation silver that stood in the centre of the serving table beneath the large window.

"Patience, my dear old chap," said Travers. "It's all part of the same thing. Fellows like Lambry have the subtlest kinds of tests for their patients."

Dryden had another alarm. "He didn't come down here specially to see Parish?"

Travers lied heroically. "Henry! you really mustn't say things like that. I induced Charles to come down. He had business this way and to get him here I promised that Palmer should drive him back to-night. I'm staying to-night, Henry, if you don't mind."

"Of course I don't mind." He smiled. "What I mean is I'm pleased—as I always am. There are times, perhaps, when I wish you'd be a little more explicit."

Travers laughed. "A hit, Henry! A palpable hit! But you can't teach old dogs new tricks." He threw in a piece of placatory information. "You knew Mould had gone? Bound for America?"

"I did gather something of the kind," said Dryden ruefully. "You and Franklin have been rather like Codlin and Short. Franklin has consoled me by saying he would know something when you arrived, and you expect me to have the information."

"It's a ticklish business," said Travers, shaking his head with tremendous solemnity. "You don't want to hear half a story, and you don't want to hear theories that end nowhere."

He threw in a certain amount of information about Mould, and waved aside the other's questions before they were asked.

"I know it's all very complicated, Henry, but one thing I'll promise you. This time to-morrow you shall know all there is to know. And now what about going back and helping Lambry out with Parish, or better still, why not start your stunt before Parish bolts?"

No sooner did they reach the lawn again than Parish rose, and this time he seemed in earnest.

"We mustn't let the vicar go without showing him your latest treasure," said Travers. "Come along, Charles. We'll let the vicar settle the dispute."

They filed into the dining-room and Dryden became the show-man.

"Well, what do you think of it, Parish?" he said, and there seemed some reason for his obvious joy of possession. The dull silver matched perfectly the black beam beneath the window, and the ancient polished wood of the table reflected the under-surface like a mirror.

Parish stood looking at it, head on one side. "It's the perfect decoration for that table," was his pronouncement.

Dryden looked at it lovingly, then picked it up and passed it over. "Now you settle the question. Is it ecclesiastical plate or not?"

Parish looked round at the perfectly serious faces before he took the bowl in his hands. When he handed it back he looked almost as enthusiastic as Dryden.

"I think I've seen something like it before. You mustn't take me as an authority, of course, but I must say I think it a very old communion vessel."

Travers was triumphant. "There you are, Henry! Now perhaps you'll give in. There's three to one against you."

Dryden took the defeat in what was for him an extra-ordinarily ungracious way. It seemed incredible that he could be so churl-ish. "Well, you may be right or you may not. If it is ecclesiastical plate there's no harm done. Far too many beautiful things already hoarded away in cup-boards in country vicarages."

"What plate have you at Bableigh, vicar?" asked Lambry.

"Very little, I fear," Parish told him. "There is a cup, but it's quite modern. Nothing like this, of course," and he looked with what was distinct regret at the bowl which Dryden was replacing on the table.

"Henry!" said Travers excitedly, "I've got an idea. You must let the vicar have that bowl! Hand it back to the church."

Parish looked as if he wanted to be anywhere but where he was.

Dryden laughed unpleasantly. "Not on your life! I haven't acquired what Parish calls the perfect decoration in order to part with it." He nodded away at it and rubbed his hands. "It'll be fine to watch people's faces when they enter this room and catch sight of it. Pre-Reformation; you'll admit that, won't you?"

Travers gave a superior smile. "I think we're agreed it's that style, aren't we, vicar? But it isn't an original. The condition is far too good for that. It's a clever copy."

Dryden laughed. "Rubbish!"

"Have it your own way!" Travers shrugged his shoulders. "As we've told you, there's a perfectly good test for pre-Reformation silver. If you're afraid to try it out, then you ought to give in second best."

Parish's head kept moving from side to side as he watched the speakers and tried to make sense out of what was for him merely the tail-end of an obscure argument.

Travers took him into his confidence. "Here's an example of the ignorance and pig-headedness of the layman, vicar. We've been telling him a sure way of testing the age of the bowl and he won't listen because he says it's quackery—"

"It is quackery!"

"Perhaps it is, Henry," went on Travers with a patience that was still more exaggerated. "It was supposed to be quackery when the village wise woman cured warts, but she certainly cured mine when I was a boy. Half the medicine in a village, whether for man of beast, is quackery—but it works, and that's the main thing."

"What is this test?" Parish asked mildly.

"Just this, vicar," explained Travers. "It's either some peculiar property of dew or something to do with moonlight. After all, we don't know everything in these scientific times. What you do is place the silver article out in the dew on a moonlight night. In the morning there should be—if it's pre-Reformation—a - curious kind of freckling all over it. If not it'll be merely tarnished."

The vicar smiled gently. "It doesn't sound too convincing."

"Well, he certainly might try it," said Lambry.

"Leave it standing on the seat in the front garden all night. It won't cost you anything."

Dryden smiled ironically. "It'll cost me nothing—except the bowl! A pretty fool I'd look when I woke up and found it gone."

Travers laughed. "Well, we'll get over that difficulty Henry. Put it on the bird-bath in the back garden. It'll be perfectly safe there."

"A capital idea," said Lambry. "It removes the last of his excuses."

Dryden looked at him derisively, then all at once his expression changed. "Very well! I will be a fool for once. To-morrow morning we'll see who laughs last."

"Splendid, Henry!" Travers took his arm. "Let's go and examine the site straight away."

As they moved, Parish cleared his throat. "I really must be going now."

"Well, if you must," said Dryden. "But bring your hat and have a look at the spot this pair of idiots are choosing for me."

There was quite a lot of good-humoured chaff as they stood round the stone bird-bath, and when Parish finally left Travers strolled with him as far as his own gate.

"I hope we didn't annoy you with all that talk about Dryden's bowl," he said. "Between ourselves, there's more in it than meets the eye."

"I thought there was something like that," said Parish. "He didn't seem very pleased about it all."

Travers explained that too. The vicar, of course, hadn't heard about that bowl, but since Dryden had had it he'd been the least bit spoiled. Justifiable, perhaps, for a man to be proud of so magnificent a possession, but one hardly expected that sort of thing from a man of Dryden's fine simplicity of taste. Undoubtedly the only place for a museum piece like that was in a fine old church, and yet Dryden had been unreasonably embittered when the suggestion had been made by Lambry and himself. That was curious, too, since there was surely a time when Dryden was much more in sympathy with the church than he had seemed to be of recent months.

Parish listened and made various comments. At the gate he held out a hand that was more limp than ever, and as he said good-bye his eyes looked out beyond Travers's shoulder to somewhere across the north valley where the distant trees were purpling in the evening sun.

Travers returned to the house in time to hear what must have been one of many protests from Dryden.

"Here's Travers now. He'll convince you. I've been trying to make him stay for dinner."

"Sorry!" Lambry shook his head. "It can't be done. I must be back to-night. But if you'll allow me, I'd like to call this week-end. Lunch on Sunday, if I may."

"My dear fellow, I'll be delighted. Come early. We must have a long talk about old times."

"And what did you think of Parish?" cut in Travers.

"Think of him?" said Lambry, and pursed his lips. "I think your own idea was right. There's aphasia certainly—and more. An operation would put him right. It'd be a highly technical one, and he'd have to be fit for it—but it'd do the trick."

Dryden was delighted. It seemed for a moment as if he was going to shake Lambry by the hand. "What perfectly splendid news! You mean you'll get him back to what he was?"

"Yes." He smiled. "Whatever that was. But there's a lot to think of before we have him on the table. This coming week-end, perhaps, we'll know more."

Franklin turned up at that moment and they all saw him off at the gate.

Travers stuck his head inside the Bentley. "Coast all clear, Charles?"

"Perfectly," Lambry told him gravely. "Let me know what happens, and don't try a second shot."

Travers nodded and Palmer moved the car off.

Dryden was in excellent spirits during dinner that evening. The news about Parish had done him an enormous lot of good. After dinner Travers suggested chess, and he and Dryden played for an hour. At just before ten Travers rose, yawning.

"Don't know when I felt so sleepy, Henry. Must be your air. Mind if I turn in now?"

"I think I will too," said Franklin, putting down his book.

Dryden smiled. "Well, we might as well all be early for once. I'm quite sleepy myself."

But he insisted on a night-cap for all that. It was nearly half-past ten when Travers shook hands solemnly at the head of the stairs.

"Sleep well, Henry. Don't forget! All your troubles over to-morrow."

Dryden smiled. "I think most of them are over now."

He watched paternally as they said good night to each other and went to their rooms, then smiled again as he remembered Lambry's verdict on Parish. That night he was asleep more quickly than he had been for days. Hardly had his head touched the pillow than he was dreaming, and in Travers's room the occasional snores sounded so clearly that he and Franklin ventured to raise their voices to more than a sibilant whisper.

It was a wonderful night. The moonlight flooded the back, lawn till all its green was lost in silver, and the shadow of the yew arch by the gate was curiously black. But for the warmth and the smell of the roses, it might have been white frost that covered everything. Everything was uncannily still.

Travers lighted yet another pipe, and kept his hand over the red glow and leaned with his arm on the sill, looking out of the opened window. He spoke very quietly. "What do you make the time now?"

As he spoke the grandfather in the dining-room struck eleven.

"He ought to be here soon if he's coming," whispered Franklin. "Once he gets to sleep he won't stir."

Travers nodded, then pointed violently. A cat had emerged from the border and was stepping across the white expanse of lawn, picking its way daintily and stopping every now and then to listen. Then it stopped altogether, by the slender shaft of the bird-bath whose shadow was a black island in the white lawn.

"Hope it doesn't start a fight and wake up Dryden!"

Franklin nodded. The cat moved on again and was lost in the near shrubbery. Franklin leaned forward.

"Can you make out the bowl from here?"

Travers shook his head. "Only see a dark patch. Everything's white."

Franklin lighted his pipe and leaned back. A quarter of an hour went by and the shadow of a tree began to creep across the lawn, to where that centre-piece of stone was standing in its white surround. Beyond the far hedge everything was black, and beyond the trees the sky an intense and oddly luminous purple. Travers sniffed as he caught the scent of the sweet briar. He thought of Jessica and young Lorenzo, and his mind floundered for a minute or two among the moonlight rhapsodizings that he had learnt at school and found that most of them had gone. Then he watched the shadow of the tree and wondered if it had been there all the time.

The grandfather struck the half-hour. Franklin groped for the flask and poured out a tot of coffee. Travers shook his head.

"I'm feeling very thirsty," whispered Franklin, and the remark sounded very trite and lame. Then as he screwed the top on again and bent to put the thermos back, Travers gripped his arm.

Something was framed in that jet-black archway beneath the yew hedge—a white circle that was perfectly still. From somewhere in the far background among the trees a match flared and was out.

"Potter!" whispered Franklin, and drew to the side of the window like a flash. Travers sat immovable, watching that white circle. It moved—then separated itself from the blackness and became the white face of a man who was walking straight to the centre of the lawn. There was nothing furtive or hurried about that walk; it was the same sort of tripping gait that he always used, with the rise at each step to the ball of his foot.

He stopped at the bird-bath for the matter of a full minute, holding the bowl close to him and staring intently at what they almost felt to be themselves. Then he turned and, with the same unhurried walk, tripped over the lawn and disappeared through the arch. Long before he reached it, Franklin had picked up his boots and was haring down the stairs in his stockinged feet. Outside the kitchen door he laced the boots up and bolted across the lawn.

Travers followed hard after. Outside the gate he caught his foot in a rut and came a cropper. By the time he had reached the vicarage gate, nothing was in sight. He listened for a moment, and thought he heard a footstep on the road. Franklin emerged from the darkness of the trees.

"Seen Potter?"

"Seen nobody," whispered Travers. "This gate's shut. It doesn't look as if he'd been this way."

Franklin clicked his tongue. "Hope to God Potter hasn't lost him!" He cocked his ear.

Somebody was running across the road towards them. A yard or so away he stopped.

"That you, sir?"

"Yes. Where is he?"

"In the church, sir. You'd better come over quick!"

They picked their way among the grass between the stones. At the porch Franklin stooped down and undid his boots.

"Potter! You go round to the vestry door and stay there. If he comes out that way, follow him till you know he's safe."

He looked round to see if Travers was at his elbow, then felt for the handle of the door. The door was open already. He got to his knees and made his way along the matting to the very end of the pew, and waved back for Travers to halt. Travers came up abreast and craned round towards the aisle.

It was amazing how much they could see—and yet how little. Above where they crouched the moonlight came in a broad shaft through the window and flooded them till they felt naked in the middle of a musty blackness. Between them and the altar was another shaft of light, on the far fringe of which something was seen to move. It was Parish; not the man himself so much as his arms that were raised high above his head. He seemed to be kneeling, then he bent towards the altar . . . and Travers knew as surely as if he stood by him that he was holding in his hands that two-handled bowl.

There was neither sound nor movement for a minute or two, and Franklin thought he must be gone. He raised himself by the back of the pew, and as he drew back out of that damnable moonlight Travers held him tight. He whispered, "I'm going to speak. For God's sake don't stir, whatever happens."

He gave a little noiseless clearing of the throat, and the voice, when it came, echoed in the hollow of the tower till it seemed a babel of voices. Franklin felt the water trickle down his face as he clutched Travers's arm and peered through the moonlight into the dark.

"Lyonel Parish!"

There was a sudden clatter as the bowl fell on the altar steps. Parish scrambled to his feet and whipped round. He stood there for a minute, his head on one side, mouth half-opened. Then he spoke—a queer, unnatural, petulant kind of squeak as he still looked into the blackness by the font.

"Yes? . . . Yes?"

"Lyonel Parish! Why did you take that bowl?"

He seemed to be nodding to himself, then stepped down and listened again. Then all at once he began to move forward, for all the world like that cat which had stepped across the lawn towards the bird-bath. Travers ducked and pulled Franklin down. Parish stopped again, almost at the end of the aisle, and they could see his face even more plainly as it came into the shaft of moonlight. On it was a look of incredible cunning—the cunning of something cruel that knows the time is almost at hand. Franklin groped back with his hand as he stepped, then tripped over Travers's foot and fell—forward into the shaft of light.

There was a shriek—a bloodcurdling, high-pitched shriek, that seemed to tear out the very bowels of the darkness. Travers saw the blackness go by into the other blackness beneath the tower and felt the rush of the body as it passed him. Franklin began to scramble up—pawing at his knees.

"Where is he? Where's he gone?"

Travers pointed. "In there!"

Before they could reach the room beneath the tower there was the sound of a door. Franklin stopped.

"Where's that? . . . Hear it?"

Travers heard nothing but a sound of gigantic mice that seemed to be scampering in the tower itself. Franklin moved forward quickly.

"Come on! He's going up the tower."

Travers seized his arm. "What can we do? We can't follow him up there. . . . Besides, he might stop half-way!"

Franklin thought for a moment, then they heard the sounds again, far up to the top beyond the line of the rope that ran upwards to the solitary bell.

"I'll go up," said Franklin. "He can't get past me. I'll bring him down. . . . You wait here and keep the door."

Travers knew something was wrong, but before he could speak Franklin had gone—and where, he couldn't see. Then a blind, unreasoning panic seized him and he began to grope his way out to the porch again. Then he ran, in his stockinged feet, till he could see the tower.

Etched black against the moonlight was the figure of a man. When Travers first saw him he seemed to be stretching out his arms beyond the parapet into space. Then he made a leap forward, caught the parapet and fell back.

Travers turned his head away with a little moaning noise. When he looked again the figure was mounting the parapet and he saw the leap, arms thrust out into space as if a man could fly and had seen a company of angels and was joining himself to their flight. Before he could turn his head away he heard the thud.

Potter padded by him in the moonlight towards the dark patch that lay in the middle of the stone walk. Travers saw him stoop, saw him straighten himself again, then came across the grass.

"How is he, Potter? . . . Is he dead?"

Potter grunted. "Dead as a door-nail, sir. And a pretty mess he's made of himself, too." He looked at Travers in a puzzled kind of way. "What do you reckon he was doing up there on that tower? Looked to me as if he was learnin' to fly!"

Travers shook his head, then looked up as Franklin came running from the porch.

CHAPTER XXI
TRAVERS EXPLAINS

DRYDEN HAD BEEN quite cheerful during breakfast that morning, and it was not till the meal was over that Travers summoned his courage for a rather difficult task.

"May we have a word with you, Henry?"

"Why, of course!" He smiled. "What's it all about?"

Travers shook his head gloomily. "It's going to be pretty hard chewing, Henry." He looked down at his empty pipe and shook his head again. "The fact of the matter is we've got some news. . . . Parish is dead."

"Dead!" Dryden stared as if he couldn't believe his ears.

"Yes . . . dead. All the village knows—and will know—is that he was walking in his sleep. He climbed up to the church tower and fell. Struck his head and was dead in an instant."

For a moment or two Dryden hardly knew what to do. Then he rose abruptly and went over to the window. He stood there looking out over the valley.

Travers went across and took him by the arm. "Come and sit down, Henry. What's done can't be undone. And we want to talk to you."

"I'm sorry. It was a bit of a shock." As he sat down something flashed across his mind. "But how did you know all this—that he was dead?"

"That's what you're going to be told," said Travers quietly. "We hope you'll understand a lot of things, Henry. . . . I mean, the reason why we've kept things back from you. We didn't want to hurt your feelings too much—and we wanted to make dead sure."

"That was good of you. . . . You saw him die?"

"Yes," said Travers, "we saw him die. Franklin has had him watched for days. That man Potter who's been at the Roebuck has been lending a hand. He saw it all and he'll give evidence—very discreet evidence—at the inquest. Franklin was there too. He fetched Sawyer, after the accident, but of course there wasn't a hope."

Dryden stared again. "You watched him? You thought he was likely to do himself an injury?"

Travers smiled gently. "Not himself, Henry. It was other people we were looking out for—after Lambry's report. You don't know who Lambry really is, do you, Henry?"

Dryden looked puzzled.

"I'm sorry," said Travers. "I can't help being inexplicable. What I mean is, you didn't know that Lambry was vice-chairman of the recent Lunacy Commission. He's perhaps the greatest authority on certain obscure nervous diseases. It was in that capacity that I saw him about Parish. It was in that capacity he saw Parish for himself. That's one thing I want you to remember. When I refer to Parish and the obscure disease he suffered from, it's Lambry I'm quoting, even though I've forgotten his technical terms. . . . You'd like to hear all about it?"

"If you'll be so good."

Travers sighed. "It's a long story and I wish it was Franklin who was telling it. Still; here goes. And the idea is to prove quite a lot of things are right because some of them are right. Suppose you're trying to follow the route of an underground passage, and you know there can be only one passage. You make a dozen chance borings and in only three of them do you pierce what you're looking for. Provided one's the beginning and one's the end, that's all you need. Even if the gaps between your borings are a mile apart, you know it doesn't matter. The passage is there, though you haven't hit it plumb each time." He smiled. "Not too good a comparison, perhaps, with this case, but you do follow what I mean, don't you? If there were five unexplained accidents or occurrences in Bableigh, and we've got the explanation of the first and the third and the fifth, the second and fourth might reasonably be supposed to form part of the same chain."

He looked at Dryden almost apologetically, but Dryden was sitting, head in hand, looking into what might have been the fire.

"We'll get the worst part over first," went on Travers, "and that's to talk about delusions. We've, sometimes laughed at them in the comic papers—people who imagine they're Napoleon, or Nelson, or Julius Caesar. Generally such delusions are harmless. If they're permanent, then, of course, the person becomes a nuisance and he has to be certified and put away. If they're only recurrent or spasmodic, that's rather different, though it depends on the frequency of the recurrences.

"The great thing about spasmodic occurrences is that they're often accompanied by aphasia—I mean, your person thinks he's Napoleon, and then, if you reminded him of what he'd said and done, he'd deny it indignantly because he'd have forgotten all about it. Or, in other cases, the very reminding might bring on a new attack—act at an impulse, as it were.

"The other great thing is that the original impulse that first made the person become deluded, occurred in the pre-delusion period. I know that sounds obvious, but I want to urge the point. The man who thinks he's Napoleon was a great reader or admirer of the life of Napoleon, or at the time of the shock or breakdown had Napoleon impressed very forcibly on his mind." He paused so suddenly that Dryden looked up. Travers caught his eye. "And that brings us to Parish."

"You mean—"

"Yes, Henry, I mean that Parish had a delusion—but a much more subtle one than that crude illustration I've just given. His great—what shall I call it?—well, hobby, was the poetry of his reputed ancestor and the poems he himself wrote in the same style. One thing you didn't tell us, Henry, but which Franklin found out by consulting the files at Hastings, is that he actually signed those poems he wrote as L. Parnell—a most informative pseudonym." Travers looked round at Franklin. "Have you got a copy of that 'Zadig' précis on you?"

Franklin found one in his pocket-book and passed it over.

"Perhaps you'd like to read this for yourself afterwards, Henry," Travers went on. "If I may, I'll read it to you myself, because I may want to emphasize a point. As you remember, Voltaire took the story of Parnell's famous 'Hermit' and altered it considerably. In my opinion he made a much better job of it. I rather think Parish was surreptitiously of the same opinion. Voltaire's version, which you may remember he had, certainly left the greater impression on his mind. In a manuscript we found in his desk last night was a distinct attempt—begun months ago—to turn Voltaire's story into heroic verse."

"Really?" Dryden frowned. "I believe I'm beginning to see a little daylight . . . a very little. Perhaps you'll go on."

"Here's a précis of Voltaire's story," said Travers, and began to read.

"'Zadig was the exiled favourite of a certain Oriental monarch, and a man of great wisdom and integrity. During his exile he underwent many vicissitudes, and at length was driven to murmur at the unequal dispensation of Divine providence.'

"You will remember that, perhaps. I shall have reason to refer to it again.

"'Walking one evening along the banks of the Euphrates, and secretly accusing providence of bringing him so many misfortunes, he suddenly met a venerable hermit, whose discourse was so sublime, whose air so benevolent and whose deportment so noble, that Zadig asked permission to accompany him. As the two were both bound for Babylon and were most attracted by each other, they swore to remain in each other's company till they had reached the city—a journey of some days.'

"You've doubtless already noticed that whereas Parnell's hermit met a youth who turned out to be an angel, Voltaire makes one man of noble character meet another of the same kind with the added sanctity of being a hermit—a most artistic transposal, I think you'll agree. After that the story follows Parnell rather closely.

"'The first night the two begged for hospitality at a castle, and were magnificently entertained. When they left the following morning Zadig was horrified to see peeping from the pocket of his venerable companion the golden bowl of which their host had been so proud. He said nothing, however.

"'That night the two received a wretched reception at the house of a miser. Nevertheless, the following morning the hermit thanked the miser most profusely for his magnificent hospitality and asked him to accept as a present the golden bowl. When they were clear of the house, Zadig felt bound to expostulate. His companion excused himself by saying that the original owner of the bowl would now be cured of the sin of pride, whereas the miser would learn to exercise the virtue of hospitality. He spoke with such wisdom and discernment that Zadig conquered his repugnance and continued in his company.

"'The next night they stayed at the house of a philosopher, and early in the morning the hermit rose and set fire to the house and then fled. Zadig followed him, and some strange attraction made him still keep in his company. The same night they were hospitably entertained by a poor widow, who had a nephew of about fourteen years.'"

He gave Dryden a meaning look, then resumed.

"'The next morning that youth was sent to show the travellers the way across a broken bridge. The hermit suddenly seized him and hurled him into the water.'"

Another look, and Travers went on again.

"'At this Zadig could no longer restrain his anger. "O monster!" he began, and then the hermit, under his eyes, assumed the form of an angel. Zadig fell on his face.

"''Learn," said the angel, "that the ways of providence are inscrutable. Beneath the ruins of the house of that hospitable philosopher will be found a great treasure which will allow him to continue his beneficence. As for that youth whom I drowned, know that in one year he would have murdered his own aunt, and at the end of two years he would have killed thee!"

"'So saying, the angel took flight for heaven. Zadig fell to the ground and adored the wonders of providence.'"

He handed the typewritten sheets to Dryden. "All that remains now is to make the application. The story's a good one, Henry, as you said yourself. It has the element of surprise. There's a para-doxical twist to the doings of that hermit, with his committing apparent evil in order that good might come. You'll agree, too, that the story shows the origin of Parish's harping on providence—"

"He agreed with that when it was put up before," said Franklin. "What we none of us saw quite so well was the connection with Parish's reference to angels."

"Exactly. That's what becomes perfectly clear. In his own delusion, Parish was both Zadig and hermit He it was who did the crimes and yet saw the symbolic figure of an angel after their accomplishment. It was a mad, chaotic, one-man show."

He took out his pipe and began to fill it very slowly.

"You'll perhaps forgive us, Henry, for what we're going to say. We're going to cut clean across certain views you have held yourself and upset some of your faith in human nature. Let's take the eve of Yeoman's death. Parish—the David to his Jonathan—was worried so much that even you feared a recurrence of his breakdown. His leisure at that time was occupied with trying to turn 'Zadig' into verse. The morning of the tragedy he went to see Yeoman with some new scheme that was to save things, and probably keep him at Bableigh. He left the garage and went through the wood. He overtook Yeoman in time to see him put the gun to his head—"

Dryden gripped the arms of the chair. "Impossible! . . . It couldn't have been!"

"Very well," said Travers patiently. "We'll say it couldn't have been. But you'll let me complete the theory."

"I'm sorry," said Dryden. "I won't interrupt again."

Travers smiled across at him. "But you must, Henry, if you feel like it. We want to be interrupted—provided we can make you understand. However, what I was saying was that Parish had the added shock of seeing Yeoman about to take the shortest way out. I may say that we had another theory that Yeoman was using some sort of apparatus to give the death the appearance of accident—and that may still be true. If so, Parish pocketed the simple apparatus or destroyed it on the spot. What he must have done was to plead with his friend and show him just what he was about to do. He got him to kneel and pray for forgiveness—and at that very second the snap came in his brain. As Yeoman knelt he handed over the gun. Parish shot him as he prayed, then dropped the gun by his side and went out of the wood. What happened from the moment he left the garage to the moment he arrived home again was wiped completely from his mind. I should have recalled to you, however, the mould that was found on Yeoman's knees, and the line taken by the shots, which are also thus explained.

"After that, when a portion of his brain had definitely snapped, Parish always knew he had forgotten something, and he kept trying to remember. It was the same when those other things occurred. When he had shot Yeoman it had probably been in the mystical presence of something that there and then became to his deluded eyes an angel. That went, too, in a flash, when the aphasia came on, but whenever he tried to think back he saw, for an infinitesimal moment of time, something that was an angel—or was it a devil? The delusion called it one; his own real, subconscious self knew it to be false.

"Still, that's all theorizing, and Lambry can explain it better than I. What I might call the killing mood passed, and didn't occur again till it received certain impulses from outside. It was I, and you and Franklin here who did some of those killings. We gave the impulses. You, for instance, had been talking to him about the boy Clark. That same morning he saw the boy's mother crying over her work and asked her about it. Later on he was using a pair of sécateurs at the gate when the boy came in. The urge came back—to do evil which should be good. Yeoman had been killed so that the insurance money could be claimed for his family, and his soul had been safe, for he had been killed in the act of prayer. If he had not been shot he might have failed in his word and killed himself later.

"So with Clark. Parish spoke to him and he promised amendment. Then Parish told him to hurry to the farm and do the errand on which Mould had sent him, but the wire that held the only brake had already been cut by the sécateurs. Parish knew all about brakes and things, even though he hasn't ridden his own bicycle since the Yeoman affair.

"Next comes something less tragic—the uprooting of Miss Rose's garden. The impulse there was deep-seated since you had long ago discussed with him the quarrel between the two women. He destroyed the garden, hoping another might grow in the hearts of those two women—and as it happened, he was right. The immediate impulse for that act was the conversation he had in this very room with us that night.

"But we also did something far more serious that night. We tried to pull his leg about his wireless set. Franklin has seen the man who installed it, and has learned from him that there's a particular warning he always gives to a new owner of an electric set—not to adjust or tamper with innards till the current's switched off. But we had also mentioned something else—that people, including, therefore, Miss Faithful, were neglecting the direct service at church in favour of sitting at home to listen to a broadcast service. Parish called to see Miss Faithful about that. He pleaded with her—poor, delightful old soul—and probably made her pray too. Then she told him about the funny happening with the plugs, and how Palmer put it right. Parish was interested and asked to be shown. Then the sudden fit came on him and he touched her hand on the metal as she pointed out something inside the set. It was only a shock of two hundred-odd volts, but it was enough for her weak heart."

Franklin coughed. "You remember in church that Sunday—how Parish guaranteed the appearance of Elizabeth Faithful in heaven?"

"Yes," said Dryden. "I remember."

"As for Fancy Frail, you and Franklin gave him that stimulus when you met him one morning. The afternoon when she was drowned Parish probably came to see her mother. He entered the garden by the back way and left it the same way. Fancy was looking into the well, and in a moment he had pushed her in. An evil thing to do, apparently—and yet a good one. No growing up for her, and marrying and perpetuating disease in a family of sickly children.

"And lastly there was the affair of Marian Crome. There the devil, by whom he was possessed, tempted him merely half-way. If thine eye offend thee, pluck it out; that's the creed that Parish teaches. When he did that diabolical trick he knew all about the kittens and the habits of their owner. He knew she would half open the shed door so that the mother could come out. It was not an explosion that should kill—it was an explosion that should blind that he was after. The eyes that offended should be plucked out. No more pictures, Henry, of the type that had so offended you and Mrs. Yeoman. You remember his distress when Mrs. Clark told him about it all, and how he overcame the aphasia sufficiently to remember—just a something that went again at once."

He seemed to realize all at once that the pipe had never been lighted. Dryden sat there as though stunned, and said never a word.

"Don't let me press you, Henry, but tell me one thing," said Travers. "Aren't you beginning to agree that we're possibly right?"

"Yes," said Dryden frankly, "I think you are. After each of these . . . these terrible affairs, there was complete forgetfulness?"

"That's right."

"And he kept trying to remember, and all he saw—when he wrestled at the altar, for instance—was something like an angel; merely, of course, part of the same delusion."

"Exactly."

Dryden nodded to himself, then turned suddenly. "Let me ask you a vital question. Lambry could have cured all this?"

Travers shook his head. "Don't ask me that. He might have said it in order to satisfy you."

"I believe he meant it," said Franklin. "He definitely mentioned to me the identification of a lesion—I think that was what he said—and the removal. The difficulty would have been Parish's consent to the operation. Then there had to be that test with the bowl, to make surety twice sure."

"The bowl?" said Dryden, and frowned. "Is there some connection with that bowl in the story of 'Zadig'?"

"That's right," said Travers. "We created a deliberate and tremendous impulse, and he took the bowl from the garden where all that gibberish about moonlight and dew had conveniently placed it. We know now, and know beyond dispute, that all the theory is right in its main bearings. Still, a telegram's gone to Lambry and he'll talk over what's best to do."

In the act of rising Dryden sat down again. "I know what's worried me. What about Mould? Why did he run away if he didn't try to kill that woman? I mean, if he merely wanted to disembarrass himself, he could have told her to go to blazes. He wouldn't lose a lifetime's work and reputation for just that."

Codlin took up the tale of Short.

"That's going to be a desperate business," said Franklin. "When you sensed something repulsive in that house last February, and sensed it in those strange pictures she began to paint, your instincts were right. Those pictures were the expression of a tremendous sexual experience."

"But she was a spinster! I mean—"

Travers smiled. "Henry, you're too good for this world! We'll put it crudely. Mould seduced her—if that's the term to use for a woman of her age."

"But his wife was alive!"

"Exactly!" said Travers dryly. "She was an ailing, mewling sort of woman who irritated Mould beyond bounds. She had nothing to offer him. There's a little servant-maid at Lewes who's related strange things to Scotland Yard. Mould got the idea that the police were on his tracks— perhaps somebody gave him an inkling. He bolted, because he knew something was likely to happen—that the police would exhume the body of the woman who died of gastric trouble, that convenient disease that gets muddled up with poison and vice versa, to the confusion of ancient practitioners and the convenience of tired husbands."

"My God!" Dryden was incredibly shocked. As he rose, face working and hands moving convulsively, Travers rose too. He gave his little chuckle of a laugh as he threw his arm over the other's shoulder.

"Henry, I'm going to make you smile. And you're going to have something to remember about that fine fellow Parish that'll stick by you when you've forgotten the rest. You know, Henry, the Parish who was fond of a joke. The man who said to you, 'Let me alone with Master Mould. I've a trick that'll cure him!' Do you know what he did?"

Dryden shook his head.

"Well, I found at the bottom of that story by Anatole France— the one about the mignonette—a pencilled note in Parish's own copy. Merely a bracket enclosing a capital M and a question mark. Don't you see the workings of his mind? To Parish in those days, art was something you see on postcards, and. the term artist not in. the least relative. Mould was a sculptor, but that conveyed to Parish the idea that he was interested in colour and the beautiful—the beautiful, that is, as Parish himself saw it."

Travers shook his own head as he smiled. "Quaint, isn't it? that Parish should destroy one garden that good might come, and when he was his normal self he made a garden that good might come! As he planned it and made that note, you can see the workings of his mind. 'Those wonderful forget-me-nots I saw at So-and-so's place! That's what I'll do to this fellow Mould. I'll make something grow under his eyes where he can't miss it; something that will get him out of the house and put a stop to his hermitry and wake all the best that's in him!

"And that's just what he did do, Henry. He went to Hastings and bought a dozen large packets of seed—cleared the shop right out, so the assistant says." He took Dryden's arm and nodded away whimsically. "We read that while a certain man slept, his enemy came by night and sowed tares in his field. While Mould slept, Parish came and sowed forget-me-nots in the waste garden of his friend. There's something for you to remember, Henry."

Dryden nodded. "Yes. . . . It's good of you. Good of you both." He looked round. "I think, perhaps, if you'll excuse me, I'll go round to the vicarage for a moment."

Franklin got up at once. "I'd like to go too, if I may."

Travers watched them through the door, then strolled across to the window. Promise of yet another magnificent day, with the sun making that valley look like a bowl of shimmering grey. Yes, a great day it'd be—and then his thoughts ran on too far. Another accident in the unfortunate village of Bableigh! Reporters by the dozen—Spence of the *Evening Record* coming for the redemption of that rash promise he'd received, when to give promises seemed the easiest thing in the world. And Franklin would be wondering who could have written to Mould and given him the tip to bolt. Travers felt a blush steal over his face as he took off his glasses and nervously began to polish them.

Printed in Great Britain
by Amazon